THE DOLL WHO ATE HIS MOTHER

They were talking about the man. Which man?
The man must have opened the door to throw himself out, or it had fallen open. The man was Rob,
then. His something had something at the first
moment of impact. But then what? Surely you
aren't saying —Clare strained forward, away from
the restraining grasp. The sharp blue beacon of the
ambulance cut through the orange glow, repeatedly
flashing in her eyes, pounding, insisting that she
hear the truth, that she admit she'd heard the
policeman's words. All he was saying was that the
man's arm, Rob's arm was *what?*

"Missing," he repeated irritably. "His arm is
missing."

THE DOLL WHO
ATE HIS MOTHER

A novel of modern terror by

RAMSEY CAMPBELL

A STAR BOOK
published by
the Paperback Division of
W. H. ALLEN & Co. Ltd

A Star Book
Published in 1978 in Universal
by the Paperback Division of
W. H. Allen & Co. Ltd
A Howard and Wyndham Company
44 Hill Street, London W1X 8LB
This edition reprinted 1979

First published in Great Britain by Millington Books Ltd, 1977

Printed in Great Britain by
Richard Clay (The Chaucer Press), Ltd.,
Bungay, Suffolk

ISBN 0 352 304987

for Kirby
a good agent; an even better friend

Acknowledgments

A great many people helped me write this book. I should especially like to thank:

Mr. McGrath of the Liverpool City Morgue, who was kind enough to describe the formalities to me

the Liverpool Coroner's Court and its officials, for their patience in answering my questions

the staff of Liverpool Public Libraries, for finding out all manner of things for me; and their cataloguing department, for cataloguing *Glimpses of Absolute Power* for me

the assembled writers, wizards of wine, culinary genies, bibliophiles, and croquet champions of LiG: particularly Tony and Cherry, for their advice on car accidents

my friends among the Liverpool cinema managers, for giving me glimpses of the job: especially Tony McCarthy, for his insights into suburban cinema management

and most of all my wife, Jenny, for sharing the birth pangs of *The Doll Who Ate His Mother*.

I cannot describe the look of the woman when I told her what I had made grow inside her. But the strength which her look made me feel, I knew was nothing to the strength I yet possessed untapped.

—*Glimpses of Absolute Power*

The Doll
Who Ate
His Mother

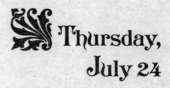# Thursday, July 24

There were no taxis.

Clare Frayn stumped back and forth on Catherine Street, shivering. The July night was mild, the entire street was orange as embers beneath the sodium streetlamps, yet she was shivering. She glanced at her watch. Four o'clock, good God. No wonder she was cold; her body was at its lowest ebb. Even Rob had never kept her up so late before. In a minute she'd chance the brakes in Ringo the Reliant and drive him home.

He was standing at the corner of Catherine Street and Canning Street, a block away, leaning his long body into the road whenever a distant motor whirred. Beside him traffic lights blinked emptily; beyond him glowed the will-o'-the-wisp of a disordered telephone box. Around them both, in the Georgian terraces of Liverpool 8, poets and artists slept—half of them drunk and snoring, no doubt, Clare thought. Rob looked back at her over his shoulder and smiled, encouraging, embarrassed. Then he leaned out again.

Who else would have such a fool for a brother, Clare thought with a kind of irritable resigned affection. Stop leaning out, for God's sake. There are no taxis. No sound at all, except for a ship's low tone drifting sleepily up the Mersey from the sea. But there was: the sound of an engine; the unmistakable sound of a taxi labouring up Myrtle Street beyond the curve, beyond the Children's Hospital. She began to run, cursing her short legs, slapping basement railings furiously with her hand, for speed. She reached the curve as the vehicle did, driving down the side street opposite, not up the hill at all. It was a lorry carrying its baby on its back.

When she plodded back as far as the traffic lights, Rob said, "I'm sorry I've kept you up so late."

"You mean you've just noticed? God, Rob, you're worse—"

"Than all the kids in your class put together. I know. But I really did need to talk, and there's nobody else I can talk to."

Except your wife, she thought. But of course it had been Dorothy he had wanted to talk about, as usual. "It's all right," Clare said. "You know I don't mind really." She was shivering again; her eyes felt as if they'd been fitted with thick lenses a couple of sizes too large. "There's nothing I have to get up for later, anyway," she said.

He saw her shivering. He stooped and put his arm about her shoulders, rubbing them. From nowhere a car came roaring up Canning Street, hooting at Rob as its occupants did, at his pigtail and leather waistcoat and checked trousers and high gold-painted boots. "I'd walk if I could," he told her.

"I know that. Don't worry." He hadn't been dressed half so bizarrely the night he'd walked home along Princes Avenue, when the youths had beaten him up and left him on the central reservation of the dual carriageway, among the trees. "But I don't think we're going to find a taxi," Clare said.

"If I could phone Dorothy I'd stay. But she might be worrying."

"She's probably fast asleep in bed." Unless she's a fool.

"She wasn't last time. That was when we had the row about having children, remember, I told you. She wouldn't go to bed until I said we'd try next year. I'm sure she'll still be up."

No man would keep me up like that, Clare vowed. "I don't see what I can do," she said.

"Couldn't you drive me home? There won't be any traffic."

"I don't want to drive until the garage has looked at the brakes."

They both heard the taxi. It was whirring purposefully toward them, so loudly that they strained their eyes at the empty street. Its sound had filled the street before it turned, tantalizingly, somewhere out of sight. "Oh Christ," Rob said, swaying rapidly and unhappily from one foot to the other, tick tock.

Clare gazed at him. He looked exactly like a child who was frantic to pee. All at once she realized that he wasn't anxious to get back to win the argument with Dorothy, which he'd abandoned along with his dinner. He wanted to go home because he was worried about Dorothy, because he loved her. She shook her head, sighing. Some things about him she would never understand. "Come on," she said suddenly. "I suppose if I drive slowly we'll be all right."

They made for Blackburne Terrace and Clare's car. Several babies were walking across the roofs of the garages opposite, crying. When Clare looked again they were cats. Rob said, "I still don't understand how Dorothy can stand those people."

Don't go through that again, Clare thought, for God's sake! She'd already heard once how Dorothy felt he was losing her all her friends. He'd arrived at midnight but had waited until one o'clock to tell her he was famished, to say nothing of his doubts about his marriage, whether he'd married Dorothy just for sex, how they'd run out of things to talk about, how working for the same people as your wife meant you were together too much of the time. To Clare, all this had sounded like one of his Radio Merseyside record shows without the records, hours of sheer nervous energy, uncontrollable words. When he'd begun to mention taxis, she'd thought he had run down at last, but here were Dorothy's friends again. "Perhaps you should ask her why she likes them," Clare said, hurrying toward Ringo the three-wheeler.

"Oh, she told that. They aren't reasons that make any sense

to me. I can't understand how she could have friends like that. I've told her before I don't like them. They're just a load of boring middle-class shit."

"Keep that for your record shows. You're never going to convince me you're working-class." In the grainy light beyond the streetlamps she squinted at the car door, fumbling with the key; her eyes prickled. "Not with parents who've retired to a spa town," she said.

"That doesn't make me any class, love. Don't try to throw me in that shit." He sounded as he did on his late-night programme, "The Working Class Hero Show": aggressive, dogmatic, secretly unsure. "You ought to meet her friends," he said. "You ought to see them, walking around the flat and looking as if this is all you can expect from a secretary married to a deejay."

"Are you sure it isn't you who think that?"

He slid into the front seat, packing as much of his folded legs as he could beneath the dashboard; then he turned to gaze at her. "No more so than you do," he said.

What, Clare despise Dorothy? Just for putting up with Rob? Dorothy, who'd married him out of admiration for his drive and his refusal to conform, who suffered him quietly most of the time now, perhaps because she knew that if she didn't contain herself he'd simply flee to Clare? Yes, Clare thought, she despised her a little. Dorothy did herself no good by keeping quiet. And all that was called love, good God.

Rob was nodding triumphantly. "I know you," he said. "I know what it means if you're more polite to someone when you get to know them better. It means you can't stand them."

"Maybe you should feel responsible for reducing her to that," Clare said sharply. "Put on your seat belt."

"We aren't going far. I don't need it with you driving."

"No doubt you'll do exactly as you please." She was determined that he wouldn't make her angry. She groped for the clasp of her seat belt.

"I know I'm irresponsible. Don't you think I know?" He'd reached another monologue, as if he'd slipped it out of a rack. "But what can I do? By the time I knew myself it was too late. Father and Mother put down everything I was, you know that. That wasn't likely to give me a sense of responsibility, was it? But there you are. I'm not even taking responsibility for what I am. That's what I'm like. Self-pitying, as well. You can hear that, can't you?"

He was retreating deeper and deeper into a maze of himself. He frightened her when he was like this; he became, in the fullest sense, beyond her. He'd had these moods more often since he'd begun smoking pot habitually. She shivered as she grasped the wheel. She must get him home quickly. She couldn't handle him in this mood, not at this hour. The car dragged its headlights over the terrace; on the porch the shadows of the columns crept out from behind their stones and across the front doors, spreading.

She tested the brakes as the car emerged between the square pillars onto Blackburne Place. "He's still not right," she said.

"Look, I'll stay if you like. I don't want to be any trouble."

God forbid, she thought. She wanted at least a little sleep. "Let's get you home," she said.

She inched the car out onto Catherine Street, grateful for the lack of traffic. The headlights gleamed on the sign of a jujitsu club in a Georgian basement, then were swallowed by the sodium glow. The car dawdled toward the traffic lights, but their green held. Clare depressed the accelerator warily. Once they'd crossed the five-way intersection at Upper Parliament Street, they would be safe.

Rob was silent now. In a way, that disturbed her more. She imagined him trapped deep in himself, with no way out, not even words. She looked sideways at him; beyond him, houses streamed by, blurred orange; the columns of a Greek Ionic porch had sprouted tubular metal scaffolding. "Soon be home now," she said, and his lips twitched.

5

Upper Parliament Street was deserted, dilapidated; its terraces soon gave way to razed waste. The green light ushered her across, and she accelerated toward Princes Avenue, past the drive-in bank and the red-brick domed Byzantine church and the Cypriot fish-and-chip shop. Ahead, at the near end of the reservation which divided the dual carriageway, William Huskisson the merchant stood on a pedestal, clutching his robe glumly about him, against exposure; beneath the sodium light he retained a faint dull-green gleam, like verdigris. Clare drove by, into the flood of orange light.

The light covered everything, thick as paint. It sank oppressively into the car, filling it with shadows that moved like submarine vegetation as the lamps sailed repetitively by. Clare resisted an urge to drive faster, to be free of the light, but she felt it clinging stickily to her. She squirmed. She shouldn't have driven without sleep, after all.

The light soaked the three-storey Georgian houses behind their stone walls and bulging orange hedges. Pools of it lay on the roofs of the line of cars which barred Clare from the kerbside lane. Ahead, along the edge of the central reservation, trees and tree-coloured lamp standards bunched, pulling lingeringly apart as they approached. Around the high lamps, papery orange leaves were tangled in bright branches like orange web. Soon be there now, Clare told herself. She might ask to sleep on the couch at Rob and Dorothy's. At the ends of pedestrian crossings, globes on poles pulsed: orange, orange, orange.

"Dorothy and I want you to come to dinner next week," Rob said. "We haven't seen you for nearly a fortnight."

A tree, a tree, a lamp standard, a gap in the reservation. She glanced at Rob's orange face, staring solemnly at her. He'd found his way out of himself, and the last few hours might as well not have happened. "Rob, you're hopeless," she said, giggling uncontrollably. "You really are."

He frowned at her, even more solemn. Behind his head,

Christ leapt from the wall of a church, tattered arms clawing high, fleshless ribs blackened by the sodium light. She started and turned back to the road, still snorting. A lamp standard, a thick tree. A man stepping straight into the path of the car.

She had time to stop. He was yards and yards away. But the brakes weren't responding, the car wasn't slowing safely. The man turned and saw the car; he clapped his hand over most of his face in a theatrical gesture of shock, and began to dither between the two empty lanes. The kerbside lane was occupied. There wasn't room for Clare to be sure of passing him.

Rob stared at his sister, apparently driving straight at the man. "Oh Christ," he said, and tried to pull the wheel over; the car yawed wildly. "Get off, you fool!" she screamed, turning her whole body to regain possession of the wheel. She swerved the car toward the central reservation. There ought to be room for her to steer between the trees. Her short legs had slipped from the brake. She trod hard on the pedal, but it was the accelerator.

She heard Rob clawing at the door release, in panic. The car bumped over the kerb of the reservation, toward a lamp standard. She dug her heel into the brake pedal, dragging at the wheel. The swerve threw the door open. The door struck the lamp standard at once, and chopped shut again with a strange, unfamiliar sound, knocking Rob back into his seat. She heard the window shatter.

She was still fighting the wheel as the car crunched across the gravel, toward the other carriageway, toward a passing car, too fast. She slewed the car round, and its left rear wheel thumped a tree. The car halted there at the edge of the kerb, shuddering.

There was silence, filled by the sound of Clare's blood in her ears. Blood thumped in her limbs; her throat was full of the threat of nausea. Rob lay silent, slumped against the door, his head leaning out of the shattered window, his shoulder pressed against the edge of the door. Someone was staring in at him: the driver of the passing car. No, he couldn't be the driver, because now he was running away toward the lamp standard, before Clare could see his face. Here came the driver, hurrying back from his car as she fumbled slowly, abstractedly, with the clasp of her seat belt.

He was thick-set, red-faced; he was like the man who'd owned the butcher's shop when she was a little girl. He looked angry and bewildered, as if he'd just been awoken rudely. "The man must be mad," he said. For a moment she thought he meant Rob. "Should be locked up. Walking in front of you like that. Are you all right? Look, there he goes," and in her mirror someone was running away up a side street, hunched over as if carrying a prize.

"My brother," she said, searching for words. "Needs help."

He went round to Rob's side of the car, then hurried back, paler. "I'll get help," he said. "Don't move. Whatever you do, don't touch him."

Curtains blinked warily in the bystanding houses; one house lit up its six flats, one by one. A third-floor window opened. "Do you need an ambulance?" a man shouted down.

"Quickly, yes!" the driver shouted. He turned back to Clare. "I'll get that swine," he said, furious again. "Running off like that," and he ran toward the side street, amazingly fast for his build.

Clare managed to unclasp her seat belt. Her blood was slowing; the threat of nausea seemed to have passed. Rob still lay against the door. She reached toward him, then drew back: mustn't touch. She was surprised at how calm she felt. But there was nothing she could do, after all: Rob was unconscious, she couldn't comfort him, she must wait for the ambulance. She climbed out of the car and almost fell into the road; her legs were unstrung. She propped herself against the side of the car. She was still calm. She only wished daylight would hurry up, to wash away the clinging sodium glow.

Something was dripping beneath the car. She bent and peered. It was fluid from the brakes; the hydraulic link had snapped. Never mind that. It was Rob she should be looking at.

He was leaning out of the window. His head lay on one side, resting against the outside of the door. Blood and the shadows of branches blotted out his face, his eyes. He lay as if gazing down at the hailstones of the shattered window, scattered over the gravel in a thickening trail back toward the lamp standard. The few hailstones beneath him, and the patch of gravel, glittered restlessly with black blood.

Clare gazed at all this calmly. She'd seen children bleeding in the playground, after all. But something was wrong. The sight of Rob she had now didn't quite fit together with the way he looked from inside the car. She went back to her side of the car to look. But all at once the ambulance was braying to a halt beside her, its siren sinking; people were surrounding her—the helpful red-faced butcher, a couple from one of the flats, ambulance attendants, police.

"A man walked straight in front of me," she told the police. She only had to speak quietly, they would know she was telling the truth; shouting did no good, teaching taught you that. They couldn't know about the brakes. "Straight into the road," she said.

"That's right," the butcher said. "I saw him. A bloody madman. I chased him, over there, but he got away."

An ambulance attendant was taking her arm. "I'm all right," she said, giggling at his look of concern. "What do you think's wrong with me? I'm only shivering because it's so late. It's my brother you've got to look after." But they had, she saw; the car was empty.

"He was out in the middle of the road. He wouldn't go one way or the other. He distracted her completely, and I don't wonder," the butcher told a policeman who was writing down the butcher's name. They would believe him, Clare thought gratefully. But another policeman was examining the car, the door, the interior, the brakes.

"Come on now, love," the attendant said, steering her gently toward the bright white box of the ambulance, away from the orange glow. "You don't know how you are yet. Anyway, you'll want to be with your friend."

Her brother, not her friend. But let the man have his own way; he was only trying to be kind. Except that she wanted to hear what the other attendant would say to the policeman who had beckoned him urgently over to the car. She was sure they were talking about Rob. There was something they didn't understand, that much was in their faces—perhaps the same thing that had confused her as she'd looked at the outside of the car. The policeman was urging the attendant over to the lamp standard, to the parked cars; they were peering beneath the cars, gazing about at the pavement. They looked like children hunting for treasure. "Wait a minute," she said, wriggling her arm in the attendant's grasp.

They were walking slowly back toward Ringo, poor old car. She couldn't hear their voices yet, but their faces and gestures were talking. There? the policeman said, including everywhere they'd searched in a sweep of his arm, pointing to the car, the ambulance. No, the attendant admitted, shaking his head doubtfully. Well then, the policeman said, looking as if he liked the idea even less. But surely, the attendant said, looking shocked, actually ill. They were nearly in Clare's earshot. She strained her ears, herself, toward them.

They were talking about the man. Which man? The man must have opened the door to throw himself out, or it had fallen open. The man was Rob, then. His something had something at the moment of first impact. But then what? Surely you aren't saying—Clare strained forward, away from the restraining grasp. The sharp blue beacon of the ambulance cut through the orange glow, repeatedly flashing in her eyes, pounding, insisting that she hear the truth, that she admit she'd heard the policeman's words. All he was saying was that the man's arm, Rob's arm, was *what?*

"Missing," he repeated irritably. "His arm is missing."

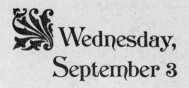 **Wednesday, September 3**

"Tell me about Bob," Dorothy said to Clare.

They were sitting on the balcony outside Dorothy's, on the fourteenth storey of a stack of flats overlooking Sefton Park. Ahead of them lay the playing field, like green baize worn through in black patches. Beyond the park and the huddled chimneys and church towers of Aigburth, a tanker slid over the glittering shattered sunlight of the Mersey. Beyond that, except for the occasional factory chimney standing smoking on the far bank of the river, there was nothing but the enormous open early-evening sky.

"I remember when Rob and I were kids," Clare said. She'd never been able to call him Bob, which he'd rechristened himself for the BBC. "He wouldn't play with his friends unless they let me join in. Usually they liked me to." She gazed out across the playing field, toward the iron-and-glass dome of Sefton Park Palm House, packed deep in trees. She was glad of these memories. She'd had them for years, and she loved to remember them. She was grateful that even now they weren't spoilt.

"But once they reached adolescence he changed toward them completely," she said. "He became all serious and protective, wouldn't let them near me. There was one boy, Lionel. I thought he was all right; we used to have some good fights when we were younger. He asked me out once, to the pictures. When Rob heard, he nearly knocked him down. He stood in front of the house that night to make sure Lionel couldn't get at me, and wouldn't tell Father and Mother why. I was upstairs sobbing my heart out, you can imagine. It was years later Rob told me Lionel had used to boast about all the girls he'd had, all the details. I don't think he could have had so many, though. He was only twelve."

Dorothy was leaning forward, alert, ready to learn. Her wide eyes were black and shining as her wiry curls, on which the sunlight rested softly. Clare could see why Rob had found her attractive. But then, she'd never denied that Dorothy was pretty.

"He could be really tough when he was looking after me," Clare said. "You wouldn't have thought it was Rob. I remember the first time I ever went to the Cavern, when the Beatles were on. Did you ever go? It was an experience." Beneath the warehouses, dark thick stone overhead and close around her, musty-smelling, a crowd squeezed in so tight she could hardly lift her arm to drink her Coke, dense smoke hanging low beneath the ceiling: beyond the crowd she could just see four figures on a stage, making loud blurred sounds. "There was a boy there I knew from school," she said. "He only touched me, only just below my shoulder, here, but Rob gave him such a push he nearly got trampled. I must have been about thirteen then."

Dorothy was shaking her head, wide-eyed, smiling, engrossed. To Clare, she looked a little like a teacher pretending to be interested. You should be interested, Clare thought. It's a side of Rob you never knew.

"Oh yes, and there was one other boy," she said. "This was a few years later: I thought he was nice, at the time. We used to go for walks, and he'd tell me all his plans, all his dreams. Then one day I heard Rob had nearly broken his arm with a piece of railing because of what he'd been saying about me. All the time he'd been laughing at me with his friends. Rob never told me what about." But she'd heard from someone else. Little Stumpy, he'd been calling her. Little Noddy. Little Stumpy-legs.

"Poor Clare," Dorothy said. "You must have been really unlucky with boys."

"Unlucky? I don't think so. I'd say they were about average." She gazed ahead; the light on the Mersey trembled against her eyes. "The funny thing was, he kept on, Rob did, even after we had our own places," she said. "If I ever had a boyfriend I had to bring him up here for inspection, or Rob would be at me until I did. We had a row once. I'd told him I was inviting my latest to my flat, for dinner. I'm not making this up. We were just sitting down to dinner when Rob arrived, and he stayed until this bloke had gone. God, did we have a fight then. But the bloke wasn't any great loss, when I think about it—a bit snobby and know-it-all."

"It's incredible you didn't lose your temper with Bob more often."

"Oh, he didn't bother me really." Sometimes she'd been grateful to him, when he'd arrived just in time to interrupt a planned seduction—or at least what she was sure had been threatening to be one. Not that she couldn't have defended herself if it had ever come to the point. "I haven't much time for going out with blokes," she said. "Too much to do at school. When I've been teaching I just like to go home and flop. But I don't mind that. It satisfies me."

Dorothy was nodding, smiling warmly. "No doubt I sound as if I'm deluding myself," Clare said coldly.

"Of course you don't. I was just thinking, perhaps Bob was jealous. Maybe that was why he kept getting in your way, because he needed you."

Her voice faltered. She was coming up out of memories now, toward what had happened to Rob. "I suppose so," Clare said hurriedly, searching for a change of subject. She felt uncomfortable. She always did here, trying to pretend she didn't know everything about Dorothy, everything she'd said to Rob. All her mind would offer was that Rob had certainly seemed to need her since he'd married Dorothy.

"Obviously I don't mean he needed you, you know, sexually," Dorothy said. "You used to look after him, didn't you, as well as the other way round. Maybe he still needed that."

And why not sexually? Clare demanded. Why is it so obvious? Just because Dorothy was prettier! She remembered Rob at the age of eleven, saying, "Look what I can do!" and brandishing his erection. It had been empty, though, and she'd failed to see the point of all his red-faced manipulation. So she'd been the first, in a way; Dorothy needn't feel so smug.

Dorothy was gazing at her. Were her thoughts showing? She shouldn't be scoring off Dorothy, not now. She stood up, pretending to abandon the conversation for the view. Around the park the long curve of Victorian villas and pointed spires, the occasional high-rise block that had shouldered itself a space, rose with her like a congregation. Some of the trees were heavy with children; a park-keeper shook them down with a flourished fist.

Below her—a couple of storeys below, as it sounded—she heard passing cars. She looked. The world fell away with a soundless sucking gasp, down, down, to the tiny cars. Though the balcony wall was almost as high as her shoulders, Clare stumbled backwards. She imagined Dorothy resting her elbows on the wall, gazing down at the waiting concrete. It was morbid of Dorothy to have suggested coming out here. The sky tugged Clare toward the edge. "I'd like to go in now," she told Dorothy.

They carried the folded chairs into the flat, down the hall that always felt to Clare like a low concrete tunnel, dressed in striped gingham. On the right, the door of Rob's workroom and record library was a lid, closed tight on the walls taped full of aggressively middle-class complaints, aggressively working-class complaints, and the newspaper report: THE RECORD SHOW MILLIONS OF FANS LOVE TO HATE. They laid the chairs in the hall cupboard, whose door promised a room.

The living room seemed empty to Clare now. It had seemed so when she arrived, after the lift had given its usual joyful little leap at the fourteenth floor. It seemed deserted because it was full of Rob's things—the rattle he'd bought when he'd joined the working class in watching football, the team photograph above the electric fire, the red lapel rosettes, the book by a local poet on top of the television, eager to show visitors its dedication to Rob. Must be leaving soon, Clare thought. She'd done her duty. Besides, they were running short of memories to discuss.

"I liked your parents," Dorothy said. "But I think I can see why Bob didn't."

"Did he ever tell you about them?"

"He never wanted to."

"You mightn't have liked them so much if he had."

Dorothy was moving about the flat, flicking a duster. The flat always seemed alert for visitors. Now she sat down, turning her heart-shaped face eagerly up to Clare. The first time she had done so Clare had thought she was trying to compensate for Clare's height, and had been furiously annoyed. Later she'd realized the woman only wanted to be told everything, to know, to understand: a good pupil. Now, deep in Dorothy's eyes, Clare saw a plea. She must be going soon. Dorothy's friends would look after Dorothy; she couldn't.

"Oh, I don't suppose Father and Mother were that bad," she said. "It was just that Rob was never what they wanted him to be. But that's part of adolescence; they couldn't understand that. They wouldn't let him grow out of it. It was always: My God, you're not going out wearing that. Or: Don't let me see you with that girl again. Or: I won't have that cacophony in my house—that was his records, of course. The worst thing was, if he tried to be what one of them wanted, the other didn't like it—it was always: Don't be so affected."

"Yes," Dorothy said. "I understand him better now."

No doubt she was remembering the shifting, self-contradictory arguments he had used to hurl at her. Clare remembered them too, though she hadn't been present. She hurried on. "The strange part was they believed they were going to win. They were sure that whatever phases he went through, he'd join Father in the jeweller's eventually. When he kept telling them he was going to work in broadcasting they just treated it as something else they'd talk him out of. They never really believed him, even when he went to work at the Cavern. When Radio Merseyside opened they behaved as if he'd betrayed them, hardly spoke to him. I used to get furious with them. I was two years younger than Rob, and their favourite, of course. They often blamed him for things I'd done. I could say anything to them and they'd listen. But then they went on doing exactly the same things to Rob."

"That's what I meant, about your looking after him," Dorothy said. "He needed it. I liked to look after him. But I didn't do it too much, because I thought it mightn't be good for him. Maybe I should have looked after him more."

Her voice was shaking. Her emotion was building, charging the room; Clare felt suffocated. She must go. Dorothy probably wanted to be alone.

"Your mother wrote to Bob after we were married, you know," Dorothy said. "She wanted us to go and stay with them. Even though he hadn't invited them to the wedding. He wouldn't go, of course. He didn't even answer her letter. I suppose she wanted to see what I was like. I wonder what she thought of me finally. I wasn't exactly at my best at the funeral."

There it was. She'd touched it. Perhaps that had earthed her emotion. "You looked fine," Clare said, and indeed she had: she'd glided through the funeral, artlessly graceful and poised.

Rob's death hadn't made her forget how to walk, Clare had thought—unfairly, no doubt. I must be going, she prepared to say. But Dorothy was gazing up at her, eyes moist.

"There was only one thing I couldn't bear," she said. "When I had to go to identify Bob. There's a little window that you look through. They had Bob lying on a trolley, under a sheet. He looked as though he were asleep, because, you know, all the injury was under his hair. They'd put him with his left side away from me, under the light. But I could see how the sheet hung straight down from his shoulder, just flat against his shoulder. I couldn't understand at first what was wrong. Then I kept saying, 'Where's his arm? Where's his arm?' " She turned away from Clare and pressed her face into the back of her chair, shoulders writhing. After a while she said, "I'm sorry. I'll make some coffee." She hurried out, and Clare heard her sobbing in the kitchen.

Clare listened, detached. Best to leave her alone. It was odd: she couldn't feel what Dorothy was feeling. No doubt that was because her own reaction had overwhelmed her physically, all at once, and purged her.

In the ambulance one of the attendants had poured her a drink of hot sweet tea from a flask. She hadn't liked to say that she hated sugar. He'd stood over her while she drank it, blocking her view of Rob. The sugar and the motion of the ambulance had made her feel sick again.

She had been sitting in the hospital with an old magazine lying slack on her hands when she'd heard her pulse. It was huge and soft; it was slowing like a run-down record. As she fell forward her mouth opened and the hot sweet tea spilled out, over the magazine.

They gave her a sedative. She'd awoken in the evening. She'd felt fine, but anxious to telephone her parents. She mustn't write; it would be bad enough for them to hear the news over the phone. When someone had reluctantly brought her a phone, she'd described the accident, which she'd variously imagined full of grief, outrage, disbelief, a broken connection. Then her father had said, "When are you coming down?"

She'd gone down to Cheltenham the next day. The Radio Merseyside people were looking after Dorothy; she didn't need Clare. Neither on the phone nor later had Clare been able to tell her parents exactly what had happened to Rob. Thank God they disliked most of the news too much to buy newspapers. What could she have said? "They couldn't find one of his arms"? "Someone stole his arm"? She'd tried once or twice, with her father, but it had sounded so ridiculous she'd thought it was best not to try. The absurdity of it had helped her not to brood. She admitted to herself she was glad. She wouldn't care to feel like Dorothy. Here came Dorothy, behind coffee mugs muttering together on a trolley.

"It's past seven. Why don't you stay for dinner?" Dorothy said. "Some of the people from Radio Mers will be coming up later. You haven't met Tim Forbes, have you?"

"I've a chop in the fridge, thanks, Dorothy. I don't like keeping meat too long."

"Come and have dinner before you go back to school. I'm sure you'd like someone else to cook you a meal."

I'm quite satisfied with my own cooking, thank you. "I'm afraid I'll be busy getting ready for the new class."

Dorothy nodded, sipping. "Did you go back with your parents?"

"Yes." Straight back to Cheltenham after the funeral; her mother had wept all the way on the train, as if she'd saved up all her feelings during Rob's life. Passengers had grabbed the adjoining seats triumphantly, then had hastily retreated. Clare's father had leaned forward at intervals to pat his wife's hand; he'd gazed grimly at the rushing landscape.

"I stayed for a fortnight," Clare said. "It took my mother that long to begin to recover. My father asked me to stay, because he couldn't cope. She did love Rob, you see. It just shows, love isn't the point, it doesn't mean anything. It's what you do that counts. When I was coming back they gave me all sorts of things—money, a handbag because mine was tatty, a new carving set. I just wished they'd given more to Rob, more of themselves." She shook herself: in a minute she'd have them back at the mortuary again. "What about your parents?" she said. "Wouldn't you feel better if you went to live at home for a while?"

"This is my home. I love my parents very much, but I won't live there again. That would be admitting defeat. Particularly when they're in the same town, that would make it more of a defeat somehow. This place is cheap enough. I've got my job, and Bob had quite a lot of insurance, you know—he bought some as soon as we got married. But I want to make my own way. That's why I went back to work as soon as I could. I've got to be able to fend for myself completely. I don't want looking after."

She was looking steadily at Clare. Clare thought: You're not implying I need looking after, are you? Suddenly an idea caught her. All through her visit she had felt Dorothy preparing tensely for something: her tale of the mortuary, of course. But had the mortuary anecdote been aimed at her? Had the woman wanted to upset her in order to comfort her? Was Dorothy looking for someone new to look after? My God, she thought. The woman is sick. "I must go home and get on with my work," she lied, gulping her coffee.

Dorothy came down in the lift with her. The silver-grey box sank slowly, slowly; it smelled of scrubbing. "Do try and come again soon," Dorothy said.

"I'll have to see." Through the tiny rectangular window the rough walls of the shaft drifted up sluggishly, grey-crusted smoke; doors sailed lethargically up, scratched like the inside of a coffin lid in a film Clare had once switched on by mistake. She could feel Dorothy wanting her to promise; the wanting filled the lift oppressively. "The beginning of the school year's always hectic," she said. "I just go home and doze."

When Dorothy made to follow her to the car, she said, "Goodbye, Dorothy. Thank you." She watched her stride gracefully back toward the lifts as if she were entering a hotel foyer. If it keeps her happy, Clare thought, shaking her head sadly. She was glad she didn't need illusions. She stumped toward the Reliant as she imagined a hobbit might walk, to show she didn't care.

The passenger door was new; around the edge of the doorframe someone at the garage had scrubbed pale a large irregular patch. Aside from the door and the new rear axle, he was mostly the Ringo she'd had for years. The seat leather burned her through her thin dress; she rolled down both windows, flapping her arms at the inert heat. Then she fastened her seat belt and drove home.

Her father had paid for the repairs. "Good for you," he'd said when she admitted she might continue driving. She'd fought not to take the money he offered, but he'd stuffed it into her purse. She was still determined it would be only a loan against the insurance. It had been like taking money for killing Rob.

Even when the car was repaired she hadn't driven. She'd made an excuse and had had the garage deliver the car. She'd sat in the driver's seat a few times, beneath the shifting trees in Blackburne Terrace. Each time her gaze had been drawn to the scrubbed patch; each time she'd left the car hurriedly. She couldn't drive that car again.

A bus ride had changed her mind. She disliked buses; if she sat upstairs the stench of stale tobacco smoke clung to her clothes all day, while the lower deck was often packed full as a lift with nonsmokers. She had been on her way to visit Dorothy, to get it over with, the day after she'd returned from Cheltenham; she was rather hoping Dorothy would be out. The driver had been playing ninepins with the press of passengers in the aisle; the bus swung a child screaming at the length of his mother's arm, too far ahead for Clare to reach. As the bus laboured past the lamp standard Clare had heard the car door chop shut. All at once everything had swelled up in her like nausea; the cramped ventilation whose breeze came nowhere near her face, the soft thighs that thumped her shoulder as passengers rocked in the aisle, the flaw in the window glass that pinched thin everything that passed before letting go with a jerk, the tobacco smoke trickling down the stairs, the screaming child, her own sticky body, her helplessness. She'd pulled at the bell cord as if it were a lifeline and had struggled to the folding doors, which parted with a gasp of relief. Once home, she'd climbed into Ringo and had driven for miles. After a few days she'd hardly noticed the scrubbed patch.

She was driving past the lamp standard now—at least, she was in that area. From this side of the reservation she couldn't be sure, for someone had removed the bloodstained gravel. Weren't there darker spots scattered over the reservation even now? Never mind. It wasn't good to dwell on such things. But she knew she had only shrugged it off until next time, for she had to drive this way to school.

Christ leaned out from the church beyond the reservation. She'd never liked that Christ; he looked famished, poised to leap on anyone who came too close to the wall. Now she liked him even less. He should have saved Rob. But she knew she was trying to shift the blame. Rob's death had been her fault, of course.

Her parents hadn't blamed her. Her father had blamed Rob for talking to her while she was driving. Dorothy hadn't mentioned the accident at all; she'd kept gazing at Clare with a large, warm, forgiving expression, sympathetic, encouraging, until Clare could have screamed. All of them made her feel more guilty. They refused to blame her only because they didn't know what had happened. She was so guilty she had lied to the police.

She'd said the brakes had been working before the crash. She'd blamed Rob, for grabbing the wheel. At the inquest, when she stepped down from the witness box once she'd sworn that the statement they'd read out was hers, her face had been burning. The kindly, quiet-voiced coroner had told the jury that she wasn't allowed to answer any other questions, lest she incriminate herself. She was sure then that everyone knew she was guilty. None of the policemen in the court would look at her. She knew they were biding their time to prosecute.

But she hadn't heard from them yet. Either they were waiting for her to assume they'd forgotten, or they hoped her guilt would build up until she was eager to betray herself; then they'd pounce. They knew that she started guiltily when the doorbell rang, that she peered fearfully downstairs whenever the new postman fumbled at the letter slot. She only wished they would get it over with. She couldn't bear much longer the sense of having wronged Rob.

She coasted into Blackburne Place, past the Byzantine church of St. Philip Neri, humpy with tiny domes. Behind her in Catherine Street the orange lamps were dormant. She steered the car into Blackburne Terrace. Shade gathered softly beneath the house-high trees; the dimming trunks sailed slowly past her. Beyond the tree nearest her front door stood a man.

He had halted near the stone pillars, staring back toward her car. He was staring at the car itself. He was walking toward it. He reached it as, struggling in vague panic, she managed to open her door.

"Miss Clare Frayn?" he said. "I wonder if I can have a word with you?"

He must have been six feet tall. He was broad as well, big-boned. He towered above the car; the pale blue of his suit seemed to fill the whole of her window. His hand closed on the door handle. Red hair sprang up as his wrist emerged from his sleeve; red hair sprouted from his fingers. She could imagine him winning a wrestling match with the power of that arm alone. For a moment she thought he was going to trap her in the car. Then he was opening the door for her.

"I'm sorry. Did I startle you?" he said. "I didn't mean to."

Perhaps he wasn't a policeman, after all. She snatched the key from the ignition and hurried toward her front door, fumbling with the key ring. She heard him slam the car door tight. The key. Not that one, fool.

With two strides he was beside her on the stone steps of the shadowy porch. "You are Miss Frayn, aren't you?"

The key. Got it. She was angry with herself for having left Ringo at his mercy. "What if I am?"

"I'd like to talk to you."

"That depends very much on the subject, I'm afraid."

"Well, of course it does. But look, are you all right? You seem worried."

"I'm perfectly all right, thank you. What exactly do you want?"

"I was wondering if you would help me. I'm a writer."

She turned to examine him. His face was large, well-fed, blue-eyed, wide-mouthed, bespectacled. He looked earnest and hopeful, though behind that she thought he was faintly amused. The bridge of his disproportionately small nose was dented, as if someone had once broken through his guard. Beneath the neat, discreetly fashionable suit he wore a mauve shirt and tie; the tie was fastened with a tiny platinum dagger, and the shirt bore a motif of minute pistols. He was about thirty. He didn't look like a writer to her, but what did writers look like? "Here's my card," he said.

Against the glossy white, the black embossed letters said EDMUND HALL: RESEARCHER AND WRITER, and an address outside London, in Surrey. "Why should I be able to help you?" she said.

He glanced toward an open ground-floor window beside the porch. "Would you mind if we talked inside?" he said.

It was her landlord's window. She had her flat cheap, as a favour to her father. If the landlord heard her helping a writer he might think she could afford to pay more. "All right," she said. "If it doesn't take too long. I have a lot of work to do."

"I'll keep it brief," he said. His large voice boomed dully in the hall, among the filigreed mirrors, the vases of flowers. "Are you working tomorrow?"

"Not until next week. I'm a teacher."

"Yes, of course," he said gratefully, as if she'd helped him.

She was acutely conscious of him behind her on the stairs. No doubt as a writer he was noting everything about her. Well, she could walk gracefully if she tried. She climbed the stairs lightly; she strode across the landing straight-backed, with poise. "Do you teach your kids ballet?" Edmund Hall asked.

"No. Movement and drama, we do."

"Did you go to ballet lessons when you were a kid?"

"Yes, a few." As a teenager she'd used to pirouette when she was happy, until she'd heard herself called Stumpy-legs. "Why do you ask?" she said.

"It shows in the way you walk."

She turned from unlocking her flat to smile at him. "There, that's better," he said. "What was wrong with you before?"

"Nothing. You made me jump, that's all."

"I thought that was it. I am sorry," and he looked so: even his faint, lingering amusement seemed dampened.

"No, I shouldn't blame you. I just thought you were a policeman."

The flat was a mess. George the guitar and his music were sitting on one chair; the other chair was crowded with carrier bags full of spray cans and bottles—shampoo, lotion, disinfectant—which she'd cleared out of the bathroom that morning. The couch was a jumble of books and newspapers and letters, her sewing machine sat on the dining table, clothes lolled patiently on the dining chairs. He must be noting all this. Well, she couldn't help it. Let him take her as he found her. "Sit anywhere," she said. "Just put that stuff on the floor."

George thumped the carpet, his strings emitting a muffled protest within the canvas bag. Yes, Edmund Hall would love some instant coffee, if she had to go into the kitchen anyway. Was she sure he couldn't buy her dinner? Well, in that case he'd be out of her way before she ate.

She stirred sugar into his coffee and carried in the mugs. He laid aside a Merseyside tabloid as she entered. "Used to work for that lot," he said, slapping the newspaper. "Tell me. If I had been a policeman, why on earth should that have bothered you?"

"My brother was killed in a car crash while I was driving."

"Yes, I know. To be honest, that's why I'm here. But that's not a police matter, surely."

"It is if they decide to prosecute. They could get me for dangerous driving, or driving without due care and attention, at least."

"Haven't they let you off the hook yet? They need sorting out. I've got a few contacts; I'll see what I can do. God, that's typical. Wasting their time with the petty crimes and the innocent. If I can see you're innocent, they can."

He almost convinced her, he seemed so sure of himself. "You think I'm innocent?"

"I know you are. I only wish I were a policeman. Believe me, I'd hunt down the man who killed your brother."

For a moment she didn't understand. Then she remembered the inquest, remembered the other driver swearing that her crash had been the fault of the madman who'd walked in front of her. But Edmund Hall meant more than that; she could hear more in his voice. "Which man?" she demanded.

"The man who made you crash, and who did," he gazed at

her with a kind of furious sympathy, "what he did to your brother afterwards. I know there's such a man, perhaps even better than you do. Because I've met him."

She stared at him. He gazed back at her, frowning slightly as if unsure she'd understood. Of course she had. He meant that after the man had caused the crash, he'd—when he'd stooped by the lamp standard, he'd—no, it was too ridiculous to think about, or too horrible, or both. It was up to the police to find out what had happened; it would do no good for her to think about it. Now here was Edmund Hall, saying it out loud. One thing was certain: she wouldn't react like a wilting female, not like Dorothy. Just give her a minute to prepare herself. "Excuse me a moment," she said distractedly, heading for the kitchen. "My vegetables."

A saucepan lid chattered nervously beneath her hand. She turned on the gas for the vegetables, then stood unnecessarily watching them. She was realizing that she might not want to hear what Edmund Hall had to say. At last she ventured back into the living room.

"I want to be completely open with you," he said. "First, I want you to know exactly why I'm here. I write books about crime."

"Hence the shirt," she said, gazing at the reiterated pistols. She was both impatient with the change of subject and glad of it: mostly glad, she thought.

"You may have read some of my books," he said. "I wrote a series first, that everybody liked. *Secrets of the Psychopaths.*"

"No, I haven't, I'm afraid," she said, pacing restlessly. She'd abandoned her gracefulness and was stumping glumly, because she'd caught him glancing about the room, taking mental notes; she couldn't fool him, he was a writer. She was damned if she was going to bother trying.

"*The Homicidal Heart?*" he demanded, with an air of faint disbelief. "*Sinister Sirens?*"

27

"No, I don't think so." Perhaps he was glancing about for the bookcase, like a too-polite child looking surreptitiously for the toilet.

"Love Has Many Weapons?"

"Oh yes. At least, someone told me that was good. I've been meaning to read it," she said, to forestall further embarrassment. Let's get to the point. She plonked herself down on the couch. "You were going to tell me about this man you'd met," she said.

"I will. But first I want you to understand my motives, Miss Frayn."

"Call me Clare, for heaven's sake," she said. "You're making yourself sound like a criminal."

"Call me Ted. The trouble is, some people don't like the way a writer has to work. Their attitude gets to me sometimes." He sat forward. "I've sold the idea of a book," he said. "It could be a bestseller. It'll have a damn good publisher, and one of the Sunday papers wants it as a serial. It's to be about how the man who killed your brother was caught, written almost as it happens. There's never been a book like this one's going to be. I can write it with your help."

"How can I help?" she said, not at all sure that she wanted to give him Rob to use in a book with a title like those he'd mentioned.

"Well, do you remember what the man who killed your brother looked like? Average height, I see. Not as tall as me, then? Don't worry, nobody could expect you to be certain in the circumstances. What about his clothes?"

"I thought you were supposed to have met him."

"Yes, but years ago. I'll tell you about that in a moment. You can't remember anything at all specific? Never mind. Still, you never know what you may have noticed that might come back to you. That could be one way you'd help me, but if you can't, it doesn't matter. Also, if I can be a bit cheeky, I wondered if you'd be able to help me investigate a little. A woman might spot things I'd miss, you see. Besides, there might be sources of information you'd know that I wouldn't. All that is no reason for you to help, of course. But it struck me you might want to help catch the man who killed your brother."

Of course she would. If there really were a man who had done all that to Rob, then he would be the guilty one, not Clare. But there was something missing from Edmund's sales talk. Yes. "Isn't it up to the police to catch him?" she said.

"Yes, it is, and they will. But they won't want us tagging along while they do so. Don't get the idea I want us to arrest the man. All we're going to try to do is track him down and tell them. But, generally speaking, the police here won't help me, and I don't intend to help them at my own expense. I shouldn't think you're too fond of them yourself. Let me reassure you on one thing, though. This man doesn't kill, so we're not putting anyone at risk by keeping away from the police. I'm sure he didn't mean to kill your brother, though he certainly meant to do what he did afterward. So I've no qualms about keeping quiet. You see, I have information the police don't have."

He waited until she said, "What information is that?"

"I'll tell you. Just one more thing." My God, she thought, he's a writer all right. He's making sure the suspense is killing. "Tell me honestly," he said, "does the thought of my making money out of this offend you?"

"No, I don't think so. It's your job. Now come on, Edmund." She'd call him Ted when she was more sure of him. She sat forward, prepared at last. "What exactly do you know? What is this man like?"

"He wasn't a man when I knew him. He was about eleven years old," he said. "I was in my last year at school. Both of us went to St. Joseph's in Mulgrave Street. You know Mulgrave Street, off Princes Avenue by the statue of Christ—of course you do, sorry. I didn't make grammar school—not quite good enough in the exams. I lived a few miles away, in Aigburth, but my folks had heard St. Joseph's was a good school. Besides, we were right in the middle-class prejudice belt in Aigburth; they didn't want me learning it at school too. So they dumped me in working-class prejudice instead. Still, it helped me to learn about people.

"Now, I must have seen this lad around the school for years without noticing him. Six years, if he was eleven. But you know how boys are—someone that much younger was beneath my notice. Then one day I did notice him, on the bus to town one Saturday.

"He got on a few stops before Mulgrave Street. I had the impression he lived near the school; maybe he'd been visiting a friend—he had a lot of friends, though I never spotted any really close ones. I was sitting at the front of the upper deck, and he sat a few seats behind me. I was trying to think where I'd seen him before. There was one of those mirrors above my head, that the driver uses in a kind of periscope to see upstairs. So I looked at this lad in the mirror, trying to place him. He didn't see me looking. The bus was just coming up to Mulgrave Street when his expression changed."

He leaned forward at Clare, gripping his knees; she sat back involuntarily. "I've tried to describe that expression for years," he said. "You've seen lads of that age. There he was, picking his nose while nobody was watching, staring out the window, looking a bit aimless and bored. And all of a sudden, just as we came to Mulgrave Street, this other expression came welling up—welling up, and I don't care if this sounds melodramatic, like poison. It was the unhealthiest look of anticipation I've ever seen in my life.

"But that doesn't make you even begin to see it. He looked eager, dreadfully eager, to do something he wanted to keep secret even from himself. He looked apprehensive and somehow secretly delighted all at once. His eyes were shifting about as if he were afraid to see himself, and he was licking his lips, really, licking his lips. He didn't look that way long. We were only a few blocks past Mulgrave Street when the expression went back into him. But believe me, it was hotter than today, yet it took me a while to get warm again. And he had that expression at the spot where your brother was killed."

He was gazing at her. "Well, that's strange," Clare said, "but even so—"

"Oh, that isn't all. That was only what made me begin watching him. And you know, that look was there most of the time. Not as blatant as that, obviously. But it was there, a kind of tension and anticipation. He was waiting for something.

"Now, I never thought it related to the school. School doesn't make kids look like that. Once or twice the expression looked as if it might surface. I pointed it out to some of my friends, but all they could think of was he'd left his glasses at home, his eyes were strained. But he never wore glasses. I'd found out that about him, and his name, Christopher Kelly. Nobody else seemed to see what I saw in his face. I began to get as tense as he looked, with waiting.

"The first thing that happened was the cat. This cat lived in one of the houses opposite the school, or it may have been a stray that begged its meals round there. It used to come and howl outside the playground, and we'd feed it when the masters weren't looking. We were trying to entice it in to have it off with the school cat, though I don't think anyone was even sure what sex it was.

"One day it got run over. Someone was waving a sandwich at it through the railings, and it came straight across the road and under a car. The driver just left it twitching in the middle of the road. Most of the younger boys were terribly upset. Most of the older ones too, though we tried not to show it. But not Kelly.

"He stood and watched that cat twitch and die. And then he held on to the railings and watched the dead cat. I think he'd have stood there all day if a master hadn't made him leave off. As it was, he must have stood there for ten minutes, because the masters were busy cheering people up. When they took the cat away he was still trying to see, past everyone else who was trying not to hear the shovel scraping it up."

He squirmed a little at the memory, but his amusement was less faint now: Clare could see he enjoyed storytelling. "That wouldn't have been much by itself," he said. "I mean, he was a nasty morbid child, but nothing that could bring me back to Liverpool this way. But there was something else. What he did to the school bully."

Clare felt herself grow tense. This was what had brought Edmund to see her. He was about to give form to the figure which had loomed up through the orange glow, peering in at her.

"The bully's name was Cyril," Edmund said. "With a name like that, perhaps he had to be a bully. He was in my year, but he behaved years younger. He was a big lout, though. He picked a fight with me once, I think because someone had dared him. He got in a couple of good ones before I knocked him down," and he tapped the dent in his nose.

"He had to pick on Kelly sooner or later. Kelly was a fat boy, you see. Now the whole school had one playground, juniors and seniors together. It was supposed to make the older boys take responsibility for the younger. But most of the time you got the older ones bullying the younger or feeling them up, and those of us who didn't tended not to interfere. So it meant that Cyril could follow Kelly around the playground every day, calling him Billy Bunter, Fatty Arbuckle, trying to nudge him into a fight.

"Now Cyril was a butcher's son. He always used to smell of raw meat, him and his clothes. When he was younger we made fun of that, holding our noses, you know. That probably helped make him a bully.

"Well, I wanted to see what Kelly would do, you can imagine. I followed them all over the playground. Cyril kept it up for a week at least. Until one very hot day, when he smelled like a butcher's all by himself. And Kelly turned on him. Cyril had said something, 'You look like a tub of lard,' something like that. And just as if he were answering a remark, Kelly looked at him and said, 'You stink.'

"That was odd, you know. Kids aren't that unemotional. He looked just as if he'd had the thought and said it. Of course Cyril thought he'd got his fight at last. So he said, 'You what?'

" 'You stink,' Kelly said.

"Well, Cyril brought his arm back to belt him across the mouth. He'd flung his jacket off, and Kelly must have got the whole of that butcher's smell. And I saw that expression come rushing into his eyes. I think I might even have warned Cyril, if there'd been time.

"You've seen kids fight. Girls fight worse than boys, they tell me. But you haven't seen anything like this. Cyril never managed to hit him at all. Because Kelly went straight under his guard and fastened his teeth in his upper arm, just above the elbow.

"And he wouldn't let go. Cyril tore at his hair and clawed his face, but he wouldn't let go. They must have been able to hear Cyril screaming in the school, because half the masters came running. The one on playground duty was strolling about with a book, but he threw that book away and ran over so fast he knocked someone down. But even he couldn't get Kelly to let go, not until he dragged him off. When he did, Kelly took a piece of Cyril's arm with him."

He searched Clare's face for horror. She was wondering how she would have coped if it had happened at her school. "The worst thing," he said, "which I think you need to hear to understand, is that when he'd dragged him off, the master had to hold Kelly's nose and take hold of his jaw to force him to open his mouth."

"God," she said. "Poor kid." She realized she meant both of them.

"Kelly's mother came to the school that afternoon," he said.

"If she was his mother—she was pretty old. A woman, anyway. Our classroom was opposite the headmaster's study. My desk was by the window. I could see Kelly and the head sitting in there, waiting. Then the woman and Kelly's class teacher came in. The head had told us to close all the windows, so we couldn't hear. But we could see him telling her what had happened. Then she began to tell him something.

"I don't know what that was. But I saw the effect it had on the class teacher. They'd moved Kelly to the back of the room, where I couldn't see him, and the head was out of sight round the window. But that teacher—I've never seen anyone so crippled with horror. He just stood there going white. The woman was pointing her thumb back at Kelly as if she couldn't bear to look at him, and the teacher was staring back at him as if he were trying to feel pity but couldn't get through the horror. He was off school for weeks after that, that teacher. He was always fond of his kids."

What could a child of eleven have done, so to affect a teacher who was fond of him? Clare felt the horror now, close to her amid the murmur of the evening. Suppose it had been one of her class—what could be so horrible about a child? "Didn't you ever find out what she'd said?" Her voice shook before she could take hold of it.

"Never. That was his last day at that school, you see. Oddly enough, he moved to a school near where I lived. And I left school for good a month later. I saw him once or twice on buses. In fact, it was wondering what there was in his past to make him behave as he had that got me interested in the kind of thing I write about. But when I saw him on the buses, that expression of his had gone. I thought the business with Cyril must have cured him. Now I'm sure he was simply biding his time."

Clare stared behind her at the open window, at the murmuring dark. He was somewhere out there. He had leaned toward her in the orange light, peering, hurrying back to the lamp standard in the mirror and stooping. "You've got all that written down, haven't you?" she said harshly. He couldn't have Rob to use in his glib storytelling.

"Does it show? I'm sorry if I seemed unfeeling. I've had twelve years to think about it, remember. I send off the chapters as soon as they're written, in case they want revisions." He was searching her face anxiously; his nose twitched. "As you say, it's my job," he said. "I told you this in all good faith. You know his name now, which is more than the police do. I can't stop you telling them."

He looked like a child confronted with betrayal. "Of course I won't tell them," she said impatiently.

"Then you'll help me? It isn't only for my book. He needs to be caught for his own sake as much as anyone's."

"I don't know." All right, she was wrong to condemn him for doing his job: she was still uneasy. The spell of his story was wearing off, and she knew that something had been missing. "I see how all you've said fits together," she said. "But I can't see why you're sure he was the man who killed my brother. I can't see how you can have been sure enough to come down from London."

"Because of your brother? That wouldn't have brought me by itself," he said. "Don't you read the papers?"

"I buy them mostly for the crosswords. Why?"

"Because your crash wasn't the only thing. There was an old lady and her dog, nearly four weeks ago."

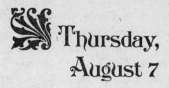# Thursday, August 7

He was lying in the earth.

There was a house on top of him.

He was gazing down at the earth beneath which he lay. He began to dig. He had to find himself, beneath the moist sucking earth and the wriggling insects. He felt the dark, still house alert above him, behind his back, and dug faster in panic, spitting out mouthfuls of earth. He could feel himself coming closer, coming up out of the earth. When he saw himself, the two of himself would be one. He forced his face deeper into the earth, seeking impatiently.

The man awoke snarling. He lay in the dark for a moment, then snatched at the light. He didn't like lying in the dark. It was too much like lying in earth. He lay trying to subdue his heart.

He wouldn't be able to sleep again. He never could, after the dream. Somewhere a bell tolled four in the morning. He laughed, a mirthless grunt. He didn't need to be told. That was always the time of the dream.

He went to the window, but darkness lay thick as mud in the backyards; a dim glow crawled on the houses. He closed the window and drew the curtains, but the flat was already too hot. When he tried to read he was constantly aware of the dark beyond the curtains, sucking him down.

The book struck the wall and fell, broken-winged. He thrust himself into some old drab clothes, which always felt right for this hour. He had nearly slammed the door of the flat when he caught the handle and eased it quietly shut. Then he tiptoed downstairs and out of the house. He would have used the fire escape outside his window if it hadn't been for the dark in the yard.

The inert sodium light hung about him. The gravel beneath the trees squealed underfoot. A breeze touched him, but the light never moved. He had to reach somewhere, or flee somewhere. Of course he knew where. Abreast of Mulgrave Street he halted, staring past Christ posed like a starving diver on the wall.

He wasn't going there. Whatever was up that street, he wasn't going. It was pulling at him, pulling him into the desire to cross the carriageway and walk up the deserted street among the windowless houses, pulling him into a tiny intense point of impulse, stretching him as if through a pinprick in darkness. He felt it pulling every time he passed the street. But it was worse now; it felt like the time he'd eaten dope. He climbed back out of himself in panic, grabbing at the orange light, the breeze, the trees along the central reservation, the squeaking gravel.

The gravel. The gravel had squeaked as he'd walked across toward Mulgrave Street, moments before the car had come hurtling at him. He heard the car thud against the lamp standard, the scattering of glass. He saw the car thump the tree, the dark eye-catching splash of blood. He turned his back on Mulgrave Street and began to hurry toward North Hill Street, opposite.

It was all right. He hadn't hurt anyone, after all. The crash hadn't been his fault. He had been preoccupied. What he had done afterward hurt nobody. He walked past shuttered corner shops, past the dark open mouths of a launderette, their lids ajar. Beneath the flat hats of the lampposts hung conical drops of cold white light.

This was no good. He was simply becoming more restless. His mind was shifting uneasily, snatching feebly at passing thoughts, vainly searching the deserted street for something to grasp. He hurried into one of the side terraces of little two-bedroomed houses. The houses were closer; he might feel less isolated. They must have outside toilets, like his childhood home.

Beneath the white glare of the streetlamps, curtains hung faded, dead. Between the lamps the houses lay under shadow like dusty glass. The icy light stood close to him; he felt all the more isolated. His footsteps tapped on the still houses.

He emerged onto High Park Street. It was wider, and emptier. Even the sodium glow of Princes Road at the end seemed more welcoming. He hurried toward the orange carriageway. Beyond the trees he saw a disused church, its blackened rose window like a fossilized plant behind barbed wire.

To his right, beyond the locked gates of Princes Park, ducks squawked amid the mud and litter of the lake. Otherwise, everything was silent, even the carriageway. He stood on the pavement of Princes Road. Opposite him, across the reservation, Princes Avenue led out of the city; the two halves of the dual carriageway bore different names. Somehow it reminded him of himself. He laughed, almost snarling.

He walked along the reservation, back toward his flat. The trees creaked stealthily in a breeze. He would have to pass Mulgrave Street again. During the day it didn't matter, but at this hour it made him feel helpless. Already it was pulling at him.

He couldn't stand the silence, nor the trees, whispering around him like visitors at a sick-bed. He began to kick at the gravel and to roar wordlessly. He hoped he was waking people up; if someone looked out to protest, he would be less alone.

No, nothing less than a crash or a car theft would bring them to their windows. If they were listening, no doubt they thought he was drunk.

He was a block from Mulgrave Street when he saw the face at the ground-floor window.

It was laughing at him. It had come to the window to jeer. The wide mouth in the flat, drooping, almost noseless face hung open; the pink tongue lolled out, shaking; the small eyes stared at him. He had to cross to the pavement before he made out that it was a bulldog.

He stared at it, over the garden into which someone had hurled a stray brick at a flower. The dog panted at him, dribbling; its claws scraped in the crack beneath the just-open sash. He felt a rush of pure cold hatred. The flat dripping face and wobbling fat body were unbearable. It shouldn't be there in the window, jeering at him.

He opened the gate slowly, minutely. Then he began to creep toward the window, hardly moving at all. He no longer felt the pull toward Mulgrave Street. It took him minutes to stoop to the flowerbed. As he straightened up the dog growled softly.

He crept across the lawn, placing his feet delicately, silently. The dog kept glancing away from his gaze, shaking its head. Its low growl grew louder, never faltering. It was gathering itself to bark as he threw up the sash and smashed its face with the brick.

He gazed down over the sill. His actions already felt like a memory. The dog lay twitching on the Persian carpet, fat and raw; its blood added to the pattern. When it had died he glanced behind him. Trees and orange lamps queued both ways along the deserted carriageway. Quickly he climbed into the room.

He heard the old woman almost at once.

"Rex?" she was calling. "Rex?" She was just beyond the door ahead of him. He heard a bed creak as she stood up.

Slippered feet shuffled toward the door. He had heard how her voice wavered. There was no need for him to run.

When she switched on the light it seemed to freeze her, like a flashbulb. She stared at him, her mouth and eyes gaping. Then she stumbled forward, one hand clawing viciously toward him. She gave a wordless furious shriek. She had taken two steps when her face squeezed tight with pain and she doubled over as if a hook had caught her heart. He gazed at her as she fell. He might have spoken, but his mouth was full.

He listened to the silence of the house. Then he went over to her. She was dead, no doubt of that; he could tell by the way her arm flopped on the carpet when he let it go, the way her head rolled when he pushed at her cheeks. He squatted beside her, pondering the way the wrinkles of her face seemed looser now.

He stepped over the dog and peered out of the window. Still there was no sound or movement on the carriageway. He thought of switching off the light. No: fingerprints. He had one foot on the sill when he turned and stared at the old woman's body. After a moment he reached out and drew the curtains tight. Then he went back across the room.

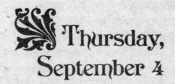

Thursday, September 4

"There's a Mr. Edmund Hall and a lady to see you," Mrs. Freeman said.

"All right, all right," George Pugh said irritably. "Tell them I'm coming in a minute, will you?"

He gazed over the stalls at the screen. Ryan O'Neal and the girl with the boxer's name gazed at each other, in love; a long hair danced between them, trying to get out of their way. A giant purple thumb groped along the bottom of the screen, trying to tweak away the hair; faint cheers from the front stalls urged it on. The lovers gazed, oblivious of the struggle. The hair leapt off the screen; its tip waved a defiant farewell from the edge. Its fans in the front stalls applauded.

George Pugh mopped his forehead. This new projectionist, Bill Williams, was worse than his predecessor: no experience, and slow to learn. The experienced men went to the theatres that were secured by distribution chains. Independents such as the Newsham had to make do with what they could get.

And we will, George thought. His mother had, with worse staff, in their second cinema. All her days had been as hectic as the one he'd had today. He shook his head, admiring her. Today—first he'd had the list of all the confectionery prices that should have been increased on Monday. He'd had to calm down Mrs. Freeman and work out the increases with her; she still wasn't happy with decimal coinage. Then next week's posters had come in, misprinted. He'd been half the afternoon trying to convince someone at the printer's, a dimwit he'd never spoken to before. "One woe doth tread upon another's heel," he thought, remembering *Hamlet*.

This fellow Edmund Hall had rung up that morning. He was a writer in need of help for his new book. "I'd prefer not to say more until I see you." If he was really a salesman he'd get a kick where it would do the most good. George would have put him off once the woes had started treading, but hadn't known where to reach him. He supposed he'd best see what the fellow wanted. The girl on the screen was dying prettily; he'd be able to lock up soon. There seemed to be nothing but death in the last few films he'd shown.

Mrs. Freeman was chatting to a friend as she counted the confectionery takings. No wonder she had to do her sums again so often. "He just bit my head off," she was saying. "That's nothing new. I think he's just using his mother's death as an excuse."

She was talking about him. "When you've finished that," he said coldly, "tell Mr. Williams to come in at eleven tomorrow so I can talk to him." She gazed at him, horrified that he'd heard, as he strode toward the man and woman waiting by the doors.

The man was tall, broad, red-haired; he looked very sure of himself. She was a young woman, about twenty-five, five feet tall or so, rather petite. Her legs were a little short, but shapely. She wore a smart blue cardigan over a faded summer dress, as if she'd determined to be smart at the last moment, too late. Her brown hair was cut very close, as if she'd wanted to forget about it; her small face looked timidly mischievous, rather afraid of being itself. It reminded George of his daughter Olivia in her first days at school. If she was applying for a job he'd be disposed in her favour so far. Now they were turning toward him.

"Mr. Pugh?" the man said. "I'm Edmund Hall. This is Clare. She's helping me."

Mr. Pugh's dark suit was sharply pressed but paler than when new; one button on his shirt pretended to be like the others. Clare could imagine him as a schoolboy, his loose-limbed frame squeezed awkwardly into a desk, his stook of hastily parted auburn hair standing among the heads, his long, somewhat horsy face gazing up at her, not down as now. He blinked through his horn-rimmed spectacles, squinting impatiently at Edmund as he might have squinted at a blackboard. The lines of strain which overlaid his young face were fifty years old, maybe more.

"What can I do for you?" he asked Edmund.

He glanced at Edmund's card as if it were an unnecessary distraction. "Shall we talk in your office?" Edmund said.

"I've got to see the building cleared. What did you want?"

"Two things. I want to write a book, with your help. And I want to help catch the man who caused your mother's death."

Girls were emerging from the stalls, dabbing self-consciously at their eye makeup. "Did you enjoy the show? Good night," Mr. Pugh said. "You want to write about the man who killed my mother, do you? Killed her," he repeated savagely. "Not 'caused her death.' "

"It was a terrible business, Mr. Pugh, I agree. But I don't think he actually murdered her, did he? I understood she died of heart failure."

"Then you know more than the coroner. The inquest isn't until tomorrow."

Several young girls with fingernails like spatulas of silver

43

plastic ran out of the stalls, pursued by a waft of the national anthem. "You've got an urgent date, have you?" Mr. Pugh said. "Betty and Anne and Linda. And I'm surprised at you, Andrea. Have a bit more respect next time, or you don't come in here again."

Edmund said, "I understood there weren't any marks of fatal violence on the lady. Please don't think I'm trying to defend the man in any way. I'm as anxious to see him caught as you are."

"Good night, Mrs. Dodd. No, I agree that word wasn't necessary, but of course we can't interfere with the films. Did you enjoy it, Mrs. Kearney? Better than last week's? Good. Good night." Clare was expecting the rest of the crowd when the front doors swung back squeaking behind the last. "Why?" Mr. Pugh demanded of Edmund.

"Why—"

"You know what I mean well enough. Why do you want him caught?"

"Because I believe society must be protected. I say so in all my books. We must consider the victims first, not the criminals. And even more important, the potential victims."

Mr. Pugh was heading for the stalls; they hurried to follow him. "Bring that to the office when you've finished," he said to the lady counting money in the kiosk, and straightened her tiers of chocolate bars—unnecessarily, Clare thought. He held the stalls door open with one foot for the duration of a stride; Edmund had to run to take advantage.

"You've had books published, have you? Such as what?"

Edmund listed them. His voice returned muffled down the long narrow auditorium, with a kind of frustrated echo. The single slope of seats was dim; above it a spread of tobacco smoke drifted reluctantly away, toward the ventilation. At the screen, curtains twitched and fidgeted, rattling; the projectionist peered through his window, trying to settle them. Mr. Pugh tugged vigorously at the chains of the exit doors. "You're not telling me you're protecting society with books like those," he said.

Clare realized how easily she had let Edmund persuade her; he had no room for faint amusement now. She felt wickedly pleased. "With respect," he said, "you haven't read them. They've been praised by criminologists."

"Experts," Mr. Pugh cursed.

They emerged from the stalls as he hurried into his office. Clare heard the lady from the kiosk saying, "I'm sorry, Mr. Pugh. I didn't mean what I said. It was a dreadful thing to say."

"All right, Mrs. Freeman. Thank you for waiting."

A few of the lines on his face had softened. Clare saw Edmund note that too. Edmund motioned her to the vacant chair, then stood gazing down at Mr. Pugh across the desk. "In my own defence," he said, "I must say nobody has ever accused my books of inciting crime. Not like some of the films nowadays. Aren't there some films you wish you didn't have to show?"

"Of course there are." He checked the lady's calculations rapidly. "But they're what the public wants these days. You can't go against the public."

"Well, that's it. You show them because it's your job."

"That's right. My job," he said, locking the safe. " 'There's place and means for every man alive.' Isn't that right?"

"Sorry?"

"*All's Well That Ends Well*. We can all see what my job is." He glanced sharply at Edmund. "But I still don't know what job you think you're doing."

"I believe I'm helping people understand what makes a criminal. And I think that may help prevent crime."

"Understand?" His voice boomed in the small office; Clare started. "You want me to understand that animal? You want me to understand the man who could do that to an old lady?"

"I know exactly how you feel. If it had been my mother I'd want to meet the man who did it face to face."

"But it wasn't your mother, so you write about it. I don't want to catch him. I wouldn't trust myself. It's the job of the police to catch him. You help them if you want to protect society so much."

"We will be helping them, by pursuing an independent line of enquiry. We'll tell them as soon as we have something worth telling. But I have to make a living too, you know. I don't always like what I have to do—you should be able to appreciate that. I have my job to do, just as you do."

Mr. Pugh squeezed his bottom lip forward thickly, shaking his head. He reached for the phone and dialled. "Yes, it's me, dear," he said. "In fifteen minutes. Bye-bye now, dear. Bye-bye." It was clearly a ritual. "Sounds as if you're doing everybody's job to me," he told Edmund. "Coroner, detective, God knows what. Just tell me this: what made you pick on my mother?"

He was tidying his desk, though it was neat already. "It wasn't only your mother," Edmund said. "There was another incident, just as tragic. Someone caused a car crash almost outside where your mother lived. We're sure it was the same man."

Mr. Pugh held open the front doors of the cinema for them, and switched off the lights. "Yes, my mother mentioned it," he said. "I'm sorry someone was killed. But I'll lose no sleep over a car crash." He gestured at the cars hurtling by beneath the sodium lights of West Derby Road. "Let the buggers—excuse me, my dear—let the drivers kill each other off. The air might be a bit cleaner. The sooner they have to use bicycles the better."

Clare watched Edmund timing his move exactly. He waited for Mr. Pugh to lock the doors and turn before he said, "Clare was the driver in that crash. Her brother was killed."

Mr. Pugh swung around to her; his face was the face of a schoolboy who had betrayed his awkwardness and youth. "My dear, I am sorry," he said. "I wouldn't have upset you for the world. I won't try to excuse myself. But I'm under a bit of a strain at the moment, as I suppose you are, my dear."

"Don't worry. I know what you must be going through. You can call me Clare if you like," she said, as a token of forgiveness.

He smiled but withdrew a little; she knew he wanted to escape them, to hurry home. "My name's George," he said, rather unwillingly.

"Like my guitar." She smiled at his puzzled frown. "I've a guitar called George," she said. She thought he looked faintly insulted. "He's a very good guitar," she said reassuringly.

His frown was fading, and she was about to say, "We mustn't keep you," when Edmund said, "Perhaps you'll let Clare tell you the background to this business."

He'd told her she might be able to help him with Mr. Pugh; now she saw how. "What background?" George said.

"The history of the man who killed your mother."

"I'm walking home through the park," George said discouragingly.

"We'll walk along with you, if we may."

"Suit yourself." George hurried away beneath the railway bridge beside the Newsham; a train went over like thunder.

Clare was about to protest when Edmund said, "Please, Clare. It'll come better from you. You said yourself it sounds just like a story when I tell it. If George still doesn't want to help then, we won't need to bother him further."

"I don't want to bother him at all," she said, resounding from the bridge.

Abruptly George turned back to them. "Go on, Clare," he said. "Tell me if he wants you to. I suppose I ought to know, since you do."

Beyond the bridge and the police station lay the park. The

sodium glow drained from George's back; Clare hurried to overtake him. Overhead opened the deep blue sky, hung with large white clouds almost as still as the small clear new moon.

George left the park road for the main walk through the trees. The tall windows of the Park Hospital blazed; the lake stretched their lights into thick pillars, supporting a slab of darkness on which the hospital rested. "Building up the suspense?" George said. "Are you a writer as well?"

"No, a teacher. Sorry, I was thinking how to start. The man we're after," she said, "we think he used to go to St. Joseph's School in Mulgrave Street. It was supposed to be quite a good school in its day. But now they're pulling all the houses down round there."

A duck jeered raucously on the lake, flapping its wings like a wet coat. There was no need to put off what she had to tell. It was only like telling the kids a story. It should be easier, since the policeman had been to question her today about the man who'd caused the accident. He'd looked uneasy, as if he hoped she wouldn't ask his reasons. She'd realized they had connected Rob's death with George's mother's. She had begun to feel someone else might be guilty instead of her, after all. He was finding out for her whether they intended to prosecute. "There was something obviously wrong with the boy before he did anything," she said, and glanced at Edmund as if he should have noticed.

As she talked George glanced about constantly, at the trees. She looked, and saw what perhaps he was seeing: great feathers against the sky, conical leafy beehives as high as a house, swelling billows like smoke from a factory chimney, a bent old man scratching his armpit beneath a covering of shaggy lumps of dust. Beneath she could make out the winter patterns, thick vertical piping, candelabras sprouting candelabras sprouting candelabras, intricate webs of twigs gliding over one another and changing, all standing still against the sky—until a branch stood still almost into her face and she slipped on a twig. He must walk home this way every night, looking at the trees.

"He sat on the bus with this absolutely horrible look of anticipation," she said. The story was reaching for her; she glanced about uneasily. Three tower blocks twenty-two storeys high squatted together close as witches on the far side of the green, beyond the trees. Light leaked from scattered windows, diluting each block grey as mist; the huge threatening shapes dissolved luminously into the sky. She thought of Dorothy, gazing down.

"And this boy Cyril kept on teasing him. That may have been what pushed him over the edge." Behind her rationalization the luridly orange face loomed toward her. Toward the tower blocks, beneath foliage that glowed dimly like sprouting clouds, an owl called plaintively; George glanced toward it. Perhaps he was an amateur naturalist; perhaps that was why he walked through the park.

They passed a shuttered kiosk, its green paint raw with slashes of red graffiti. A man came striding round it, nearly knocking Clare down, snarling, "I know what I mean, don't I?" to nobody. George caught her elbow, steadying her.

"She sat with her back to him and told the headmaster about him. She wouldn't even look at him. Have you any children? I thought so. Could you do that to one of yours?" But she hated herself for dreading, deep in her mind, that the woman might have had a reason.

They walked around the stone rim of a pond; the water sounded as if it were discovering that it had blubbery lips. Trails from streetlamps shivered in the pond; shadows of branches lay still along the trails of light. A few ducks floated, as if in a bath. Clare felt Edmund pacing behind her and George, like a chaperon.

"And after he'd caused the accident," she said, "he stole part of my brother's body." This part was more like a story, she'd heard it so many times. Suddenly, as she became more conscious of Edmund, she wondered why he was so anxious to involve George.

George's spectacles blinked as a car went by on the park road. He was looking at her for the first time since she'd begun. He hadn't really wanted to hear at all. Why had Edmund made her trouble him? It must be a masculinity thing. Because George had been difficult, Edmund was determined to overcome him, to give himself a sense of power.

"I'm sorry about your brother. At least you weren't hurt. No, I go this way," George said as she continued walking forward.

Clare looked where he was pointing. If he lived near the tower blocks, why had he come the longest way through the park? She gazed, bewildered, at the long dark curve of houses surrounding the green. She gazed at the streetlamps planted widely along the dark curve, each revealing part of a tiny house and sometimes of a tree: shrines of light, mysterious and calm. Calm. At once she knew why George had wanted to walk alone through the park on the night before the inquest on his mother.

Edmund was strolling toward George. She said, "There's one other thing we know. The boy's name was Christopher Kelly." She would have liked to grin viciously at Edmund. "Even the police don't know that," she said.

"He's certain to have changed his name," Edmund said hastily.

"The police still ought to know," George said.

"We can follow it up as quickly as they can. We've agreed not to tell them until we've finished our enquiries," Edmund said, glaring toward Clare, who was hiding in the shadows near the pond and feeling as she might if she'd distracted the villain in a wrestling match. "I ask you as a gentleman not to reveal what you've heard," Edmund said.

"I can't promise that. Why should I?"

"Because you won't be helping the police at all. You know

they're undermanned. If they have to put someone on our line of enquiry, they'll be taking him off something else. That's why we will be genuinely helping them." George was hesitating, gazing down the road like a runner anxious for the start. "At least think it over," Edmund said. "I can tell you aren't an impulsive man."

George said nothing. He wasn't going to win, Clare thought, disillusioned.

"Thank you for being so patient," Edmund said. "Perhaps I could have a word with you tomorrow. I'll be at the inquest. That is, if you don't mind."

"I can't stop you."

"You aren't forbidding me to be there, are you?"

Wearily George said, "No, I'm not forbidding you."

He hurried away down the empty gleaming road, beneath the crescent moon. Edmund began to walk back toward the Newsham, to their cars. Incredibly, he seemed triumphant. "I don't think he's the sort who'll tell," he said, and she could hear that he was forgiving her. "I don't think we've anything to worry about."

 Friday,
September 5

As George entered Castle Chambers he saw Edmund Hall on the stairs ahead of him.

He halted. He wouldn't go into the inquest with the man. All right, he had a job to do. Probably the boy's name would be more of a hindrance than a help to the police, a false trail. He wouldn't prevent Edmund from doing his job. That didn't mean he had to like the man.

As he entered the cream-coloured corridor off the landing he saw Edmund step through a doorway marked ENQUIRIES. George hurried past to the glass double doors outside the courtroom, but they were immovable, like false doors on a stage set. They added to the sense of unreality he was already beginning to feel. He'd never expected to visit such a place; he'd shown courtrooms in too many films. He retreated to the ENQUIRIES door.

At the end of an inner corridor was a waiting room for witnesses. A few people stood outside, smoking; inside sat a sobbing woman, rattling a cup of tea. George's mother's friend Ruby was comforting her, gazing at her with eyes that drowned in themselves, slapping her own heart as if to quicken its emotion. She was an actress, of course. That was how his mother had known her.

He stood outside the glass door. He didn't feel equal to Ruby's effusiveness today. As he stared at the lettering on the door he felt wholly unlike a witness—as if he'd undertaken the part without preparation. "All the world's a stage"—yes, yes, all right.

He had insisted on being a witness. He had to be there, to make sure nothing wrong was said about his mother. He only hoped the inquest wouldn't take long. Bill Williams had seemed to understand the projection this morning, but George wanted to be at the Newsham this afternoon, in case the projection went wrong again: he didn't want the children running riot.

"Will the witnesses take their places in court, please," a man said, very Scottish, and went to look after the sobbing woman.

The ceiling of the court was low. Ranks of benches and long tables stepped down on three sides of the room. Following the other witnesses to the furthest set of benches, George glimpsed Edmund leaning from the front bench opposite the coroner's dais to greet him. He walked by, unheeding.

Ruby pressed close to him on the bench. "Who's that lumberjack?" she demanded, nodding at Edmund. "Does he know you?"

"Just someone who's writing up the case." Half the people in Edmund's set of benches must be reporters: a full house. Well, they had their job to do.

"He wants to hear what happened, does he? I'll tell him. Your poor mother." She dabbed hastily at her smudged mascara, thick as makeup in an early film. "I'll never forget her face as long as I live. That terrible expression. Oh, I'm sorry. I shouldn't be saying all this to you, you poor boy."

She hadn't disturbed him particularly—too theatrical. Overhead, a chair scraped, and loud, flat footsteps crossed the ceiling. Fat mushrooms full of light sprouted from pale splashes on the ceiling. The splashes of light vanished; the lamps hung dead in sunlight. George watched Edmund glancing rapidly about, snapping up details like a camera.

Last night, walking home, George had remembered whom Edmund reminded him of: the man from the London cinema chain who had come to see him six years ago. The man had been staying with friends; he'd admired George's efficiency in running the Newsham with so little help, he'd said. George was the man they needed to run their new London cinema. But Olivia was happy in her first year at school, and Mark wanted to go to that school; George's wife, Alice, hated big cities, except for her birthplace, Liverpool; most important, the Newsham was the only cinema his mother now owned. The man had understood none of this. Leaving, he'd glared back as if George had wronged him deliberately. Beneath all Edmund's protestations of sympathy, George suspected, lay the same lack of feeling.

"Stand up, please," the Scotsman ordered.

George jumped up, startled. The rest followed him. After a pause the coroner strode in behind the jury and onto his dais: a good dramatic entrance. The Scotsman began to read from a card: "All manner of persons having anything to do at this court, before the Queen's Coroner for the county of Merseyside, touching the deaths of Lilian Pugh and Thomas Eric Hardy, draw near and give your attendance." Surely he'd rehearsed it often enough not to need the script, George thought—but the thought didn't dam the flood of shock he'd felt at the sound of his mother's name.

Everyone else was sitting down; George joined them. The Scotsman was leading the jury in the oath. "I swear by Almighty God—"

"I swur by Almighty God—" Only the front row of four men was responding, translating his Scottish accent into Liverpudlian. When he'd finished he began again with the back row. George almost expected all eight to go through a final rehearsal. But the coroner was speaking.

"We have first to consider the death of Mrs. Lilian Pugh, née Stanley, of 20 Princes Avenue. This is a very sad and tragic case, of a kind I have never met before. The police are investigating the circumstances. We are concerned only to determine the cause of the lady's death. At about four o'clock on the morning of seventh August, it appears that Mrs. Pugh surprised an intruder in an act of extreme cruelty to her dog."

His quiet voice continued. It was like the synopsis at the beginning of a serial episode. George was bewildered when he said, "I call George Bernard Pugh." Surely he'd covered George's part of the story in his synopsis. But the Scotsman was standing beside the witness box, waiting for him. "Take the book in your right hand," he said.

"Your name is George Bernard Pugh and you're the manager of the Newsham Cinema," the coroner said.

"Yes." He could swear to that.

"And Mrs. Lilian Pugh was your mother."

"Yes, she was," George said proudly, almost challengingly.

"She owned the Newsham, didn't she? Did she own any others?"

The coroner was putting him at his ease by chatting. "She used to own the Granby and the Picton, she and my father," he said. "But they closed in the sixties. The Granby closed last. That was just by where she was living. There were two cinemas there, and not enough audience for either." He was babbling; he wished the coroner would stop him with a question.

"Your father isn't alive now, is he?"

"No, he died seven years ago. The strain of knowing the cinemas would have to close killed him. That made my mother determined to keep the Newsham open. She was the business side of the marriage, you see."

"Quite right," the coroner said approvingly. "Quite right. Did your mother always live in Princes Avenue?"

"No, she moved there after my father's death." She'd said she had sold the house because she couldn't cope with it, but he had known she wanted the money to put into the Newsham, though he'd never let her realize.

"And did you often visit her there? Did you visit her on the night of sixth August?"

"Yes, I did." The jurymen were beginning to look away from him, dreading naked grief. But he felt that the coroner would lead him skilfully around that. He would be able to get back to the Newsham soon.

"I visited my mother, Mrs. Lilian Pugh, on the night of sixth August," the coroner said. That's odd, George thought: I didn't see you there. It took him a moment to notice the tape recorder to which the coroner was confiding information.

"At about what time did you leave? Midnight. Did you happen to notice whether the front window of the flat was open?"

"Yes. She often left it open a little in summer. Rex guarded it during the night."

"Rex was your mother's dog. When I left at midnight the front window was open a little, comma." By now George felt wholly detached from the proceedings. "Your mother wasn't afraid of intruders?"

"She said not." But he had been, on her behalf. Alice and he had had no room for his mother, but that hadn't made it easier to think of her on Princes Avenue, among the gangs and burglaries and racial confrontations.

The questions continued, and the echoes. Yes, his mother had had a couple of heart attacks—nothing serious, the doctor had said, provided she took it easy. No, she hadn't seemed unwell that night. Silently he remembered her saying, "Good night now, dear," turning carefully back toward the lighted hall, supporting herself with a hand on the doorknob, glancing back to make sure he was safe on his bicycle. He felt Edmund gazing intently at him—as if, he thought angrily, he had written the script.

"Do you know of anyone who might have had a grudge against your mother's dog?"

"No, nobody." The police had asked him that. "She would have told me," he said.

"Thank you very much, Mr. Pugh."

Was that all? It seemed to have petered out, like some of the films he had to show nowadays. The coroner was telling the tape recorder that he knew nobody with a grudge against his mother's dog. "I call Ruby Roberts," he said.

Ruby swept her coat about her like Caesar adjusting his cloak for an oration, and grasped the Bible, gazing up as if she were Joan of Arc yearning for a friendly voice. "Is Ruby Roberts your real name?" the coroner said.

"Yes," she said, eyes blazing. "It certainly is."

He nodded, smiling faintly. "And did you know the deceased Lilian Pugh? You knew her from the theatre, didn't you?"

Don't start on the theatre, George thought; we'll be here all day. "I knew her husband first," she said. "He was on the stage, of course, before he went into showing pictures. A fine actor, and a fine man. How he would have felt if he'd seen his poor wife there, on the floor—"

"All right now," the coroner said, holding up one finger. "We're coming to that now. You went to Mrs. Pugh's flat on the morning of seventh August?"

George switched them off. He felt almost disloyal listening to Ruby—it was like watching a play about his mother's death. But then everything about his mother's death had seemed theatrical: Ruby's telephone call to him, hinting breathlessly at horrors; even the sight of the body. At the morgue he'd waited in a small bare room. Suddenly the curtains at a window before him had parted, exactly like the opening of a first act, and there had been his mother, lying covered with a sheet beneath a cymbal-shaded bulb. He'd felt cut off from her by more than the glass. Once he and his parents had played a game to see who could feign death the longest. His mother had looked more convincing then. Behind the glass she'd looked like someone inexpertly made up to resemble her.

"She was lying on the carpet, covered with blood," Ruby said.

It must have ruined the carpet, then—his mother's favourite, the Persian. His mother's friend Mr. Billington, who had used to manage a cinema and who helped out at the Newsham for no more payment than the chance to watch films free, was sorting out everything at the flat. George hadn't been able to go there. But now he couldn't avoid hearing what Ruby had found there, what she'd held back from him.

"I could see they were bites," she said. "But that wasn't what turned me sick. It was the look on her face. She was looking at Rex, poor faithful beast." She leaned toward the jury and said in a whisper that filled the court: "She died of knowing that what had happened to Rex was going to happen to her."

That was her exit line. The coroner thanked her, but didn't repeat what she'd said. A young policeman took her place in the box, blushing. Ruby sat down beside George, holding her heart in with one hand, squeezing his hand with the other.

All at once, with a cold horror for which he was wholly unprepared, George realized the policeman was confirming Ruby's story.

The policeman wasn't playing a part. He was plainly embarrassed and disturbed by what he had to tell. The court snapped into place around George, sharp and close. He saw the intent faces. He saw Edmund gazing at the coroner, admiring his lucidity and skill. He saw the young policeman's white face, and knew he had been sick after he'd seen George's mother. He felt his own legs trembling uncontrollably. He pressed his knees together, but still they shook.

Now there was a pathologist. The coroner echoed him. Even the echo was no longer unreal; it was twice as real, unbearably so. George saw his mother turning anxiously in the doorway to watch him ride away. Yes, the pathologist said, there were numerous lacerations. The marks of teeth. Not an animal's. Portions of the flesh had been— George's horror was mixed now with helpless rage that this audience should hear what had happened to his mother. All he could see was Edmund's face, alert for every word. All he could hear was his own blood, punching his ears furiously.

"Stand up, please," the Scotsman said.

"Stand up, please," the Scotsman said.

The jury had returned; now the coroner strode in. "Mr. Foreman, what verdict do you return on the death of Lilian Pugh?"

"Pardon?" said the foreman uneasily.

"What is your verdict?" the coroner said, still as quietly.

"Death by misadventure."

"Yes." The coroner was nodding slowly, as if he knew the verdict was inevitable, even if not entirely satisfactory. Death by misadventure! George thought wildly. As if she had died in some unavoidable accident!

The coroner was gazing at him. "Please accept my deepest sympathies, and my hope that the culprit will quickly be brought to justice," he said kindly. In a moment he was standing up.

"Stand up, please," the Scotsman said.

The reporters were leaving. They'd come only to hear about George's mother. Now that the show was over they were hurrying to lunch, a pint and a pie. George glared so fiercely at Edmund that he turned and followed the reporters. George waited until the man had had time to leave the building. "I'll be in touch with you soon," he told Ruby. He couldn't bear her just now.

Reporters were crowding outside the courtroom. For a furious moment he thought they wanted to interview him. Then he saw they had surrounded Edmund. "I didn't know you were back in town," one was saying. "I'd have thought our provincial crimes were beneath you these days."

George heard the sarcasm. It fed his own rage and his dislike of Edmund. His feelings welled up beyond his control. "He's here writing a book," he said viciously. "All about the things this monster has done. No doubt it'll make him a lot of money."

He strode furiously downstairs. In a room off the landing a girl was washing teacups by an urn. He halted in the wide sunlight of Castle Street, at the edge of the lunchtime crowd. He must go home to Alice. He wouldn't be fit to run the Newsham until he'd told someone about all this. It was minutes before he ceased shaking and was able to cycle home.

 # Saturday, September 6

WHAT MAKES A MAN A MONSTER?
I'm here to find out, says writer

Most people, unless their sensibilities have been numbed by the world we live in, still shudder when they hear of a murderer at large.

But one man who has reason to rejoice at every new atrocity is Edmund Hall.

His first book, *Secrets of the Psychopaths*, which he describes as "a serious study of the criminal mind," contained detailed descriptions of sadism, incest, cannibalism, and necrophilia. It sold 100,000 copies.

"Crime has fascinated me ever since I was a child," says Mr. Hall, who describes his books as "helping people to understand crime."

Now he is in Liverpool, researching his new book on a psychopath. Yesterday he sat in on the inquest on Mrs. Lilian Pugh, whose death last month is being investigated by the police.

One man who is less than happy about Mr. Hall's research is George Pugh, the son of the deceased Mrs. Pugh. After an angry scene with the writer outside the coroner's court yesterday, Mr. Pugh told our reporter that the book was "bound to make a lot of money."

"Is *Secrets of the Psychopaths* only one book?" Clare said. "I thought you said it was a series."

"They've deliberately misrepresented me," Edmund said. He was gazing impatiently at the hotel-room phone, though it hadn't been long since he'd rung for drinks. "Can't you recognize the tone? They're the lot I used to work for. It's pure jealousy, just because they had to stay in this grubby little town while I made it big in London. They haven't changed. There used to be incredible petty rows because I wouldn't join their union. God, I'm glad I'm out of that. Half of them couldn't even spell."

He picked up the telephone receiver, then clubbed the cradle viciously with it. "Now half the people we trace won't want to talk. And no doubt the police will be warning me off their patch. Thank you, George Pugh. I can do without his help in future."

"Won't he be here?"

"Not if I can help it. Not if he can either, to judge by the way he behaved after the inquest."

Walking back toward the Newsham, he had said he would invite George too. She had been looking forward to a return bout between the two men. Now here she was, alone with Edmund in his bedroom. She was wondering wildly if he'd engineered the situation, when someone knocked at the door.

It was a porter. "You took your bloody time," Edmund said.

"I'm sorry, sir. We had to send out for this brand of bourbon."

"Never mind the backchat. Leave them, I'll pour. Wait a minute. Take that empty with you; don't leave it for the bloody maid. I don't want to sit and look at it, do I? Christ, these people," he said to Clare as the porter strode silently out.

The empty bottle had been of bourbon. Surely he hadn't drunk all that today? At least, she thought (remembering a bit of Shakespeare they'd all used to giggle over in her teens), he wouldn't be able to do much, if he planned to seduce her. "Never mind, Edmund," she said. "It can't be that bad."

"What can't?" he said, snarling at the stiff cap of a gin bottle.

"I mean, that report won't stop you writing your book. They still don't know that you know his name. Maybe some people will be more ready to help, now they know about your books."

His fist was still clenched, wrestling with the cap.

"I'll help you if I can. I feel better about helping now," she said, "because the police told me today they've decided not to prosecute, now that they've realized the psychopath was involved. They said I should have heard from them already. It must be our new postman's fault. So anyway, I can help you now."

"You're a nice girl, Clare." He was filling her tumbler with gin, well past her cry of protest. "We're going to get on well together. I'll tell you one thing I don't like about London: it made me forget there were girls like you."

"Oh yes?" she said, laughing uneasily.

"Yes. You're not like the women down there. Too bloody sure of themselves, all of them. And half of them are fake inside and out. Listen," he said, "I haven't bought you that dinner yet. What night are you free?"

"Oh, I don't know, Edmund." All she could see was his small dented nose, twitching a little like a sleepy rabbit's amid the solemn frowning friendliness of his face. "Not for a while," she said.

He brought her her gin and tonic, rocking stormily in its tumbler. "Oh come on, Clare," he said, putting one large hand on her shoulder. It leaned there, hot and moist as a patch of fever. "You're not doing anything tonight," he said, stooping his face at her.

She edged forward on her chair. He tottered sideways to

keep hold of her shoulder, almost overbalancing; his eye had pulled free of his face and was caught in the lens of his spectacles, blinking in front of itself.

"I'm very busy tonight. I must straighten up my flat before the school term starts." At once, like full stops forbidding him to add to her paragraph, came three sharp knocks at the door.

"You bugger," Edmund said. He levered himself away from her and strode furiously to the door. Surely as a writer he ought to appreciate dramatic timing. "What's your problem?" he demanded.

At the end of the hall, beyond the bathroom, a young man's voice said, "I hear you want help from the victims of the man you're hunting."

"Oh yes," Clare cried. "We do, don't we."

The young man strode lithely into the room and gazed at her with unconcealed delight. His shoulder-length fair hair swung against his face; he shook it back impatiently, gazing at Clare as if she were an unforeseen bonus. "Hello," he said. "Who are you?"

Edmund appeared from the hall, nose twitching with displeasure. "Her name's Clare," he said.

"I didn't catch your name," the young man said to her.

"I'm Clare. Who are you?"

"I'm Chris Barrow."

She felt uncomfortable beneath his gaze, yet not unpleasantly so. Somehow it was too open and childlike to be embarrassing. His clear-skinned, shaven face looked very young, late teenage; but that might have to do with the sense of innocence she felt in him. He'd strode into the room as if nothing bothered him, like a child who has yet to learn self-consciousness. Even his clothes—a wide-sleeved Oriental shirt, joining his flared trousers snugly at his tight heavy crotch, drawing her gaze there—seemed part of a little boy's inoffensive delighted exhibitionism. His eyes were surrounded by thin silver frames.

Nobody had ever looked at her like that before. When Edmund had said she looked like a ballerina she hadn't seen his face; but there was no sign of flattery on Chris Barrow's.

Edmund gripped the bourbon bottle, staking his claim. "Who told you I need help?" he demanded.

"The newspaper that interviewed you."

"They would. What makes you think you can help?"

"I'm a victim. Well, my cat was." His pale gaunt face was flushed now.

"Your *cat?*" Edmund said, snorting mirthlessly. "You're joking."

"No, why? They found her in the alley, half eaten. Not far from where Mrs. Pugh lived."

"Strange I didn't read about it."

"It was in the paper. I've still got the report. I'll bring it to show you if you like."

"I'm not that interested." Edmund rolled the neck of the bottle between his fingers, as if it were a good cigar. "I can't offer you a drink," he said happily. "No more glasses."

"You can finish mine if you like gin," Clare said.

"It's okay, I don't drink."

Edmund stared at him, stretching the silence, clearly hoping he would leave. "What do you do?" Clare asked Chris.

"I'm with TTG. Total Theatre Group."

She could see he thought she was distracting him unnecessarily, but Edmund seemed determined to ignore him. "What sort of things do you perform?"

"Street theatre mostly, and in the parks. Stuff for kids particularly."

"Is that all?" Edmund said. "Sounds more like a game to me."

"Oh, right. But everything's a game really, isn't it?"

Edmund stared at that contemptuously.

"Do you visit schools?" Clare said.

"Yeah, sometimes."

"Maybe you could visit mine. I'd like my kids to see some of that kind of theatre. It would help them, I think."

"Oh, right, yeah. Get in touch with TTG at the Upper Parly Arts Centre. Anyway," he said to Edmund, "I'd better tell you about my cat."

"I don't think it's any use to me."

"Why not?" Chris asked. Clare sensed his impatience, uncomprehending as a child's.

"Did you see the man do it?"

Chris gazed at him speechlessly.

"You see what I mean," Edmund said. "You've no proof it's connected with this case. It's not worth putting in my book, a dead cat in an alley."

Chris's shoulders shifted restlessly. In that moment he seemed to Clare hardly more than a vulnerable little boy. "She was worth a lot to me," he said. "I used to play with her."

Edmund stared at him. "The people who are helping me have lost relatives," he said, "not bloody cats!"

After a moment Chris whirled and stalked out, slamming the door; the bottles chattered on the tray. Edmund poured himself another bourbon, sniggering. "Bloody prima donna," he said.

"Was it necessary to be so nasty to him?"

"I'm sorry, I can't stand his type. London's full of them, poncing about, pretending to be artists. I doubt he's ever done a proper day's work in his life."

"I still think his story sounded genuine."

"Oh, it was. I wasn't going to tell him, but I'd read the report he mentioned. I just couldn't have stood having him around. Besides," he raised his voice as she turned her back on him, "a dead cat could have been anything. A mad dog might have done it. That area's full of strays."

Clare gazed down ten storeys at the Saturday crowd in Elliott Street, a swarming multicoloured beehive. Behind her,

Edmund said plaintively, "You're not going to walk out on me as well, are you?"

The cathedrals challenged each other above the roofs: the red sandstone Gothic tower of the Anglican, the spiky glazed lantern crowning the concrete drum of the Catholic. "I've said I'll help," she said without turning. "But you won't tell me how."

"Well," he said. "Are you back at school on Monday?"

"Tuesday."

"Then you've got yourself a job. Try to find out the address of Kelly's mother or whatever she was. If she's still alive—she looked pretty old when I saw her. I've tried ringing the Education Offices, but they wouldn't tell me. Seemed suspicious."

She moved away from the window, leaving the half-full tumbler behind the curtain. "I think they'd read about me," he said. "But the school won't associate you with me. You'd better tell them you're a teacher. Then you ask to consult their records—"

"I know what to do," she said impatiently, feeling patronized.

"Fine. I'll leave it to you, then."

In the lift, she shrugged off the offers of the menu, angry with herself. Fool. She'd talked herself into going to lie at a school less than a mile from her own.

 **Monday,
September 8**

"Go all the way up them stairs," the boy said. "The staffroom's at the top."

Clare leaned against the railings, trying to fan away some of
the still, oppressive heat. In a minute she would go up. She was
from the Vale School in Aigburth. A relative of Christopher
Kelly's guardian needed her address urgently. She didn't know
why. The Education Offices had mislaid the address, the Vale
School didn't have it; St. Joseph's was the relative's last hope.
Since Clare had had to come home this way, the head had
delegated her to fetch the information. They'd felt they ought
to send someone personally; certainly her school, the Vale
School, would never give out such information over the phone.

Irrationally, she dreaded meeting someone here from her
own school, Durning Road Primary. Nonsense. The staff would
be making the most of this last day of their holidays. But she
couldn't rid herself of the dread. If she met them, what could
she say?

She gazed out through the railings. The sky was overcast;
fragments of china blue were trying to pierce the slow grey
wool. Around the school the windows of derelict terraces were
curtained with corrugated tin. Facing her at the end of a side
street, one house had been torn down; four of its hearths still

clung to the next house, black shrines to soot. She could smell houses smouldering. Against the dull sky, birds rose and swooped like black tatters of ash.

Uniformed boys were staring at her, this alien creature. Some of them towered above her, gangling. She felt dwindled. She couldn't go up those stairs. One of the older boys swaggered by whistling loudly, to show his friends he could. She remembered that they were only boys. And she'd let them deter her. She strode through them to the doorway in the long Victorian building, to the stairs.

The stairs were wide black stone. They made her footsteps clank however carefully she walked, like children shouting a message she'd wanted to keep to a whisper. She clanked upstairs loudly, defiantly, feeling hemmed in by the railings that barred children from the stairwell. I must have this address urgently. I'm from the Vale School. In fact she had just come from there; they'd said they would need a request on headed notepaper for the information; they had seemed suspicious. Round and up and round and up, clank clank. I'm from the Vale School.

At the top, a notice on a dauntingly tall door said KNOCK AND WAIT. The door was ajar; she went in.

She thought at first that the staffroom was empty. Nobody sat at the long central table, which was bare except for a Bible and, lying in a pool of ketchup on a plate, the chewed stump of a sausage roll. Even the greenish walls seemed deserted. There was a smell of charred baked beans; saucepans gathered in the sink, wearing dirty plates. Men, Clare thought angrily. She was as angry with herself for having dared the stairs for nothing.

Then a grey-haired head rose above the end of the table and demanded, "Yes?"

The man had been sitting back in an easy chair. She guessed him to be in his early sixties, but the lines that pinched his eyes and mouth were less lines of age than of weary cynicism, the kind of cynicism she'd seen turn to vindictiveness. She had hoped for a young man, so that she could make him feel masculine for helping her. But if she didn't go through with it now she couldn't come back. She was reaching for her story when he said, "If you're here for David, he'll be back at one."

The large clock on the wall said twenty-five to one; the minute hand sprang up a minute. Before she knew what she was risking she said, "Has David told you all about me?"

If he had, she could say, "Well, you can see that's not me," laughing, passing it off as a joke, she didn't mean any harm, please let her go now, only a joke. But the man said, "All he said was that if a girl came up she'd be for him."

"Aren't men conceited?" She was beginning to enjoy the game even though she felt light-headed, almost weightless. She floated to the easy chair opposite the man. The clock's hand twitched, as if the nostrils of its winder holes were tickling. Twenty-three minutes. "Have you worked here long?" she said.

"Since you were in your cradle, I should think."

She toyed with a magazine that had perhaps been confiscated. HE CUT UP YOUNG VIRGINS AND LAUGHED. *His Potency Came From Not Having Orgasms.* "You must have been here when Christopher Kelly was," she said, gazing blindly at the magazine.

His bright sharp eyes were scrutinizing her. "What do you know about Kelly?"

"Well, er," she said. She had to chance it. "David," she said.

"David wasn't here then."

"No, someone told him about it. Perhaps you did."

"I shouldn't be surprised." He'd completed his scrutiny; she managed to look up. "That terrible boy," he said, shaking his head. "These children today are bad enough, but I don't think anyone who was here then will ever forget him. I only hope he had no lasting influence on the other children. He had too many friends, that boy, he was always riding someone else's bicycle.

He shouldn't have been allowed into an ordinary school at all. That's not our job, that kind of case."

She nodded eagerly. Perhaps he would tell her something new about Kelly; he might even give her a cue to ask to look at their records. "I pity whoever had to deal with him after he left us," the teacher said. "And his poor grandmother having to look after him by herself, oh dear. Do you know, I think he was even worse when he came back."

"Came back here?" Her surprise was showing. "To this school?"

"That's right." He frowned at her. "Why are you so interested in Kelly?" he said sharply.

"Didn't David tell you what I do?"

"He told me nothing. Not even your name."

"It's—" (Oh God, a name, a name!) "It's Clare," she said. "I'm a teacher too. That's why I'm interested."

"Haven't you a surname?"

She'd anticipated that; she grabbed the last name she could remember having heard. "Clare Barrow," she said.

"And you've come into teaching? May God protect you, then. The law won't. Or are you one of those who don't believe in upsetting the little dears? Let me tell you, I used to teach them more with a clout round the head than half of these people teach them in years. But now it's oh no, you might damage their poor little brains. Brains! Half of them haven't got any, and most of the rest are warped beyond repair. These days they're sending them up from the junior school not even able to read. And as for spelling, oh dear me. The teachers want teaching themselves these days."

"Have you tried teaching a class of thirty-five lately?" Clare said furiously. "Maybe if they gave us enough staff for a sensible pupil-teacher ratio, you wouldn't have so much to complain about."

He relaxed visibly. "Yes, you're a teacher," he said. "I

71

thought for a while you were trying to delude me. We have to be careful in this district, you see. Last year we had a man pretending to be an electrician. He didn't get past me. I don't exercise every day for no reason. He must have been thirty years my junior, but I held on to him until the police arrived."

Seventeen minutes to one. Clare smiled, nodding. He doesn't suspect any more, she reassured the cold hole of fear in her stomach. "You were saying Kelly came back," she said.

"Yes, he came back. Dear me, he did. When I saw him in the playground I thought it must be his double, until I saw his expression. No one else on earth ever looked like that. He always looked as if he were listening to something no one else could hear. Like Joan of Arc. But it must have been a devil he was listening to.

"I went straight up to him, among all his schoolfellows, and took him by the collar. His school had sent one young girl in charge of the whole group, supposed to keep discipline. She didn't look much older than her charges. I told her in front of them: 'We've thrown this one out once, don't think we won't throw him out again if he isn't on his best behaviour.' "

Clare smiled down at the magazine; she didn't trust herself to look at him. Interfering old maid. She'd have liked him to try that on with her. "Am I boring you?" he said.

WAS HIS POWER OVER HIS VICTIMS BLACK MAGIC? "No, of course not," she said, forcing herself to lay aside the magazine and smile at him. "Please go on."

"This young girl told me they were from the Vale School. They'd come to give us an end-of-term treat," he said. "I wasn't interested. That's not why the country pays for schools. Of course it wasn't up to me to challenge the head's decision," he said rather bitterly. "So here was Kelly back again, as if he hadn't entertained us enough when we had him.

"My class had to go to watch their treat, but I didn't. I wasn't going to let that boy have me as an audience, though some of my colleagues had no compunction. I came up here and marked homework. And that was how I came to see Kelly chasing the cat.

"The caretaker had a cat called Felix. I was opposed to letting him keep it in the school, but of course that was the head's decision; he didn't consult me. Half the boys here would set fire to a cat, given half the chance. But Felix had managed to escape injury.

"I presume they didn't need Kelly for a while, otherwise he couldn't have slipped out of the hall unnoticed. I might not have noticed him myself if I hadn't found this room stuffy and got up to open the window. I was about to do so when I saw Kelly down there in the playground, chasing the cat. But chasing isn't the right word. He was stalking it, like an animal.

"I once saw a film on television. I don't watch as a rule, but I don't think a little does harm. They showed a lizard which had lived underground all its life, an eyeless thing. They showed how it walked, slowly and delicately, with its fingers stepping along, feeling its way. I had never seen anything so furtive and horrible—until I looked out of that window. Because out there in the sunlight that enormous fat boy was stalking exactly like the lizard, on all fours. And on his face was a sort of hungry joy I shall always hope to forget.

"When I knocked on the window he looked up at me. You know I'm a strong man, but I was glad there were two floors between us. Then he fled back to the hall. Afterward I told the girl in charge what had happened. Do you know what she did? Nothing. Oh no, the cat had distracted people's attention from him or some such nonsense, and he hadn't done anything really. She wouldn't admit what he was, you see. She wanted to believe he was just a boy."

"But what was he?" Clare said, frustrated. "Did anyone know why he was like that?"

"Three people did." She suppressed a giggle; it was like a banal thriller—perhaps written by Edmund. "The head," he said, "and Kelly's class master, and his grandmother. It was she who told them all about him. One of my colleagues asked the head afterwards what she'd had to say, but he made it clear that was none of their business. As for the class master, he was off a week recovering; no one needed to be told not to question him. He never recovered completely. He used to run away from the sight of blood, and once I had almost to carry him into the school just because he'd seen an expectant mother going by. I've no idea what that meant to him. But as for Kelly, I believe he was possessed. Such things do still happen, you know. Science has yet to find a cure for them."

Perhaps, perhaps, Clare was interrupting. Five to one. "Is Kelly's class master here now?" she said.

"Dear me, no. He left years ago; he could never teach properly after that. He never trusted the children again, once he knew what Kelly had been hiding. You wanted to question him, did you?"

Question? Did he know why she was here, after all? She snatched at the only thought left in her suddenly dull mind. Records. "I was just thinking how much trouble he must have had filling in Kelly's record card," she said.

"Yes indeed. I recall he was very glad to see the record go."

"Go where?"

"To the Vale School, when Kelly went there, of course."

"Yes, of course," Clare said dully. "You wouldn't have kept any record of him here at all."

The clock's hands twitched, a nervous upturned moustache. At least she could leave, knowing she'd teased out all the information to be had. "I think I'll go down and wait for David," she said. "It's too nice to be inside."

"I imagine he's on his way up now. That clock is slow. It's well past one."

When she grabbed its strap her handbag almost vomited its contents; she knew how it felt. "I'll catch him on the stairs," she said. "I must get back to work. To school, I mean. Where I work." She was at the door when the grey-haired master said, "Odd you should mention Kelly. I bumped into a friend of his grandmother's only a few weeks ago."

"Which friend was that?" Don't sound so eager, don't waste time, don't wait, run, it's past one.

"A woman who would sometimes collect Kelly from school. I've no idea of her name. She works in a launderette on Lodge Lane."

But Clare drove that way to work! "Which, the one on the corner of, of"—oh God, David would open the door in a minute, the door was too thick for her to hear him coming—"of Cedar Grove?"

"No, the one next to the Bingo Hall." He turned toward the window as a motorcycle roared below. "Here's David now," he said. "David!" he called.

He was calling, "Your friend is here!" as she ran stumbling downstairs, her heel slipping from a stone edge. A young man appeared in the doorway from the playground, unstudding his crash helmet, as she caught herself back by the railing from the sharp stone edges below. He glanced curiously at her, seemed about to speak—but she was past him and out, across the playground and through the gates with a shouting gasp, almost suffocated by her panic.

Ringo was parked a hundred yards away, on Princes Avenue. She had calmed down by the time she reached the car. She'd done what she had set out to do, and no thanks to Edmund's patronizing advice. There was something else she could do now, without his approval. She climbed into Ringo, pressing herself determinedly against the hot leather, and drove away.

The Upper Parly Arts Centre was a terraced Georgian house covered with cheerful graffiti, largely red and blue. Clare was fascinated long before she was close enough to be sure what it was. A red and blue front door, red and blue walls beyond the windows: the paint was bright despite the discolouring gusts from passing traffic. But the building seemed empty, hollowed out by echoes. She was leaving when an enormous man on the opposite pavement caught sight of her and shouldered his way pugnaciously through the traffic, brandishing a movie camera like a gun. His bare stomach smacked its stack of fat lips above his trouser belt. "TTG?" he shouted, wheezing. "They're on location. Church Street."

By the time Clare reached the city centre they had finished performing, except for Chris. He was pacing around the stubby concrete tubs of sprouting earth, pretending not to know that his prey, a dozen children, had almost caught up behind him. Crowds of shoppers hurried by, glancing furtively at Chris or refusing to look; a few gazed, fewer smiled. Though Church Street was a shopping precinct now, its roadway paved over and forbidden to traffic by the scattered tubs and a handful of saplings, the crowd still huddled together on the pavements. Only Chris and the children played in the road.

She sat on a bench to watch. The sun had cleared itself a space now; everything was dazzling. She kicked aside pebbles of chewing gum the colour of doll's flesh, scrawny coins of milk-bottle tops. Today Chris wore a mauve singlet and elaborately patchworked trousers; she could tell he was proud of the pots of ginger hair under his arms. Two shopgirls from Woolworth's pointed at him, cawing. He didn't falter; he was wholly engrossed.

She watched his pale intent face. Down a side street, a drill chattered harshly in stone; next to her, the plastic cover of a hotdog stall folded open with a thick gasp of onion. More strongly than in Edmund's room she felt how young Chris was —whatever his physical age. But now she could see how he'd made this a virtue. She could never play so freely with kids. If these kids weren't enjoying themselves so much, she thought, some of them would be shoplifting. She wondered if Chris had ever wanted to teach.

The children pounced. Chris was shouting, laughing, collapsing beneath them. She watched his face. Before, she'd thought it strange, a little spectral, with its long pointed nose and chin; now, as he gasped—as flushed and excited as the children—she found it attractive. Its long, clear, simple planes looked sculptured, uncluttered. But beneath the simplicity she was convinced lay depth.

As he heaved himself and clinging children upright, he saw her. At once there was nothing in his face but delight. She couldn't help feeling it too. "Hey, fantastic," he said. "I didn't know you were watching."

"I only saw the end. I enjoyed it, though. You'll have to do it for my kids sometime."

A little girl was tugging at his arm. "Play us a hide and seek," she pleaded.

"Right. But let's do that later, okay? You come to Upper Parly later and we'll play."

"When shall we go?" she said, hopping impatiently. "In ten minutes?"

"Hey, you want me to starve? You go home and have your tea, then we'll play."

Kids! Clare said in code with her smile, and felt needlessly secretive; his smile included the children as well. "It's fantastic to see you," he said. "What are you doing downtown?"

"Looking for you." At once her abdomen felt as if she'd stepped off an edge.

"Yeah? That's amazing." He didn't even seem anxious to know why.

A man was thrusting his way through the crowd, frightening people with his spongy red-and-purple grimacing face, since that was what they seemed to expect him to do; the children fled, squealing. "You know I'm helping Edmund Hall," Clare said to Chris, to reclaim his attention.

"Right." He watched the crowd flinch from the man.

"He thinks the man who's committing these crimes went to the same school he did. I went to the school today and talked to one of the staff. He was a horrible man, absolutely horrible. He shouldn't be in charge of a zoo, never mind children. I don't wonder this boy Christopher Kelly went mad if that's the kind of thing he had to put up with."

"Yeah, I know what you mean."

"Anyway, what I was going to say—this man said he once saw Kelly stalking a cat, really stalking like an animal. So that shows you were right about your cat. I'm sure it must tie in. Dogs don't *eat* cats." All at once she remembered how vulnerable he was; she'd interrupted his enjoyment just to remind him of this. "I was angry with Edmund for saying what he did," she said, but it sounded like a feeble excuse.

"About my cat? Yeah, well. She's gone now. Anyway, she was only a cat."

She was delighted he was taking it so well—though perhaps he had sensed her anxiety and was pretending. "That's all I came to tell you," she said.

"Yeah? You came just to tell me that? That's really nice. Thank you. Listen, come and eat," he said.

She slumped inside herself. After the tension she'd felt with Edmund and at St. Joseph's, Chris was almost too much of a relief. She felt exhausted; she had to sit quickly on the edge of a concrete tub. Maybe food was what she needed. "I'd love to come," she said.

The other actors had been packing props into a nearby van; now they came back for Chris. "This is Clare," he said. "She's a friend of mine. She teaches. We're just going to eat. I'll see you back at Upper Parly."

"You be sure you do," an actress said. "Rehearsals later. Then we're going to my place to get stoned. Hey, when are we coming up to yours? You never invite us."

"Yeah, I'll tell you when. I'm involved in a few things right now."

When the others had returned to the van, Clare said, "Is that girl chasing you?"

"Kind of, yeah. I mean, she's all right. They're all good people. But I'm particular who I invite up to my flat."

Clare blocked her answering thought. It was presumptuous; she didn't know him. Still, she could tell he liked her. "Where shall we eat?" she said, to shut herself up.

"Anywhere. You say."

"It's too late for the cheap lunches. There's the Master Mariner's. That's self-service, not expensive."

"Listen, don't worry about the price."

Was he offering to buy her lunch? He mustn't do that. His acting couldn't earn him much. She'd argue when the time came to pay, if she needed to. "The Master Mariner's food is good," she said.

They headed for a side street; the sun rang blindingly in the metal sign of a corner shop, set with computer type. Off Church Street it was slightly cooler. Clare hurried to keep up with Chris before she realized he was strolling. He was strolling as though he enjoyed it, as though he weren't forced to slow down for her. Her self-consciousness faded. When he caught up she began to stroll too.

She gazed in shop windows. She slowed, gazing at a heavy necklace of smooth, richly brown beads, darkly glowing wooden ovals; it hung on the reflection of her African-print dress. "Yeah, that really goes with your dress," Chris said. "That's perfect," and he hurried into the shop.

She was still gazing into the window, waiting for Chris, when a girl lifted the necklace from its hooks. Clare glanced wistfully beyond her and saw Chris holding out his hand for the necklace. Clare thumped the window, shaking her head vehemently. She shoved the doors open, shouldering her way through a wall of rock music as thick as the heat. "No, Chris," she cried. "No, no, really!"

But he'd stuffed money into the girl's hand and was placing the necklace around Clare's neck. "Come on," he said. "I want to."

She sensed his frustration. He'd released her from her tensions; she couldn't bear to cause any in him—besides, she was exhausted. She couldn't cause a scene. "Thank you," she said. "It's beautiful." At the door she kissed him on the cheek. The convex mirror overhead sucked up their heads from their dwindling bodies.

When they reached Williamson Square, Clare gazed about at the crowd, proud of her necklace; the beads touched her nipples tenderly, like fingertips. Thin trees sprouted from uneven chessboards of grey stone; pigeons nodded rapidly at crumbs among the benches; a man with a trayful of birdsounds warbled liquidly; Punch and Judy squawked at a dog. People were handing out pamphlets beneath the boxy metal walkways, beneath the cantilevered glass-and-concrete cylinder stuck to the side of the Playhouse, which still looked like a music hall. A man was bearing down on Chris and Clare.

Clare clenched inside. He was a Child of God, or something similar. He extended a friendly smile and a pamphlet toward them. She always disliked such encounters—felt rude .if she hurried by, didn't want to get involved in a discussion. But he was looking at Chris. "Stuff that fucking shit back up your arse," Chris said without breaking his stroll.

She stifled her gasp, of shock or of mirth. "Chris!" she said, but it didn't sound much like a rebuke. Her ears were throbbing with the surprise. "You're terrible," she said.

"Oh, right." Four hundred feet above their heads a restaurant spun slowly on its pole. She took his arm to steer him toward the corridors of St. John's Precinct; his forearm was soft and furry beneath her fingers. "We go through here to eat," she said.

The restaurant was on the second level. As they crossed the balcony above the enclosed market Clare gazed down at the roofless stalls: boxes full of colours—no more full of colours than Chris's patchwork trousers. "I like your trousers," she said.

"Yeah, they're all right." He held back the glass door for

her. "A girl I used to know made them. She made a lot of my clothes. I lived with her for a while," he said with no change of tone, as if there were no reason for one. She could tell he wasn't trying to shock her, and he hadn't.

Chris scanned the plastic menu above the metal counter. "The fish and chips aren't bad," Clare said.

"You mean the 'large deep-fried fillet of codling and fried potatoes,' " he said loudly enough to make heads peer over the edges of booths. Rob had used to trap her in this kind of public spotlight. "Don't, Chris," she said, nudging him. In fact her embarrassment was rather delicious; a few people were pointing out her necklace, her dress.

"Anyway, that stuff's not for me," he said. "I'll have a salad. I'm into health foods, strictly vegetarian."

A woman moped over their glasses of milk, sniffing. Clare tried to push past Chris to the cash desk, but he blocked her way gently. "Come on, I'll pay," he said almost impatiently. "I want to give you something. You gave me something, right?" He was loosening the drawstrings of a little leather purse. She hadn't realized he'd been so pleased to see her. Maybe he had been more upset by Edmund's attitude than he'd admitted, and therefore more grateful to her.

They sat in a booth of heavy, dark brown wood and red-and-orange deck-chair canvas. "Listen, I wanted to pay," he said as she frowned a little at her tray. "Really, you came down just to tell me?"

"Well, I felt you ought to know," she said around a chip. "After the way Edmund treated you. You offered to help, after all. Do you still want to?"

"Yeah, I'd like to."

"I'd understand if you didn't. But we might be helping the police as well as Edmund."

"Right. You think he'd let me?"

"I don't know." Now that she had to think about it, she thought not. "If I can make him, I will," she said.

Below the window, shoppers stumped grumpily up a paralyzed escalator toward the market balcony. Across the road, a marquee said, "Come to Me, all you that labour and are burdened, and I will give you rest." Clare remembered the building as a cinema, offering *Girls in the Sun and Women by Night*, which she'd taken a while to recognize as a double feature.

When Chris stopped spluttering with laughter at that, he said, "Do you like teaching?"

"Yes, I do. More than anything else that I do."

"Yeah. That's really the way to be, right?"

"Yes, it is. You like your job too, don't you? You like kids."

"Right. You saw that. I like playing with them." When he saw her expression sour he said, "Huh, what?"

"I was just thinking of that teacher. He was so horrible. You couldn't imagine him playing with kids. He really hated them." Her brow pinched at a memory. "I got one more thing out of him. I was trying to find out where Kelly's grandmother lives, his guardian—oh yes, Christopher Kelly is the name of the boy we think we're after. Well, I couldn't work round to that. But there was a friend of hers who collected him from school sometimes. The teacher told me she works in a launderette."

"Yeah? Fantastic! Let's go and talk to her!"

"I haven't thought what to say yet."

He'd stuffed the whole of a lettuce leaf into his mouth and was chewing vigorously. "Don't worry," he said, his mouth sprouting and retrieving green. "I'll get the address out of her, if that's what you want. You watch me."

He might be more convincing than Clare. But just now all she wanted was to eat her meal leisurely. "All right," she said, "but not today. You promised to play with those kids."

"Yeah, right. I can do both. It won't take long. I just feel right for it now. I mightn't tomorrow," he said, casting his cutlery loudly on his plate. "I mean, don't hurry. I can wait." He shook his hands impatiently in what she took to be an attempt to calm her. "We'll go and see her when you've finished. Then you'll be able to tell Edmund I helped, right?"

She could feel his frustration, almost like a threat of violence. She ate slowly, determined to do so; she felt him urging her faster, faster. She laid her knife and fork beside a few chips. "Come on, then," she said, "I've had as much as I want," unable to bear more.

Ringo was parked behind Church Street, by the Bluecoat Chambers. Birds in trees shouted above the cobbled courtyard; a traffic warden had trapped a motorist and was lecturing him ponderously before issuing a ticket, confidently dictatorial in her uniform. Clare resented the woman, and resented the way Chris was making her hurry to keep up with him.

When he saw Ringo he said, "That's a sweet little car."

"That's about the word for it," she said. "A Noddy car."

Her tone made him glance at her. Although he was a head taller, she didn't feel he was looking down. "Don't you like your car?" he said.

"I don't like me."

She fastened her seat belt, started the engine, and swung rapidly away through the side streets, up a hill of warehouses and nightclubs. "What don't you like?" he said.

"Oh, I don't know. Dwarfs are all right in Walt Disney." She didn't bother to make it sound like a joke.

"Who's a dwarf? You're small, but you're no dwarf."

"Small, and out of proportion."

"What's this out-of-proportion shit? You don't look deformed to me."

"Well, I feel it."

"Fu-uck! Listen, last year we had a girl in TTG. The kids wouldn't go home when she was there; we had to throw them out. She'd play with them all day; they loved her. And then she'd help us in the evening. We'd work out parts for her to play because she asked for them. It got so people came just to see her. Right? She was a spastic. Couldn't even hold a cup without spilling it. She's gone to London now, doing a one-girl show in an arts theatre. She could do all that, and you're kidding yourself you've got problems? She hadn't even got a pretty face like you."

She frowned at the road ahead. "You're just saying that to have your way with me," she said.

"Yeah. I wouldn't mind, either."

She felt as if she'd lit up red as the lights ahead on Canning Street. Yet the feeling in her stomach wasn't embarrassment, wasn't fear. Apprehension, anticipation? She should be anticipating the road. She frowned ahead.

They passed the flats of Canning Street, the blackened columns and iron balconies; vague patches of music tossed on the car's wind. She swung widely right at the lights, through more lights at Upper Parliament, and past a cinema which now offered HALF A MILE OF FURNITURE. "Hey, it's good to be with someone who can drive," Chris said. "The guy who drives our van, they should never have let him see *Bullitt*."

William Huskisson shone green in the sunlight, except where the birds had given him leprosy. "For a while I thought I wouldn't be able to drive," she said.

"Passing your test, you mean?"

"No, I mean after my brother was killed."

"Oh, right. I can imagine."

She didn't want him to stop her talking. "I felt responsible," she said.

"Yeah?"

He sounded indifferent, but she went on: "I was driving with faulty brakes. I knew they were faulty before I had the accident."

"Well, it's good you can still drive."

He still hadn't said what she wanted to hear. "I'm not so sure now it was my fault," she said. "Now I know that the man who caused the accident was insane."

"Yeah, you shouldn't blame yourself." She relaxed gratefully, and he said, "I live on the other side there, on Princes

Road. It's weird, right? You don't know how close I might be
to the guy who's doing these things."

"Yes, you should be careful," she said anxiously. "Especially
at night."

Children were playing ball against the church; Christ held up
his arms for a catch. "This is where it happened, the accident,"
Clare said. "I have to drive along here to school. That was one
reason why I thought I couldn't drive."

"Where do you teach?"

"Durning Road."

"Where, the other side of Lodge Lane? You don't have to
come along here."

"You do now. They've blocked off all the shortcuts."

"No, you could go down Upper Parly."

She gaped at him. "You're right," she said. That was a more
direct route than this. "Why couldn't I see that?" she said, bewildered.

"Maybe your head wouldn't let you. I mean, things can screw
you up half your life if you look at them the wrong way. You
feel better now, right?"

By God, she did. She swung Ringo into Lodge Lane, hooting
at a man laden with a typewriter, a Richard Strauss opera, and
an armful of bottles of hock. She felt ready for anything. "Let's
go and grill this woman," she said.

She manoeuvred the car along the narrow swarming street.
Cars squeezed past parked cars, vans hung open outside shops,
buses muttered impatiently. Litter flapped across the road, ap-
ples rolled from stalls to be kicked by children, a dog darted
through the traffic, a cat watched superciliously from a hill of
onions. Clare braked as children were chased out of the library
by a red-faced man in uniform. On the next block was the
launderette.

They parked in an alley; two men sat in a doorway, sucking
bottles wrapped in newspaper. As Chris reached the launderette a woman in a pink-checked overall, her hair like a rusty

poodle's, glared through the window at him. "Someone doesn't like you," Clare said.

"Right. Bet she thinks I'm gay."

"She doesn't like me either." The woman glared at her over a row of infants like reluctant ornaments on the window ledge. "It doesn't look worth trying, does it?"

"Hey, anything's worth trying. If she thinks I'm gay then that's what I'll be," he said, smoothing his hair, limp-wristed.

"Oh, Chris," she said, snorting. But he'd gone in; she could only follow.

The launderette felt overcast; the heat was heavy with the smells of soap and hot cloth. A shirt reared up almost shapelessly at a porthole, flapping empty arms; vortices of clothes pressed against glass. A young man filled his plastic sack from a dryer, feeling a girl's underwear furtively for damp, like a fetishist hastily fingering the contents of a chest of drawers. A child went out dragging a sack, an early Christmas gnome. "Leave the door, will you," the overalled woman shouted as the child slammed it.

"Ex-*cuse* me," Chris said, bowing limply toward her. "Are you the friend of Christopher Kelly's granny?"

Oh my God, Clare thought, disguising her mirth as a sneeze. Women turned to stare at Chris; their children scrambled over the machines. "Eh?" the woman said, as if that were all she intended to say.

"Christopher's a dear friend of mine. I promised I'd visit his old granny if I was ever in town."

"He doesn't live there now," the woman muttered. Next to her, a pair of knickers sailed up and were snatched back.

"Oh, I know. That's why he asked me to look her up. He tells me she's a *lovely* lady."

"She doesn't like strangers. Doesn't trust them." She stared at him.

Clare knew he'd failed. Kelly would never have called his grandmother a lovely lady, not if the way she'd behaved at St.

Joseph's was typical. Nor would he have asked Chris to look her up. They'd betrayed themselves and Edmund. She looked away, at the young man with the sack, who had retrieved a loose button and was gazing at it as if it were a miserly tip.

"But I *prom*-ised!" Chris protested. "I can't go back on a promise, not to him. He'd be so upset."

"He wasn't any friend of hers. She wouldn't have taken him in, except he was her daughter's boy. I wouldn't have taken him, not after what his mother done." Her tone had changed; something about it walled Clare in, away from the sunlight. "There's no wonder he was what he was, not after what his mother was, the things she was mixed up with. He wasn't born human." She ducked quickly and kissed a saint's medal sewn inside her overall. "It's no use you going round there," she said, having conjured back her old tone. "She wouldn't want to see you."

"Oh, she *would*. All the things I could tell her—she'd want to hear them, I just know she would." His voice rose hysterically; Clare could hear his frustration. "You wouldn't want to upset him. Did you ever know him? Do you know what a sensitive boy he is?"

"That wouldn't be my word for him. Now go on, stop bothering me. I won't tell you, whatever you say."

"Oh God. I don't mean to upset you, but I *promised*. You do look ill."

Clare suspected he was simply playing now, as he had with the kids. "It's you that's made me ill, then," the woman said; Clare saw her in a porthole, looking for help from the audience, but the women had returned to their washing. "I've got a weak heart," the woman said. "I mustn't be upset. The doctor said so."

"Oh God. Me too, I need treatment. Is he good, your doctor?"

"He's the best there is. I've known him all my life. You can trust him, not like some people I know."

Come on, Chris, give it up. But he said, "What's his name? Where's his surgery?"

"Dr. Miller in Boswell Street. But he won't have you. He only has local people."

"He should have Christopher's granny. Then there'd be someone she could trust."

"He has got her."

"I thought he might have," he said, gaily but no longer gay. "Well, thank you. You've been really helpful."

Her face closed, trapping her with the truth. She stood up, shaking, but Chris dodged her. In the doorway he swung his hips as a farewell. "I've wanted to do that ever since I saw Lauren Bacall," he told Clare as they fled to Ringo.

"How did you know about the doctor?" she demanded, snagging the key in the ignition.

"Well, it made sense, right? For that woman to collect him from school she must have lived near them. So it sounded like they'd have the same doctor."

The car shuddered out of the alley. "You could act your way through anything, couldn't you?" she said.

"Yeah. But it sounds like you did pretty well at St. Joseph's."

"I suppose I did." She felt rather pleased with both of them. Edmund couldn't do without them now.

As she drove past the launderette toward Upper Parliament Street, she saw the woman glaring out. What had she meant about Kelly, about what his mother had done? Clare was suddenly all the more glad to be with Chris. For a moment she'd wondered what their prey might do if he realized they were hunting him.

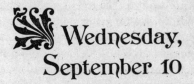 # Wednesday, September 10

It's only a mound, he told himself. Only earth. But the mound was rising, slowly as a sleeping breath. It split lethargically open, and what had pushed it up emerged with a maggot's gropings, its unsteady head nodding. He was surrounded by the mounds. Several pale shapes were already crawling feebly, lopsidedly toward him. They were babies, scaly with earth.

When he opened his eyes the darkness piled on them. That, and his terror, trapped him in himself. He lay trying to gaze out. Sounds of cars, infrequent waves on the distant beach of the road. The dark was too huge for him to dare making for the light switch.

He burrowed under the blankets. At least his own warmth was down there, instead of the dull suffocating heat of the darkness. His breath was huge, trapped. The dream had brought back more than terror. It had brought back his grandmother's voice, unmuffled.

"I was never going to tell you what you are," she said. "But you've shown your true colours today. You're a child of the Devil. Do you think I'm exaggerating? Then let me tell you something. Your mother promised you to the Devil before you were even born."

She went on, and on. The past was dragging him down, like

exhausted sleep. He tried to snatch himself back, and for a moment was lying not beneath blankets but in the earth, lying contented and waiting.

He writhed. The feel of his skin, the taste in his mouth were hideous. He forced himself to relax. There was no use struggling. He had come through the horror before. He had only to remember how. He let himself down into the past.

He remembered his grandmother, remembered her telling the headmaster, the doctor; he remembered the slow thick shame swelling him, until he'd thought he would burst. At night he had lain awake, shrinking away from the loathsome horror in his bed, himself. The house had echoed with his grandmother's voice, praying for him. He had buried himself under the blankets, but a memory had always crept into his hiding place: the way he'd grinned to feel the piece of Cyril's arm inside his grin.

Only a child of the Devil could have enjoyed that. He would clench himself tightly, as if to squeeze out the poison of what he was. He would grind his teeth in self-disgust until, insidious and tempting, there had come the taste of blood.

Then, one night, he had realized there was no God.

He'd been suspicious for a while. He had been noticing things: the boy who passed around nude photographs during school mass and who had somehow not been struck down by Heaven; Mr. Nicholas, who prayed ringingly, and who spread-eagled naughty boys against the classroom cupboard, so that he could watch them while teaching. There had been books on biblical archaeology, films by Buñuel, the way the masters condemned communist persecutions but didn't want to discuss the Spanish Inquisition. "No book has caused more torture and murder than the Bible." All of this accumulated in him, until the night it had flooded out.

He had been listening to his grandmother's hollow prayers, to stop himself remembering Cyril. All at once, as he heard the echoes stretch out her prayers only to drop them into reverberating silence, he'd realized she was praying not out of love but out of fear. She was trying to fill the vast waiting silence. She was holding back her awareness of death. She couldn't risk being alone with herself in case, fatally, there might be a moment during which she failed to believe.

He'd lain gazing at the dark, allowing the implications to flow through him. He had known them already; only his grandmother's apparent absolute faith had made him deny them uneasily. If there was no God, there could hardly be a Devil. But then he wasn't a child of the Devil. He wasn't a monster at all.

The horror was fading, the past was losing its hold on him. Why had he thought he was a monster? He reached for the memory, happy now with the past. Because of what he'd done to Cyril? It hadn't been much worse than what Cyril had done to him. As for the other thing his grandmother had said he'd done—well, he hadn't hurt anyone. She'd made it sound worse than the Spanish Inquisition. He'd thrust his head out of the sheets, grinning at the dark. Cyril had got what he deserved. He'd grinned at the desperate voice surrounded by its own echoes.

He'd needed no more reassurance until he had begun to dream of lying in the earth.

It was a childhood dream; he had had it many times. But once he'd left home it had vanished—only to return without warning a few months ago. He had figured out why. Since returning to Liverpool he had become increasingly restless; he'd moved several times, usually away from landlords who seemed too inquisitive. He had been moving always nearer Mulgrave Street.

At least that explained the dream. Probably the last traces of his childhood guilt were luring him back toward the school. It was disturbing, but bearable. The dream must be returning along with the memories Mulgrave Street prompted. He didn't know what the dream meant, but that didn't matter. His guilt and its source were past.

But the pull of Mulgrave Street had increased. At night it was worst; he couldn't go into that dark. During the day he'd considered visiting the street, to be done with it. But he didn't want the staff at the school to recognize him. He'd begun to wake at four in the morning, his nerves jagged with the problem. He'd been trying to walk it off when there was the car hurtling at him, the car slewed against the tree, the orange-painted meat on its bed of blood and gravel.

He had felt no guilt. It was only the same as Cyril. When the man had chased him he had been annoyed. He'd been uneasy when the man had forced him to dodge into Mulgrave Street, but he hadn't had to stay there long. Half an hour later he'd returned to his flat and had fallen asleep at once.

Afterward he hadn't quite known how he felt, until he saw the newspaper reports. They were enormously reassuring. They had the tone of schoolgirls whispering in a haunted house; none dared mention what he'd done. As if it were so unspeakable! Why, it had been more the driver's fault than his.

The cat hadn't upset him. It had been lying there dead in the alley, after all. He had kept remembering the man chasing him; he'd felt vulnerable. The cat should have given him back his freedom.

As for Mrs. Pugh—well, he shouldn't have gone near Mulgrave Street at night. But the newspapers had made him laugh again, with their screams of horror—WHAT MAKES A MAN A MONSTER? He'd felt happy: Mrs. Pugh had been so easy that it seemed to have left him completely satisfied.

He slid up through the sheets, stretching comfortably. He felt refreshed—he grinned: reborn. He only wondered why he had had the dream about the babies. He'd had it a couple of times after his grandmother's outburst, then it had faded away. Still, if it had come back he could deal with it. He felt ready for anything.

He bared his teeth at the dark. Most of all he felt ready for this writer who was hunting him.

It reminded him of the cat he'd stalked in the playground that day. No doubt the cat had been proud of its hunting, yet it had never noticed him behind it, stealthily following. Only the master at the window had saved it. He grinned, and chewed his tongue to taste blood. There would be nobody to warn Edmund Hall, nor anyone who was helping him hunt.

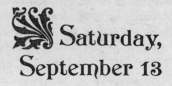 **Saturday, September 13**

"Oh God," Clare said. "I forgot to tell George you were vegetarian."

She was driving along Prescot Road toward Newsham Park, the far side from the cinema. It was nearly six o'clock. Beyond the wire fences at the edge of the pavement, people emerged from small shops with the evening newspaper. Buses honked; ducks flew over them back to the park, honking. Children watched a large green maggot writhing in televisions.

Clare turned at a film library that looked like a corner shop. A willow swept past on her right. Silence settled on the street a hundred yards down, except for Ringo's whirring. Ragged tousled gardens rolled by; trees and low walls were painted with moss. A shampooed poodle and a lion gazed from the window of a flat.

"Edmund hadn't even mentioned you to George," she told Chris. "I rang George to thank him for the invitation. He's decided he may help Edmund after all. Well, I told him about you, and he said you must come to dinner too." She drove slowly, gazing at the street plaques. "I don't understand Edmund," she said. "He seemed grateful when I told him how you'd helped."

"Yeah, well," Chris said. "So it goes."

That was from a book Rob had liked. "I think you'll like George," she said. "And I bet his wife's nice."

The three-storey terraces passed, their front doorways buttoned with strips of doorbells; Dylans, singers or dazed stuffed rabbits, gazed from posters through windows. At the end of the street the park opened out with a flourish of trees, making room for a sky that was largely covered by twin wings of white cloud. Ah, Hampstead Road. Clare turned right, and there was the Pughs' house.

It was one of a terrace. Its front bay was held back from the pavement by a low wall, painted crimson. The front door was painted orange, as were bricks around the windows; the curtains, beyond which George stood up as he caught sight of her, were orange and red. All of the colours still looked quite bright. Through the curtains Edmund turned to wave, faintly amused again.

The front door jammed briefly. "This is Chris," Clare said. "This is George." George gazed at her quizzically, and she took the risk. "Like my guitar," she said.

"She always says that. Come and meet the wife. Alice!"

It was a long thin house. A door opened far down it; sunlight fell out. "This is Clare. And Chris," George called. "My wife, Alice."

She stepped forward from her blur in the box of light. Beneath slightly greying hair her face was wide-mouthed, smiling; her bright eyes wrinkled, they'd had some wrinkles already. Her hips were wide; children had taken the shape from her breasts. Under her apron her summer suit was rather old-fashioned, clean but faded. Clare liked her at once. "It's nice to meet both of you," she said with a laugh that went with the smile. "Excuse me if I don't shake hands, mine are greasy. I'll come through to chat with you soon."

"Oh, Alice," Clare said. "I'm awfully sorry, I completely forgot to say Chris was vegetarian."

"Don't you worry about that. Do you eat eggs, Chris? Well

then, no problem. I expect you're fond of animals? You'll enjoy yourself here, then. It's a menagerie."

So it seemed. In the front room, which was two rooms run together, a cat sat looking fat and lazy, waiting for a nearby fly. Fish gaped at the air or shook themselves into golden glides. A rabbit's black and white nose ventured over the arm of a chair, twitching its pink Y. Two children were calming the rabbit. "Look at Flopsy. You scared her," the girl (twelve years old?) said.

"There you are," Edmund said to Clare, leaning back expansively. Dozens of tiny daggers on pink cloth bulged tightly over his stomach. "Come in, come in," he said.

George poured her a sherry. "No, thank you," Chris said. "A glass of milk would be really nice."

"I'm Olivia," the girl said, admiring his patchwork trousers. "I'll get you some milk."

"Don't you drink beer either?" Edmund demanded, faintly amused. "What's the matter with you?"

"Nothing's wrong with a man for not drinking," George said. " 'O thou invisible spirit of wine, if thou hast no name to be known by, let us call thee devil!' And it's Iago who contradicts him. You were saying you came from Liverpool, Ted."

"Do you want to hold our Flopsy?" the boy (eleven?) said to Chris.

"Yeah." But the rabbit had hardly been dumped on his lap when she leapt off and thumped the floor with her back legs, growling. "Don't do that, Mark," Olivia said, returning with the milk. "She won't be comfortable with so many strangers."

"Oh, all right," Mark said grumpily. He looked at Chris and brightened. "Do you like astronomy?" he said.

Clare remembered not to grin secretively at Chris. "Do you remember the trams going along the middle of the carriageways?" George was saying to Edmund. "And the overhead railway along the dock road? Did you use to go to the pictures all over town? I did when I was a lad, in case my parents didn't book them. And then when I came into the business, my friends would let me watch their shows. I'll never forget some of those places." The rabbit galloped around the room, twisting in mid-leap to come down backward. "The Mere Lane, where they never turned the lights on—I never saw what it looked like properly. And the Essoldo Litherland, where they'd start the film before they opened the doors. And oh, the Winter Gardens in Waterloo, where they put on all the old Hammer films for their last week and let all the little kids in. I suppose they felt they had nothing to lose. It did the kids no harm; they chased about and only sat down for the monsters. Ah, those old theatres. They may have better projection today, but they've lost the personality. Don't you have memories of Liverpool?"

"I suppose there are good things about the place," Edmund said. "If you're a pop singer or one of these Liverpool poets. But it's no use to anyone in my line of business. You have to sever all ties and go where the money is. And that's London."

"Do your parents still live here?" Clare said.

"Yes, in Aigburth. I bought them dinner last night," he said, gazing at Clare as if she should have let him take her. "Oh, I must tell you," he said to George. "There was this incredible queer at the next table that some poor sod had had to buy dinner. An actor, he sounded like."

Clare faded out the anecdote. Chris was admiring a Japanese doll which Olivia had handed him.

"And he stood up and said, 'Oh I *can't* eat this, I *can't*. Please, please take it away.' Seems to me," Edmund ended loudly, "if you're invited to dinner you ought to eat what you're given."

"If I'm cooking," Clare said sharply, "I like to know people will enjoy it."

"That's amazing," Chris said, handing back the doll. There was an awkward silence. "That's where Flopsy pees," Mark shouted, unaware that his voice needn't compete. "In that box. She used to pee on everyone." He looked up at the silence, confused.

Clare smiled at him. "Right," Chris said, and Alice opened the door. "Come and get it," she called.

Beyond the long dining table a tap ticked in the metal sink; Alice tightened it. A pudding in a tin raised itself feebly from a pan of boiling water and fell back, fell back, fell. Alice carried over bowls of homemade chicken soup; George opened bottles. "We must thank Ted for the wine," he said.

"Thank you, Ted," the children said in chorus.

"Oh, it was nothing. The least I could do. Pass the salt."

Olivia was reaching for the cruet when Alice said, "Let's just say grace first, Olivia."

She and the children whispered. George bowed his head, but Clare could see it was a token gesture. Chris smiled at her across the table; next to her she sensed Edmund's impatience.

"Would you like some grapefruit juice?" Alice asked Chris.

"That'd be fantastic. Thank you."

"Actually, it's quite real. Not at all fantastic."

"Olivia!" Alice said.

"Well, that's what our teacher said when I said something was fantastic."

Edmund slurped the last of his soup. "That's something wrong with Liverpool," he told George. "The food. I haven't had a really good meal since I got back—apart from this, I mean. Last night they tried to say they couldn't cook Steak Diane at the table. I soon sorted that out, I can tell you. And told them how much brandy to use. That looks good," he said as Alice hurried over with a steaming casserole of shepherd's pie.

"Chef's special for you," Alice told Chris, and watched approvingly as he ate a large omelette and salad. "Is it fun acting?" she said.

"Right. It really is. Half the time I'm just doing my own

thing, being myself, you know. I reckon I'm most myself when I'm acting. Whoever myself is."

"Have you played Shakespeare?" George said.

"Yeah, at school. I'm not really into that kind of acting. I do more improvisation."

"Oh, George," Alice said. "You and Shakespeare."

"Show me a greater playwright and I'll buy you a yacht. It's true, though, isn't it?" he said to Chris. "Everything is in Shakespeare. He makes you feel things as if you've never felt them before. Whatever it is, he says it best. You describe a book to me, I'll show you the story in Shakespeare."

"There's a few he didn't write," Edmund said.

"All the ones that are worth writing, he wrote. All the films I used to show had Shakespeare stories. That was when they bothered with stories. My father acted most of the plays locally," he told Chris. "He used to rehearse with us, so I knew half of it by heart when I was Mark's age."

Clare glanced at Mark. He frowned at his fork, as if it were a problem in mathematics (astronomy, rather). He smiled shyly to himself when the adults laughed; if he understood the joke he looked up, laughing, and was his mother.

"Then I fell in love with the pictures. I remember looking forward to managing one of my parents' cinemas. I wanted to give people what the pictures gave me, take them out of themselves, make them feel things they'd never feel otherwise. The pictures were magic to me. They still are, sometimes." He poured more wine. "Of course I didn't know then how much work goes into running a cinema. But sometimes when I talk to people coming out of the film, the magic's there."

"Yes, I've finished, thank you. That was very good," Edmund said; his plate was still half full. "Only when you talk to people?" he asked George. "Not when you watch the films?"

"They aren't making films for me any more. Oh, a few. But I'm not there to please myself." Alice was serving tinned pudding to the children, fruit and cream to the adults. "The thing

I had last week, supposed to be a horror film," George said. "It was horrible all right. About an actor who kills off his critics. I wouldn't have minded, but he was a Shakespearean actor, supposed to be copying his behaviour from Shakespeare. There was one," he said to Chris, "where he cooks up a man's pet dogs and makes him choke on them. Oh, I'm sorry," he said as Clare froze. "My table manners aren't all they should be."

"It isn't that," Chris said. "I think Clare's worried because the man Edmund's hunting ate my cat."

George slapped his forehead. "God in heaven. 'I am a very foolish fond old man,' or I might as well be. I'm sorry. One day I'll learn to keep my mouth shut."

"Shit, no. It doesn't matter. Clare told me about your mother and her dog."

"*Ate* your *cat?*" Mark said.

"Yeah."

"That's enough, Mark," Alice said.

"But I want to hear about who ate his cat."

"No, you don't. And I'm sure nobody wants to talk about it, either."

Into the silence Edmund said, "It's presents time." He took several books from his attaché case. "I thought you should know what my books are like, since you're going to be in one. Here you are, Clare. I wrote that one with ladies in mind."

Love Has Many Weapons. The heart has its reasons for murder, and here's Edmund Hall with a dozen of the best. Opposite the blurb Edmund had written "To Clare, who still owes me a dinner date." The row of kisses might almost have been stylized graves. She wondered if he meant her to remember the awkward scene in his hotel room.

"I couldn't leave you out, Alice. That's one for the ladies too." He dealt her *The Homicidal Heart.* "Here's George's. That'll give you some good dreams." He winked at George, who stared at *Sinister Sirens.* "Oh, I didn't know you were coming," Edmund said to Chris.

" 'Was ever book so fairly bound?' " George said. "I've left a bit out of that. Never mind. Thank you, Ted."

"About my book—there's something I wanted to say while we're all together. It would be heartless of me not to put in something about your loved ones. Well, you're the ones who can tell me what to put. But it isn't the sort of thing I should take notes of. Write it down for me, anything you want to say. Oh, Clare, can you tell me where I can contact your sister-in-law?"

"Dorothy? I'll ask her if she wants to get in touch with you."

"Sell me to her as hard as you can. Now there's one more thing. I expect this book to make me a lot of money. Jesus."

The rabbit had been rubbing her chin on his attaché case; now she was nibbling a corner. Clare made a grab—she didn't want Edmund to get his hands on the rabbit—but the animal fled under the table. Olivia picked her up. The girl's long face had been morosely introverted throughout the meal, rather like George's in his office; now it softened as she carried the rabbit out, stroking her ears. "Naughty Flopsy," she said softly. "Naughty girl."

"I expect to make a lot of money," Edmund said. "I want the book to make you some too. You're contributing; you get paid as contributors. Now, George, no arguments. You'd pay a man if he helped you run your cinema."

George was gazing into himself. "Say it, George. Whatever it is," Edmund said.

"I was thinking of my mother. She worked in a music hall when she was eight. She helped my father start the cinemas. She brought me up and looked after him, and kept the cinemas going. And—I never told you this, Alice—she sold her house to subsidize the Newsham."

"I know she did," Alice said, smiling for him alone.

"You'd think she'd earned a peaceful death, wouldn't you? Instead of—"

"I know," Alice interrupted. Clare sensed her heading him

off before he upset himself. "Why don't you show them the music hall scrapbook?" Alice said.

"There's a bit of business I want to discuss," Edmund told George.

"Mark, see if Olivia wants to play in the park. Will you wash?" Alice said to Clare. "My nails break easily."

She switched on the fluorescent tube; it stuttered like lightning. Something rattled loudly in the front room. "Come and help me sort out the children," Alice said.

The children had drawn the partition which stood in for the dividing wall; it rattled as Alice pushed it back. "Is the funny little car yours?" Olivia asked when she saw Clare.

"Now, Olivia. They're good little cars, those," Alice said. "Don't get settled in here, children. We'll need all the room."

"Oh, why?" Olivia said.

"Because Daddy and his friends want to talk about Grandma Pugh."

"What about her?"

"Just about her, Mark. It wouldn't interest you." But Olivia was sobbing. "Oh never mind, lovey," Alice said, putting an arm about the girl's trembling shoulders. "I know, I know."

The television shouted; interference or a flaw plucked at the image, pinching it inward. "No, Mark. Not when we're going to talk. Tidy up your books, now. It's too nice to stay in. Why don't you go for a ride in the park?"

Mark gathered up books about astronomy. "I can't ride my bike," Olivia said, picking up books on costume, sniffling. "It hurts," and she ran upstairs.

"Take Olivia to feed the ducks, Mark."

"I want to play football."

"Go on, Mark. Your sister isn't well; she needs cheering up. Until she gets used to it," she said to Clare.

"Used to what?"

"Something that only happens to girls, Mark. I'll tell you

about it later if you promise to be nice to her. And don't ask *her!*" she shouted after him.

Clare gazed at the rabbit, which had dozed through the whole thing, squashed small on an armchair, nose buried in the fur of her chest. "Let's do the washing up," Alice said. In the dining room she said, "You boys had better take your seats in the other room before the children and animals steal them."

Which meant she would be excluded from their talk, Clare thought, frustrated. It annoyed her, this assumption that men must talk while women did the washing up.

"That's got rid of them," Alice said. "Actually, I wanted to talk to you alone. Is Edmund a friend of yours?"

"Not particularly. I'm helping him."

"What's your opinion of him?"

Clare gazed into the yard, which was almost full of a coal shed and four bicycles. "I don't know," she said guardedly. "What's yours?"

"I don't like him."

The tap coughed up ropes of water. Clare dropped cups into the suds; the washing-up bowl plopped like a pond. "Why not?"

George appeared, seeking glasses. He took three as Alice wiped them. "What about the kitchen staff?" she said.

"Oh, we're not drinking yet. Just getting ready." He began to tidy the draining board, until Alice shooed him away, flapping her towel.

" 'Away, you scullion!' " he shouted, dodging. " 'You rampallian! you fustilarian!' " and slammed the door just ahead of a ball of towel.

"Why don't I like Edmund. Because he uses people. I didn't like him when George told me about him. He made you do all the talking to George, didn't he? I think he uses people so he won't get involved himself."

"Did you make him dinner so you could examine him?"

"No, it's just that George is more relaxed at home, especially after dinner. I thought I'd make sure he was a match for Edmund." She rubbed a plate, preoccupied. "And I wanted to be nearby when they talked. I don't want George upset again. He loved his mother very much, you see. So did I." She turned away. Suddenly she smiled widely at Clare. "I'm glad I've met you, though. And your friend is nice."

"Yes, he is rather." Clare was surprised how proud she felt to say so—prouder than she'd ever felt while defending Rob to her parents. Rob made her think again of Dorothy. Poor Dorothy. Here with the Pughs, Clare could see how unsuited Rob and Dorothy had been. She must go and see Dorothy. God, how bitchy she'd been to her last time! Maybe she could find Dorothy a man. Her mind listed couples: Rob and Dorothy, George and Alice— It stopped, because she'd stopped it. "Yes, I'm fond of Chris," she said, to get him out of her mind.

But she found she had been in his. "I'm not surprised you showed it twice," he was saying to George. "*Bonnie and Clyde,*" he explained to the late-comers. "My favourite movie. The first part, anyway. Before they all start to get killed."

"Can we get on now?" Edmund demanded, impatiently laying aside one of several scrapbooks and photo albums.

"Oh, right. I just thought we should wait for Clare. And Alice."

"Thank you, Chris," Alice said. Clare found herself blushing and was bewildered.

"All right," Edmund said, sitting forward sharply. "George says he wants to help."

His amusement had faded. Clare was sure he'd wanted to take George aside and persuade him. His nose twitched, but behind him the rabbit had won that contest. Clare jammed her handkerchief into her face and glanced hastily away, toward the goldfish hanging from their gulping mouths.

"You know after the inquest I opened my mouth even wider than usual," George said. "I didn't know they were going to quote me. Well, the other day they sent a reporter to get me to say Ted had used me against my will. I won't repeat what I said to him. But that doesn't make up for what I said after the inquest."

"Still, it did some good," Clare said. "Otherwise Chris couldn't have got in touch with us."

Edmund made an ambiguous sound. Alice said, "But now he knows you're after him, the man you're hunting."

"That doesn't matter. He doesn't know how," Edmund said. "He'll assume we're following the police. That's what the police must think themselves; they haven't been in touch with me. He won't see us coming from another direction."

"If I hadn't opened my mouth he wouldn't know anything," George said.

The rabbit had been lifting fire-irons off their stand with her teeth, dropping them on the rug. Now she hopped into Chris's lap and chattered her teeth, shoving her nose under his hand to be stroked. "She makes that sound when she's happy," Alice explained. "She's a funny little thing. Isn't she, George?" But she couldn't get hold of the conversation.

"You could be very useful, George," Edmund said. He and the cat gazed loftily at the rabbit. "You could see what you can get out of Kelly's doctor, his grandmother's doctor. If anyone knows what's behind this, he must. You're the man to find out."

"Why is George the man?" Alice said.

"Because he'd be one professional talking to another. Chris is no use, too young. Clare might do it, but what he might have to say could be pretty horrible. As for me, I'd be too busy worrying whether he'd read about me."

"Don't you tell people who you are before you question them?"

"Certainly I do, Alice. But they haven't usually been turned against me beforehand."

"Then he'll feel the same about anyone who's helping you."

"Now, Alice," George said. "I've offered to help. I'll feel better if I do."

"I don't want you to. I wouldn't feel safe. Suppose this Kelly still has the same doctor? Suppose he hears you've been asking about him?"

"I think he'd stay away from that doctor," Edmund said.

"But the doctor might tell his grandmother. Suppose Kelly finds out where we live?"

"Don't be silly," George said. "How could he?"

Clare felt Alice's despair. Suddenly she knew why Alice had sent the children to the park: so that the horror couldn't touch them in any way. Now the horror was threatening to come closer. So long as it didn't touch Alice's home, her children, it was bearable; but now she couldn't be certain of keeping it out.

"I know how you feel, dear," George said. "I'll be careful. I'll want to be certain the doctor won't give us away."

Alice slumped back, closing her eyes wearily.

"Now, how do we get you into his surgery?" Edmund said. "You wouldn't know anyone who might be on his list?"

"I know people in the district. There's an actress friend of my mother's, and the fellow who helps me out at the Newsham."

"You'd just need to go to the surgery on their behalf, you see. That would be perfect. Let's see if we can figure you out an approach once you get in."

If George borrows someone's medical card, Clare thought, he can be traced through them. She glimpsed Olivia and Mark in bed, the orange face bobbing at the window, climbing in. Well, tell George he can be traced! she prompted Alice. She glanced round to grimace at her. Exhausted, Alice was asleep in her chair.

Clare was debating whether to make the point herself when George said, "I think I've heard Ruby mention a Dr. Miller.

I'll see. Now if you'll excuse me, I'll just ring the Newsham to make sure they've no problems."

"Don't be long. You deserve a treat," Edmund said, producing and brandishing a hip-flask of bourbon. "Wake up, Alice," he called. "You don't know what you're missing."

 Monday,
September 15

A woman was emerging from the doctor's house as George rode up. "Are there many waiting?" he called.

"Half a dozen," she said, and had to take a wheezing breath. "No, one just   went in. There's   five. No, wait a   moment, there's a woman   with her   son. They might both be here   for treatment."

"Thank you," George said when he was sure she'd finished. Five or six, either was worth a ride around the side streets. Cycling relaxed him. Ten minutes and he'd be ready for the doctor. He rode away down Boswell Street.

The houses were Siamese twins. One pair shared a shallow porch supported by a thin stone pillar; the left-hand house was pebble-dashed as far as its half of the pillar, leaving its twin drab with various faded shades of brick. Some neighbourly pairs supported each other with timber struts. Beyond a crew-cut hedge and dusty curtains, George saw a vase of flowers that looked as if they'd sat in an attic for years.

"Tell the doctor your friend is a friend of Kelly's grandmother," Chris had suggested. "Say his grandmother is anxious about him, you don't know why. Say your friend told you and you promised you'd try to help. That way you don't have to know anything else, right?"

It seemed all right. Ruby Roberts had turned out to be a

108

patient of Dr. Miller's. She had been tearfully glad to see George, had talked about his mother for hours, strengthening his will to help Edmund. She needed more medicine; George had every reason to visit the surgery. He cycled by the old Smithdown Picture Playhouse, a supermarket now; the noses of shopping trolleys nested inside one another. At least Bill Williams's projection was improving, he thought, gazing at the lost cinema. Ten minutes and he'd go into the waiting room.

Down Tunnel Road was Fred Robinson's old cinema, the Avenue, a bingo hall now. Once George had leaned forward to watch a film and the front row of the circle had collapsed beneath him. He rode into the terraced side streets that would take him that way. But there were no side streets. As if the main road were a film set, there was nothing behind except a waste of pale clay and grit and odd bricks, a few scrawled walls, a heap of flame, a cloud of smoke wide as streets resting almost inertly on the orange clay. Specks gathered on the lenses of George's spectacles. He cycled quickly back toward Lodge Lane. The landscape had made him uneasy, irritable.

The stopped clock in the Lodge Lane library tower pretended it was 8:24. George glanced angrily at his watch, wobbling. At Boswell Street a clown was sketched on an ice-cream van, wearing the contents of a cornet as a turban. Five minutes. Children ran out of the baths, thumping each other with rolled wet towels. A cat sat on a butcher's slab. ECONOMY O was books, George gathered from the window display. In the side streets, many houses had tin instead of windows; it was like one of those horror films where people turn to reveal eyes full of white makeup. A baby with a red rubber stopper sat in a pushchair outside a dilapidated house. George swerved around a child's red boot, a pram wheel, a clutter of young black footballers. He felt nervous, out of place.

One minute. All right, no hurry. Cars were hunting along Lodge Lane, eyes bright in the evening; children ran in front of them, for a dare. Down the side streets to his left, a frieze of clouds curled, sharp against a band of orange. In a window a rabbit hung by its feet from a metal hook, its head wrapped in a bloody plastic bag.

For some reason, that upset him. He almost scraped the doctor's gateposts. The house rushed at him, twin windows peering over the downstairs bay, long eyes above a longer snout. He padlocked his bicycle and hurried through the arch of the porch into the hall.

A woman slammed a filing drawer and turned in the same brisk movement. "Yes, what is it?" she said, her upswept spectacles glinting pointedly at the clock.

"I'm here on behalf of Ruby Roberts."

She nodded once at the medical card; the bits of glass decorating her spectacles blinked. "The usual? I'll ask Doctor to write the prescription," she said. "Then you needn't wait."

"Ah, no. If you don't mind," George stumbled, "I'd like a word with him myself."

"What did you want to speak to him about?"

He'd recovered. "I'll tell him that myself, thank you," he said.

But in the waiting room he found that his chest was pounding. He gazed at his interlocked fingers, forced himself to breathe slowly. Gilbert and Sullivan chattered cheerily behind him. A bell rang. A man shuffled coughing through a side door; the hem of his overcoat trailed after him, dragging toffee-papers. George wished the music would stop babbling, wished that the two small children wouldn't clatter among the chairs out of reach of their dull-eyed mother. He rummaged in a pile of magazines. Ah, the *Beano. Biff! Yow! Oof!* The bell rang. "Come on, you little buggers," the woman said, shoving her children toward the side door. Ruby was a friend of Kelly's grandmother. Of Mrs. Kelly? No, that mightn't be her name. *Thud! Aargh!* The bell rang. The bell rang. George started. He was alone in the waiting room. The bell was ringing for him.

He strode onstage, as his father had used to describe himself striding—and halted, taken aback. The doctor's room, his chair and desk and the rest of the furniture were enormous. When he saw the flowers beyond the flowered curtains, George realized that the room was ordinary: it was the doctor who was small. But he'd lost his poise.

The doctor swung round in his swivel chair: sixty years old, or older. The cords of his neck sprang taut; his bald head shone unwrinkled. "For Ruby Roberts, is it?" he said, already scribbling.

"That's it." All George could do while he tried to regain his poise was speak. "She asked me to—"

"Yes, all right, all right. Her usual." He glanced up quickly, frowning, as George sat opposite him. "Isn't that right?"

For a moment George wanted to take the prescription and leave. He could feel the man's impatience; its momentum would carry George away if he didn't slow it down. "I think so," he said slowly. "She said she wanted a tonic—"

"Yes. Yes. Her nerve tonic." George had made him more impatient. The tendons of his hand stood out, working beneath the almost-translucent skin. He was a framework of cables, exposed by his energy that had burned away the flesh, the superfluity. Even his head looked as if it had dispensed with hair.

George took a slow deep breath. "Dr. Miller," he said.

"Yes?" He snapped his pen into its cap, then glanced up at George's silence. "Yes?"

He couldn't tell his lies. Not while battling the doctor's impatience, not beneath the scrutiny of his quick pale-blue eyes. In his job the doctor had to read people all the time. George saw from the doctor's expression that some of his thoughts had spilled onto his face. It didn't matter. "It doesn't matter," he said.

The doctor sighed and sat forward. "Whenever people tell me that," he said, "it always does." Beneath the impatience

George saw the beginning of concern. "Now, what's the trouble?" Dr. Miller said.

George teetered on the edge of the doctor's readiness to listen, and said, "I'm looking for Christopher Kelly."

"Are you now." Emotion flickered unreadably on the doctor's face. "You're this writer," he said.

"No, I am not." In a moment he realized: "You read about the inquest."

"So I did."

"Then you read about me. I'm the son of the lady who was killed."

"Ah, the man who didn't like what the writer was doing." He peered into George's eyes. "And why are *you* looking for Christopher?" he demanded.

"I want to see him suffer. I want to be there when he's caught. If I can hurt him I wouldn't mind going to prison for it. They should bring back torture for him. It wouldn't bring back my mother, but it would make me feel better. I'd help mutilate him, I can tell you."

A bird twittered. For George the silence was full of his own surprise. Until he'd spoken he hadn't known what he felt. There had been nobody he could tell, not even Alice. He felt weak with relief.

The doctor gazed at him. George picked up the prescription and stood. "I'm sorry," he said. "I know your patients trust you. I came here to try to make you betray that trust."

He was at the door when the doctor said, "Have I refused to talk to you?"

George turned. A secret emotion was flickering over the doctor's face. "I gave my word about some things," he said, his voice as private as his gaze. "But that isn't the same as a vow of silence. Is it?" he demanded.

"I suppose not."

"Sit down," the doctor said. His purposeful rapidity had returned. "I can't tell you where to find Christopher," he said as a preamble. "I don't know."

"I don't suppose you'd tell me anyway."

"No, certainly not. But I'd like you to know a few things about him. About his background."

"Does that explain what he did to my mother?"

"Perhaps." For a moment George was sure that the doctor's relief at the chance to talk was as great as his own. "It depends whether you believe in black magic," the doctor said.

George thought of Christopher Lee shouting at a skeleton on a horse; he thought of Barbara Steele, the girl from Birkenhead, with her face painted green. "I don't believe in the supernatural," he said.

"Nor did I," the doctor said, gazing inward. "Nor did I."

The woman in the launderette had told Chris and Clare something—"Was Kelly's mother mixed up in black magic?" George said.

The doctor nodded. "But I didn't know until years later that she was involved. I heard about the black magic from someone else."

The doctor sat back. He seemed less to relax than to anticipate strain. "Tell me what you would have done," he said. Hearing the start of a story, George relaxed—realized that Dr. Miller had freely admitted that Kelly was the man they were hunting. He managed not to react visibly.

"There was a woman, one of my regular patients," the doctor said. "This was twenty-five years ago, but I won't tell you her name. A hypochondriac. Every doctor has them. It's a disease without a cure." He shook his head rapidly, as if to dislodge something. "The mind can be a terrible thing, you know. The suffering it can cause.

"This woman, she suffered. Terribly. The joke of it was, she didn't believe in medicine—not the kind she could get here. She was one for the miracle cures. I had to calm her down when they didn't work. I had to cure her of them sometimes, some of the things they fooled her into swallowing.

"She used to catch complaints from the medical dictionaries. I thought the library shouldn't let her read them, but she'd only have invented something. The trouble was, she wasn't bright. Once she got an idea in her head, it took ten men and a bulldozer to get it out again. I never really convinced her my medicines weren't addictive.

"Now then. All of a sudden she didn't come in for months. I almost thought she'd found her miracle. Then back she came one day. But she stopped me writing her prescription; she didn't want that. She wanted to ask me something.

"She was worried. More than usual, much more. I honestly felt that if I gave her the wrong answer she'd panic. It took her a while to get the question out. Well, she wanted to know if anyone could say in advance that a baby would be born deformed.

"No, she didn't say 'deformed.' She said 'monstrous.' "

He nodded sharply. George wondered if he should have heard more meaning than he had. "You say she wasn't Kelly's mother?" he said, to say something.

"Oh no. That was another business entirely." The doctor wrinkled his brow hard, as if trying to squeeze something out. "I never saw Christopher's mother at all," he said, but for a moment an emotion peered from behind his poise; it had gone before George could make it out. The floor-length plastic curtains shuffled, creaking.

"Well, I wanted to know who'd been telling the woman rubbish like that," Dr. Miller said. "But she wouldn't say. I could see she suspected I was ducking her question. Well, I didn't take the question seriously, but the anxiety behind it was another matter. I told her there was no reason why she should have a deformed child. She was in her early thirties; there were no medical complications. I told her not even her worrying could harm the child. I hoped that was true. I'd seen some bad accidents of birth in my time. Very, very bad." He pressed his eyes with his fingers. "Then I packed her off home, told her not to listen to any more rubbish.

"She didn't come back for a couple of months—which was

unusual, of course. When she did, she was nearer to panic, much nearer. I thought she'd been sitting at home, getting herself worked up, but do you know what she told me? Her husband had forbidden her to come, because he said I'd been lying to her. The baby was going to be born monstrous.

"I wouldn't like to tell you what I called that man. I told her if he thought he could do my job he could come in here any day. I told her to send him anyway, if he dared come; and if he didn't, to stop listening to his drivel. I honestly believe I got through to her for once. When she left she actually looked happy."

George's attention was wandering. This story couldn't be the vital link he'd hoped for. The doctor seemed so relieved to talk that he was rambling. George glanced about, mentally tidying the office. Prescription forms lolled from a pigeonhole; he restrained himself from pushing them in.

"The next time she came," the doctor said, "she was completely terrified."

His voice was harsh; his eyes gleamed like glass, held still by memory. "You see, it wasn't her husband who'd told her originally what would happen to her baby. It was another man, who had power over her and her husband. Those were her words: had power. And he hadn't just said the baby would be born a monster. He'd said he would make it be born that way.

"I didn't lose my temper with her, not even when she wouldn't tell me his name. I'd have arranged for the police to call on him, I can tell you. She did tell me how she'd heard of him. She'd seen his notice in a shop window, among the other postcards—wouldn't tell me where. It promised youth, new vigour, perfect health, the meaning of life, the usual nonsense. She told me the slogan: The Way of Absolute Power.

"So she went to the address on the card." The doctor gazed aside at a memory, as if glimpsing something from the corner of his eye. "She would never describe him, that man, even when I asked her. It was as if I'd asked what God looked like, or the Devil. That kind of pure terror. That was part of what he did to her.

"She said he asked her first of all why she'd come. He was finding out how gullible she was. Then he said he was going to model her. And he made a model of her, in some kind of clay. She had to sit absolutely still for an hour. If she so much as moved a finger he would look at her, and she'd feel as if she'd committed the worst sin in the world.

"That was her first taste of his power. He was a witch-doctor, even if he was an Englishman. That's what they do—show their victims they've been cursed, to make the curse work on their minds. But this swine was an Englishman.

"She said the model looked exactly like her. Not *very* like —exactly. As if she were lying there in his hands, gone grey and shrivelled up. He said that was what she was like, but he was going to change it.

"She said he made her younger, just by smoothing out the clay a tiny fraction. Everyone told her she looked years younger. Well, she always looked older than her age, because of the worry. But you know, it seemed to me she'd looked younger the day she came back here after vanishing for months. I couldn't be sure, though, because I'd been looking at how worried she was.

"The next thing was, he made her healthier. He dipped the model in some herbs. And of course she hadn't come to me for medicine for months. You could see why she believed in him.

"Then she roped her husband in, because the witch-doctor asked her to. Now, he didn't need miracles. He wasn't bright, but he'd never needed me in his life. I should have realized there was something wrong; he wasn't the kind to get mixed up in that sort of thing, but I thought he must be doing it to please her. Well, she said he felt like a new man. So they both began going to the meetings.

"She wouldn't tell me much about the meetings—or at least, I knew there was a lot she wasn't telling. They met in the basement under the witch-doctor's house, about a dozen of his victims. And he made them do things.

"Even the things she told me, she didn't understand. He made them stand in a ring and he'd stand in the center with all the models. He moved the models as if they were dancing, and everyone danced round him. She said one odd thing, and she wouldn't look at me—she said she didn't like to dance so slowly, but that was the way he was moving the models.

"She showed me how they danced. She said she didn't mind it, but I'm not so sure. They lifted their feet as high as they could and strutted about with their legs wide open. But slowly, very slowly. I didn't like it; there was something very nasty about watching this pregnant woman dancing like that, here in front of me—something degrading. He said it was to help his power, some such rubbish. But I think he was showing the contempt he felt for them.

"I could tell she didn't like the meetings. She went to as few as she dared, I think. She didn't like some of the things he did with the models. He gave one woman an abortion without even touching her—well, that was probably a pseudocyesis, a hysterical pregnancy.

"I think she'd have refused to go to the meetings if he hadn't had that model of her. She didn't like some of the things he made them all do. He made her think things about herself, or about the others. He made her do things so that he could watch. But she couldn't stop herself; she said she didn't want to. It was only afterward she was disturbed.

"The last meeting she went to, he made one of the others do something. Whatever it was, it decided her never to go again. But she'd just decided that when he told her she was pregnant."

The doctor leaned forward; his chair creaked sharply. The sounds of the room flooded back around George. The curtains shifted, half awake. "What scared her was she hadn't known she was pregnant herself. Yet he did, as if he could look inside her. He told her that if she found she wasn't, she need never come to another meeting. So when she found she was, that scared her into going back.

"Then he said she must promise the child to him."

"But what about her husband?" George demanded. "What the devil was he doing?"

"Keeping quiet. You see, he hadn't believed the witch-doctor at first; he'd had to have the power proved to him. So she said. And after that he didn't dare open his mouth, whatever the proof had been. Well, she still wouldn't promise the child. The witch-doctor didn't argue. All he said was that if she didn't give it to him she would bear a monster.

"Well, she didn't know what to do. If she went back she would have to promise; if she didn't she was making her baby be born a monster. I'll be honest, I didn't know what to believe. And she didn't help by going on about the things he could do, how old he'd told her he was, the things he knew that no one else did. And, oh yes, how he could sing without words in a terrible deep voice and make her feel something behind her, coming out of the earth or the basement wall or some such nonsense. I mean to say. Would you have believed her?"

"I don't know," George said, for the story had disturbed him, here amid the smell of antiseptic. At once he saw that the doctor had hoped he would say No.

"I've seen pregnant women as good as mad," Dr. Miller said, a little defensively. "I thought there was a bit too much of her story, what with black magic and her husband plotting against her. But I felt there was more wrong than just her mind. So I told her to go home, and I'd talk to her husband.

"She didn't like that idea, but she hadn't any others. I went to their house next evening. She must have told him I was coming. I don't know what else she'd said, but she had a bruise on her face as big as your fist.

"Well, I asked him what this voodoo nonsense was about. And he said she'd made most of it up. He hadn't told her the baby would be a monster, he'd just said I couldn't be sure. Oh, there'd been a faith-healer all right; she'd even asked him once for an abortion. But all the rest was her imagination. Even so, he didn't like the effect the man had been having on her mind, so he said. She wasn't to go near him again. In fact, they were planning to move out of town.

"I believed him, because he was saying what I'd thought. The only odd thing was, he kept shouting. I remember thinking he didn't need to shout to convince me. I think he was shouting himself down. He didn't want to believe they were still in the witch-doctor's power. I think that was why he hit her, for saying what he wanted to forget.

"She didn't say a word, and I couldn't tell what she was thinking. So I told him to look after her, treat her kindly—I didn't want her having any more bruises, and he knew that was what I meant. I tried to get him to tell me the witch-doctor's name, but he wouldn't. Said the man was giving up his mumbo-jumbo. He was lying, of course.

"I must say I felt quite pleased with myself. When I didn't see her again I thought he'd begun looking after her properly. I should have looked in on them, I know, but I hadn't the time," he said harshly. "She had a midwife, if they hadn't left town before the baby was due—I'd told him to try to get her moved before then. Of course she didn't trust hospitals.

"Then her next-door neighbour ran in here one evening to tell me the baby was coming."

Though the room was thick with dusk, the doctor made no move to switch on the light. He seemed glad of the dimness, glad to be able to gaze without seeing. Outside the window, flowers nodded, bulbous on thin necks; the curtains scraped the floorboards softly, restlessly. George watched darkness fill the doctor's face.

"The midwife was out on a call. The woman wanted me to go; no one else would do. Her neighbour pleaded with me to go. She said her friend was terrified, no telling what she might do.

"I only had a couple of patients waiting. I dealt with them as quickly as I could and hurried round there. She was lying on the bed. I could see the baby was due at any moment. She was gasping, but she managed to say she could feel the baby. She could feel how it was moving, she screamed that. She could feel it was a monster.

"That was all she had time to say. And all I could do was give her husband his instructions and begin the delivery."

He had no face now, only talking darkness. "It wasn't a difficult delivery," he said. "I remember I was hearing children in the street, I could hear a football hitting the wall of the house. There was a bit of a breeze; it was an evening like the one we had today. I brought that out of her on an evening like this. Actually, the head looked almost normal."

George stared at the darkness, which had fallen silent. The only sound in the room was the faint oily creaking of the plastic curtains. The darkness was rushing at him, exploding behind his eyes. "Was it dead," he blurted, "the baby?" It was the nearest he could come to voicing his unease.

"It couldn't have lived," the doctor said. George heard shame, self-righteousness, the memory of disbelief.

The desk light glared down its cone. Dr. Miller's face was expressionless; perhaps he had prepared that in the dark. "Was it—" George said, startled by the light, and wished he hadn't begun the question. Incomplete, it sounded as if he'd repeated his previous question, like a relentless interviewer. He had to say, "Was it as bad as she'd feared?"

"Yes," the doctor said. "Yes, it was."

His eyes were blank, as if he refused to allow them to fill. George tried to look away. But the doctor took his gaze to be a question. "This is all I'll tell you," he said, and George felt he hoped it would leave him in the telling. "It was nearly two feet long."

George glanced away, at the glossy lamplit patch of yellow wall, smooth as jelly, at the greasy-looking flowers that swayed on the plastic curtains, at anything.

"She never saw it. I took it away," Dr. Miller said rapidly, anxious to finish. "But a couple of weeks later her husband came for tranquillizers, for her. She'd already known the baby was a monster, you see. He couldn't persuade her different. And she was convinced the baby was still moving.

"Not alive. Moving. She said the witch-doctor could make that happen, with his model. She said it would crawl out of wherever it was and come back to her. She'd been dreaming she'd found it writhing along the hall, covered with earth. Her husband didn't dare ask her what it looked like." He said violently into his own silence: "I gave him the tranquillizers. They moved to another house shortly after. I never saw them again."

The dim flowers peered in the window, tapping. "What's all that got to do with Kelly?" George demanded, furious with the enclosing darkness beyond the lamp.

The doctor mused, frowning. At last he said, "The woman I've told you about didn't promise her child. Christopher's mother did."

"Do you mean that worried her so much it made him what he is?"

"Perhaps," the doctor said, gazing at him as if he hadn't paid attention.

"Did you deliver him?"

For a moment the doctor's hidden emotion flickered clearly: horror, dismay. "No," he said, and it was gone. "It was nothing to do with me. There was a doctor in Wales, but he's dead. I should have liked to talk to him. Christopher's grandmother did." The dismay peered out again. "But I'm sure she exaggerates."

"Why, what happened?"

"No. I'm sorry." The doctor sat up sharply, determined. "I gave her my word. We agreed to forget the past. I thought she was making too much of it, anyway. I thought that to harp on it would only make the boy worse. He might have been all right if he'd been left alone. The witch-doctor was dead," he said defiantly. "That was partly why I promised."

"I don't understand," George said, hoping that might make a difference. "What happened to the boy's mother?"

"She died. She's dead. No more. I've said too much already." He tapped piles of forms together impatiently, rolled the desktop down.

George stood up. "Well, thank you for your help," he said. He found his legs were trembling.

"Of course," the doctor said, half to himself, "the boy's grandmother could tell you the rest."

George gazed down at the bald head. "Would you tell me her address?" he said, more in incredulity than in hope.

"Would you expect me to?"

"No, I wouldn't."

"Neither would she," the doctor mused. "Neither would anyone else. Still, I don't think I've long to run now. And if you told anyone who gave you the address I've only to say that I didn't. But I think it's time she was reminded what she's responsible for. She lives at 2A Mozart Street. Her name is Mary Kelly."

At the door into the hall, George looked back. Dr. Miller was still sitting amid the island of light, a small figure perched on a swivel chair. He looked relieved, yet unsure. Unsure whether he'd done the right thing? At once George was certain the doctor had been pondering what to do since he'd read the report of the inquest. Perhaps he had been waiting apprehensively for some such report for years. Down the hall, his receptionist, no doubt his wife, was cooking dinner. George hurried out and halted, shocked by the urban purring of the night.

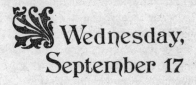# Wednesday, September 17

As they turned from Lodge Lane into Mozart Street, Edmund said, "Let me do the talking. Just to be confronted with you three might make her say things she wouldn't say otherwise. It's a gamble, but I've a feeling it'll work."

So that was why he'd let them come. Clare was sure he would have preferred them not to. If she hadn't rung George yesterday to discuss a school visit to the Newsham, she wouldn't even have been aware that they knew the grandmother's address. She'd rung Edmund at once. This woman knew why Rob had been killed; she might even be partly responsible. And Chris should meet her too; she'd shouted down the start of his protests. And George.

Each side of Mozart Street was an unbroken two-storey terrace; the front doors opened onto the pavement. A few of the houses were painted chocolate, to set them apart from the line. On some, the bricks that formed an arch around the front door and framed the windows were painted blue or moss-green. Snatches of television leaked from windows, some of which were new, with louvres. Several windows were filled with paler brick or boards; through a jagged upstairs sash Clare saw a doorway onto a dark landing. Beneath her feet the gravel of the roadway slithered, crunching.

Number 2A was the furthest from Lodge Lane. At the end of

the street, large shallow steps led down to an alley; the twilight of the street was darker there. A shouting man played football among the parked cars; he and the children with him glanced at Edmund's party. Edmund reached for the knocker on a front door that looked like part of a dead tree, mossed with paint. He halted, listening.

Inside the house, beyond the swollen, jammed sash of the grimy window, they could hear a woman's voice. "Through my fault," it said, "through my fault." A television, Clare thought, turned up loud enough to be heard through the glass. But as she gazed, a figure took shape in the grime as in fog, flickering with firelight: a woman sitting forward in a chair, dim hands clasped, blurred face confronting an open doorway. "Through my most grievous fault," she shouted, punching her breast so that her whole body shook. She was praying.

Clare saw her start when Edmund knocked. She rose and walked toward the doorway, so slowly that the grime of the window might have been thick around her. Clare gazed at the dim empty room, the colourless fat chairs. At last she heard the front door open.

The woman was in her seventies. Her thin sharp face, pinched toward the pointed chin as if between finger and thumb, peered forward on a neck whose wrinkles sagged. Her large pale-blue eyes frowned warily; her lips were gripped thinly together. Her hands, spotted like old food, clamped themselves on the doorframe, barring the way; a worn handbag hung from one arm. Her grey uneven hair stood up in spikes. She looked like a guard defending her post among her fallen comrades, or a martyr.

"Mrs. Mary Kelly?" Edmund said.

"Yes?"

He was lagging. Clare could see why; he was fascinated by the way Mrs. Kelly was dressed—green cardigan, faded purple skirt, striped yellow-and-black socks, pink fluffy slippers. "We'd like to talk to you about your grandson," he said.

He snapped his card toward her, like a dealer. She ignored it and gazed toward the man with the football. "Good evening, Mr. Wright," she called.

"Hello there, Mrs. Kelly. Got visitors, have you?"

"We'll just see about that. How many are there?"

"Three men. I think it's three men; you know how they are these days. And a girl."

"Thank you, Mr. Wright." As she turned back to them Clare saw that the large pale eyes never moved. They gazed blindly at her. "Say your names," Mrs. Kelly said.

"Clare Frayn." When the blank intent gaze moved on, she shivered.

"Chris Barrow."

"Edmund Hall. I'm a writer."

"Oh, you're this writer, are you? So that's what you want. I thought so. And who's the other one, that's keeping quiet?"

"I'm George Pugh, Mrs. Kelly. A cinema manager," he stumbled on.

"No need to sound so sorry about it," she said, grinning or baring her teeth. "Well, you sound human, anyway. A bit less sure of yourself than your friends. And you've come to try to upset me, have you?"

"We don't want to upset you," Edmund said.

"And you won't, oh no. Make no mistake about that. I'm past being upset. Not like my friend you made ill, in the launderette. So now, do you still want to talk to me?"

"Please. We'd like to hear anything you can tell us about your grandson. These people have relatives who suffered from him, you see."

Chris was hardly a relative of his cat, but Clare suppressed her amusement. "So that's why it takes four of you to talk to me, is it. Because people suffered." Mrs. Kelly smiled, then pounced: "Suffered in what way?"

"Could we discuss it inside?" Edmund said. "There are children listening." And there were, sidling closer.

"If I let you in—*if* I let you in—you're to follow me. I'll show you where to go, and you're to stay there. I won't have you excusing yourselves and wandering off. And don't think you can creep out, either. Is that understood? All right. Mr. Pugh, you come in last and slam the door."

The house smelled like dusty old clothes in a mouldering wardrobe. Mrs. Kelly's voice echoed amid the hollow clatter of feet on the bare boards. "One more thing. Just remember my friends are outside. I've only to scream. Even four of you won't stop me screaming."

Clare slowed, gazing up the uncarpeted stairs. A rusty socket hung from a flex above the landing; stripes of wallpaper stepped down toward her, almost colourless beneath twilight and dirt. "Never mind looking how bad it is," Mrs. Kelly said, startling her. "Mr. Wright's told me all about that. It's better than falling downstairs over the carpet. You'll just have to put up with it, as I have to."

"I'm sorry," Clare said. "I couldn't see for a moment, after the sun." The hall flung her voice back at her, making her stammer. As she followed Mrs. Kelly the dusty furniture muffled her words, like a hand before her mouth.

The room no longer had a door. Despite the warm evening and the coal fire in the grate, the room was cold, and almost bare except for several armchairs. A blackened rectangle of linoleum protected the floorboards from sparks, although the fire was caged. In an alcove, two framed photographs, dim with dust, stood on a small table. Large and tiny pigeons hung in flight on the pinkish wallpaper, halves of pigeons were trapped in the joins. Near the ceiling, ragged leaves of wallpaper hung down; in some of them, spiders crouched on tangles. "Sit down," Mrs. Kelly said. "I want you sitting down."

The armchair puffed dust at Clare, like a fungus. Mrs. Kelly grasped the back of the chair nearest the fire and lowered herself to sit, facing the doorway. She put her handbag on the floor beside a large portable radio, a *Liverpool Echo*, the *Catholic Pictorial*, and the tabloid which had reported Edmund's search. "Now talk away," she said.

"As I say," Edmund said, "we'd like you to tell us about your grandson."

"I'm sure you would. But why should I? Is it your business? I don't want to talk about him." She closed her eyes tight and opened them, unchanged, blank. "I'm tired. I just want to rest. I think I've earned that."

"Do you know what he's been doing?" Edmund demanded.

"No." And she smiled triumphantly. "You tell me."

"He caused a man to be killed in a car crash and stole part of the body. And he murdered a woman and half devoured her."

"You saw him doing these things, did you?"

"I know it was him, Mrs. Kelly. So do you."

"If you're so sure of yourself," and her smile was malicious now, "why haven't you told the police?"

"I've done that." He sounded totally convincing to Clare, but she knew the blind could hear lies where the sighted saw honesty. She held herself rigid, in case an uneasy movement alerted Mrs. Kelly. Dust glinted slowly, floating; shadows on the pigeons shuddered.

"Then why haven't the police been to see me?"

"Because I haven't told them your address yet. That's the one thing they don't know. But let me be completely honest. I'm writing a book about these murders. That's partly why I'm here."

Her face was as blank as her eyes now. "But I want to see your grandson get what's right for him. I used to know him at school. The police can only arrest him. But that isn't the whole answer."

Clare heard him leaving his feelings ambiguous, so that he could agree with Mrs. Kelly's. Had he done that with Clare?

"And these other people are relatives, are they," Mrs. Kelly said. "Who's the one who sends pansies to do his lying for him?"

Launderette, Clare mouthed at Edmund, pointing at Chris. "I sent someone to talk to your friend," Edmund said, frowning.

"That's the kind of person you associate with. And you want me to believe you know what's best for him, my grandson. I don't think there's anything more to be said."

Clare chewed her fingers to block her mirth. Edmund had trapped himself in his own ambiguity. At the same time, she felt helplessly frustrated. They had been close to the truth, and he'd lost it.

"Of course I don't know what's best for him, oh no. I'm only his grandmother. You should try living with him for a few years before telling me what's right. Then maybe you'd know what you're talking about."

All at once Clare's frustration said, "Since you know, Mrs. Kelly, won't you tell us?"

"You're going to have a try now, are you? Who are you?"

"Clare Frayn. Your grandson killed my brother." The empty eyes gazed at her. The silence made her say, "I'm a teacher."

"A teacher! Are you! You all think children are angels these days, don't you? He was no angel, let me tell you. He was the Devil incarnate."

Edmund was nodding to Clare, but she didn't need his cue. "Come on, Mrs. Kelly, children aren't devils," she said. "In what way was he a devil?"

But Mrs. Kelly grinned. "Oh no, you won't trap me like that. I've got all the rest of my senses left, don't you mistake it."

"I'm not trying to trap you," Clare said, full of frustration.

Mrs. Kelly hadn't waited for her. She was muttering, "I know all about teachers. They're the ones who want to tell parents how to bring up their children. I'd like to see a teacher give twenty-five years of her life to a child and then have that child betray her. I'd like to see her telling parents what to do then."

"Do you mean your grandson?" Clare said, keeping her temper. "He betrayed you?"

"No, I don't mean him." As if the silence had contradicted her, she added furiously, "I mean his mother. My daughter Cissy, Cecilia."

"Sounds like you haven't had much luck bringing up kids, right?" Chris said.

"I've had the Devil's luck. He must have it in for me. I don't know why God lets him. There must be a special place for me in Heaven. The Devil made Cissy betray me, I know. And she turned to him for help. Not to her own mother."

Both Chris and Clare opened their mouths, but Edmund gestured as if he were a conductor silencing an orchestra. In the silence the glowing embers crinkled like tinfoil. Mrs. Kelly said, "Just you have a look at her. Does she look badly brought up to you? Mr. Pugh, you look at her in the photographs."

Clare watched George rub a hole in the grime for a face. The girl beneath the glass was about eleven; her large eyes gazed out of her large face, her full lips were pressed together primly. "Is that her as a little girl?" Mrs. Kelly said. "That's her confirmation dress. It cost so much to make, we were flabbergasted. But we bought it. Just so she could go to the Devil."

In the other photograph the girl was years older. A woman in her forties—Mrs. Kelly—and a burly man stood on either side of her, arms about her shoulders. The girl's lips were fuller now; she looked sullen—trapped, Clare thought. "Can the others look at them?" George said.

"Yes, yes. Let them all see." Mrs. Kelly shook her head. "That one of the three of us," she said. "I had that taken because I thought we were such a close family, so Cissy would have something to remember us by. I shouldn't have wasted my money."

She took hold of the arm of her chair and squatted down to place coal on the embers with fire-tongs. George moved to help, but she said, "Sit down, sit down. I'm not helpless yet." She threw on a shovelful of slack; dark flames uncoiled, mostly smoke.

"Sometimes I wonder what God has against me," she said from her chair. "He's sent me some trials in my life, I know that. Cissy never had much in her head, but I'm sure the teachers made her worse. I brought her up as I'd been brought up; it never did me any harm. We found her a job in a factory, but she didn't keep that long. Still, we were used to going without; my husband was only in the post office. We looked after her and never complained. All we asked was that she was home by nine every night, and told us everything she'd done during the day. And what she was going to do the next day. Sometimes she caught herself out there; she'd contradict herself. But someone must have taught her to lie. Because she'd been at another factory for six months before we knew she was going with a man."

She looked as if she might vomit. "They used to do what they did in broad daylight, in the factory. Her supervisor found them one day. Against the wall, like animals. Her father gave her something to remember that night, even if she was twenty-five. Do you know what she did then? She ran away. Her, who couldn't even keep her shoelaces tied. She wouldn't have run away if her father had been well. But he had lung cancer, so that made it easy for her."

The shouts of children had gone from the street, which was sinking into darkness. "We knew she'd be back," Mrs. Kelly said. "Her man didn't want her, not for long. She went wherever she went for a couple of months, then she came back here. Do you know why? Because she was going to have a baby. As brazen as you please, she brought that here." Her lips were white with primness.

"Yeah, well," Chris said. "It's still life, though, isn't it?"

"You call that life, do you? I wonder if you'd think so if you heard what that thing did. I sound cruel, don't I? A cruel mother, not fit to bring up children. Oh, we thought as you do, at the time—we thought it was still a baby, after all; it deserved the same chances as anyone else. We told her she could have it, but we couldn't afford to keep it, not with her father getting worse. Of course there was no question of her not having the baby, but it would have to be adopted.

"You'd have thought we'd told her to kill it. It mustn't be adopted, she kept saying, it mustn't go out of her sight ever. We found out why later. But even if we'd known, I don't see what difference it could have made.

"She was ashamed to talk to us, and I don't wonder. At least she never talked about the man responsible. I certainly didn't want to hear about a man like that. So she just sat around the house and wasted away. Just sat and wouldn't say what she was thinking, not even to the priest. She didn't dare tell him, of course. And I had to watch her get thinner. I'm a cruel inhuman mother, am I?" she shouted at the silence. "Let me tell you, I lay awake half the night, every night, praying for her and the baby. I wouldn't have wasted prayers on that thing if I'd known. We thought it was the worry that was sapping her, but it was that inside her, eating her away.

"Then just before the baby was due, she left. And the next day there was a letter saying she was going to kill herself. After the way we brought her up, she sinned against the Holy Ghost, against hope."

She closed her eyes. The listeners waited, hoping she would answer the silence. Flames leapt through smoke. Suddenly Clare realized they must learn the contents of the suicide letter. She remembered what the doctor had told George about Mrs. Kelly's daughter. Hoping she sounded as stupid as the question, she said, "But what reason did she have to kill herself?"

"You may well ask. She had her reasons. But I don't want to talk about them. I want to forget, if I can."

Clare groaned silently. Then Mrs. Kelly said, "No, I won't have you thinking I drove her to it. I'll tell you what she couldn't tell me face to face."

Edmund nodded vigorously at Clare, flourishing his upthrust thumb.

"She wasn't satisfied having a baby out of wedlock," Mrs. Kelly said. "That wasn't enough of a sin for her. She tried to get rid of it. She'd heard of a man who could get rid of babies by black magic. God help her.

"But he didn't get rid of it. He made her promise it to him. After the way we brought her up, she promised her child to the Devil. And he told her nothing could take back that promise, not even death."

She crossed herself, squeezing her eyelids tight. "He must have seen how easily swayed she was. He roped her into all manner of filthy practices. She wrote them all down; she must have enjoyed thinking how it would upset me. I threw all that on the fire, didn't even let my husband see. This Satanist was a dirty old man, filthy, making use of gullible people.

"But he had powers from the Devil. He'd kept himself young; he told Cissy all about that. Now he was growing old, he needed someone to look after him. I'd have looked after him," she said savagely. "He wanted Cissy's child to look after him and to be taught all the filth he knew. I don't know what changed her mind, but she ended up hating him. She said she was writing to him as well, to tell him what she was going to do."

"This guy, the Satanist," Chris said. "Is he still alive?"

"No, thank God. That's one prayer of mine that was answered. He should have suffered as he made others suffer, but he died in his bed, of old age. Sometimes I wonder what God's doing."

"Your daughter," Clare said. "She killed herself after the baby was born?"

Mrs. Kelly was silent for minutes. Once she made to speak,

then her face collapsed and filled with darkness—shadows of the fire. On the walls, chairs of dark jelly danced and jerked, slowly quivering.

Abruptly Mrs. Kelly said, "They found her in a cave in Wales. Someone had seen her going up a hill. She was dead, but *that* was alive, God help us. I'd taken her letter to the police. They told me when she was found, and I had to go to identify her. Then they showed me the baby at the hospital."

Chris was squinting at the photographs. He said, "Have you got a picture of him?"

"I've got nothing of him. And I want nothing. After what he did, all I want is to hear that he's dead."

"But you cared for him, didn't you?" Clare prompted. "I mean, you looked after him."

"Oh yes. I couldn't leave him with strangers. He looked such a lovely baby. That was a Devil's trick to delude me. And I wanted him because he was Cissy's. It wasn't my fault she'd gone to the Devil, don't think that, but I thought I could save him from going the same way, make up for what she'd done. The cruel mother wanted to make up for her daughter," she said harshly.

"They kept him in the hospital for months. They said he should have died. I don't know if they meant he would have been better dead, but that's what they ought to have meant. When I went to collect him, a nurse told me— No. No, God help me, I won't talk about that." Her hands fastened convulsively on her chair.

"I tried to bring him up as if he were normal. The priest said he was still a child of God; it was up to me to put him on the right path. He said God must have let him live so that I could save him. I tried, God knows. I even called him Christopher—carrying Christ. I thought that might help."

Clare winked at Chris; shadows flickered in reply.

"We went without to bring him up. We were used to that. We even bought him special food, to change his tastes." She shuddered, or the light did. "I told him his mother had gone to Heaven. Perhaps she had. God's mercy is infinite.

"He was far cleverer than Cissy. I often used to see him watching me. The Devil had made him clever—pretending to be a little boy, waiting for the chance to be a monster.

"When he was five my husband died. I had to bring him up on the pittance they gave me. Oh, that didn't worry me, I could do without. But my sight was going. I was terrified of him, and he knew it."

"Of a five-year-old child?" Clare demanded.

"A five-year-old monster, you mean. Oh, but children are angels, aren't they? I'll tell you something. When he was eleven he savaged another boy. Did you know that, Miss Teacher?"

"I saw it happen," Edmund said hastily. "I went to St. Joseph's too."

"And you say he wasn't a monster? I took him to the doctor, but he was no use at all. Take him to a psychiatrist, he said. I'd as soon have taken him to the Satanist; not one of those men believes in God. I swore the doctor to secrecy and told him everything; then he wasn't so sure of himself. I told him prayer and faith were the only things that could save that child, and he couldn't prove they weren't. Not that they saved him. You can't save a monster."

"But did you let the child see you thought of him that way?"

"Let him see, Miss Teacher? I told him! That was cruel of me, wasn't it? When he savaged that boy I told him everything. I showed him his mother's letter."

"And that helped him?"

"Helped him? You don't help a monster, a devil! Don't you see," Mrs. Kelly said triumphantly, "he *already* knew what he was. I was only showing him I did too."

Her blank eyes flashed with triumph; she smiled bitterly. All at once Clare saw that she was imitating Bette Davis. She couldn't stand either of them.

"No, I didn't want to help him. I prayed he'd be saved. But my eyes were getting worse, and I was alone in the world. All I wanted was to be safe from him. As you would have, make no mistake. Would you have liked to see him eating with you at the table, hear him in the next room at night? I used to lie awake praying, thinking he'd crept into my room. I'm sure my crucifix kept him away. I'd told him I always carried it with me. Do you know he was here when I went blind? He'd just left school. He tried to pretend he wanted to stay home and help me. I had to scream the house down before he'd go. My throat was sore for days."

"Where is he now, Mrs. Kelly?" Edmund said.

"I don't know." Her tone was flat; she wasn't lying. "And I don't want to. I never heard from him again, and that suits me fine."

"Have you any idea where he might have gone?"

"God only knows. He had no job when he left. Gone to the Devil, probably."

Edmund shook his head, baffled. Chris said, "What was the name of the Satanist?"

Edmund nodded at Chris, alert. But she said, "Oh, I know that all right. But I'm not telling you. He died before the police could deal with him. Let him stay buried."

Clare's frustration spilled out in a long sigh.

The bitter smile turned toward her. "Oh, I'm terribly unreasonable. The cruel mother who drove her child to suicide, and made another child into a monster. Just you listen to me, Miss Teacher. I'll tell you how much of a monster he was. I'll tell you something I never meant to speak of again. When I collected him from the hospital in Wales, a young nurse took me aside. She told me there was something they'd kept from me. She told me what they'd found in the cave."

An orange face nodded forward. Clare recoiled before she recognized Edmund; in the firelight Chris and George were orange too. On the walls the chairs leapt feebly, trembling. The room shifted uneasily; firelight reached for the corners, plucking at them.

"They had to cut him out of her. Like a tumour," Mrs. Kelly said. "The doctors told me that. They found the cord was broken. That shows he was no part of her, doesn't it? Broken, or bitten through. He was born with teeth. Born," she said, sneering at the word. "And I took him, even after what the nurse told me. Because he was Cissy's. Because I thought my faith would prevail.

"They found Cissy in the cave." Around Clare all the orange faces leaned closer. "She was dead, but they thought they saw a movement under her clothes. They looked, a woman looked, and there was something moving under her skin. Do you know what that was?"

She's telling this third-hand, Clare reassured herself. The nurse wasn't even in the cave. And this woman exaggerates. But the orange faces surrounded her, and the voice said, "It was him. The maggot inside her. The Devil's child." The voice tore at Mrs. Kelly's throat as she said, "It was his mouth. He was eating his way out of his mother."

She preceded them to the front door, saying, "I'd just like to be sure you all leave." They heard her voice retreating down the hall. "Out of the depths I have cried to You, O Lord," it said.

Clare rested her forehead against the corner of the house; brick dug into her clutching fingers. The street moved as if the darkness were slow water. She heard Mrs. Kelly's muffled prayers. She heard George say, "I thought this witchcraft business was just an excuse for him, the way they find excuses for everything these days. But maybe they ought to have let him die quietly in that cave."

"I could give the police her address," Edmund mused. "But then they'd push me out, I'm sure of it. I haven't come so far just to lose the trail."

But he'd lost the trail already, Clare thought. She raised her head. At least she could think straight, now she was out of the orange light. She stared at the darkness on the steps beyond the street, stared toward Granby Street, Mulgrave Street, Princes Avenue. "Mulgrave Street," she said softly to Chris, who was gazing that way too. He was the only one who might take her sudden intuition seriously. "I'll bet that's where the Satanist lived," she said.

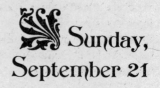 **Sunday,
September 21**

"Do you know," Clare said, "I haven't the faintest idea what we're looking for."

"Maybe we won't know until we find it," Chris said.

"I don't think there's anything to find." She halted the car beside St. Joseph's and gazed at Mulgrave Street. There were fewer houses than there had been a fortnight ago. "If he did live here," she said, "they've probably pulled his house down by now. And even if it's still standing—oh, I don't know. I thought we might be able to sense which one it was, but that was a stupid idea. Even if we found it, what use would it be?"

"Yeah, well, it sounds useless. But what else can we do? Let's go along once more, okay?"

She drove slowly back along Mulgrave Street. Terraces and scraps of terraces stood on the waste; odd single houses were surrounded by rubble and earth. Toward Upper Parliament Street, hundreds of yards were enclosed by a wall of corrugated tin. Side streets crossed Mulgrave Street; trees still sprouted from their pavements, leaves coated with smoke. Above the waste the afternoon sky was deep blue, clear except for a waning moon like the last trace of chalk on a blackboard. At one of the bared crossroads, two learner drivers juddered timidly at each other.

Clare halted Ringo at Upper Parliament Street. "Shall we call it a day?" she said.

"Yeah, might as well." But he was squirming on the seat in frustration. "Let's get a coffee," he said abruptly. "The Arts Centre isn't far."

But the building contained a couple of morose artists, annoyed by the interruption; no coffee—it had gone on a picnic. "We'll go back to my place," Clare said.

In Blackburne Terrace, birds fell from trees and swooped back onto branches, like fruit taking back its fall on a reversed film. She was unlocking the flat before she remembered how untidy it was. Perhaps Chris wouldn't notice.

He wasn't even following her. He'd stopped on the last but top stair, looking disconsolate. "Shit, I don't feel like I've done anything today," he said.

"I'm sorry," she said. The search had been her idea, though he'd joined her readily enough. "We did our best." She went to him, put one arm about his shoulders; she could feel how tense he was. "I think this whole business may just peter out as far as we're concerned," she said.

She massaged his shoulders. "At least we'll have seen the last of Edmund," she said, as he relaxed a little. "He wanted me to write to the Education Offices on school notepaper. They might know where Kelly went after he left school. But I'm afraid I won't go that far, even though I said I'd help him. So Edmund and I aren't friends anymore. Still, I think I'll get over that. Come on," for he felt softer now, "I'll make some coffee."

God, it was untidy. *Love Has Many Weapons*, of which she'd read six slickly written pages, had joined the scattered newspapers and crossword books, the children's essays, her record book, the canvas guitar case lying partly folded like a Dali version of George, a mug swarming with tea leaves, a paragraph about Rob that she'd written and rewritten for Edmund. She stood gazing, depressed.

"What's wrong?" Chris said, rather irritably.

"Oh, nothing." These things generally didn't mean so much to men. "I just wanted you to see the place looking nice. Not this mess."

"Christ, don't worry about that. You should see mine."

"I hope I shall." She hadn't known she was going to say that. Her heart quickened with the shock. When he didn't answer she fled to the kitchen, saying, "I'll get the coffee."

She felt foolish. Why had she fled? From Chris, of all people! Embarrassment was the last thing she should feel with him; it was the last thing he would feel. She considered her impressions of him: vulnerability, innocence; he needed looking after sometimes. And loyalty—he'd held back the discussion at the Pughs' for her. "You know," she called, "you're a lot like my brother was, in some ways."

"Yeah?" But no, she thought, not really. He hadn't Rob's aggressive unsureness, his self-pity—the things her disloyal mind had kept presenting when she'd tried to write her memories for Edmund. It was more that her relationship with Chris reminded her of Rob.

Why? Because she looked after him, because he was loyal to her? That hadn't been the basis of her relationship with Rob. She had realized that halfway through a sentence for Edmund, as her senile, incontinent Biro had stained her fingers. Rob hadn't needed her half so much as she had needed him. She'd needed him to fend off other people.

She'd needed him to blame for spoiling her chances with men. That was why, in her years away from him at teacher-training college, she'd never gone out with men at all. And in fact he'd shielded her from nothing except the fact of her own unsureness, her self-dislike. She had even managed to blame him for her dislike, her jealousy, of poor Dorothy.

None of these insights had seemed like a revelation. She'd sat calmly, Biro in hand, gazing into herself as they slotted easily into her awareness. Her mind had known all the time, had been waiting for the chance to let her know.

Chris had given it the chance. She had never felt so much at her ease with anyone, not even with Rob. Chris made all that had happened worthwhile. She mustn't lose him now the search was ending.

She loaded the tray, shaking her head at herself. She was so much at ease that she hid from him in the kitchen, as she had from Edmund! All right: she'd prove her ease to herself. She prepared her mind as she prepared the coffee.

She prepared herself too rigidly. She walked up the hall toward the living room, gracefully. Delicately. Prettily. Tinily. Like a pixie. Like a gnome. Stop that, she demanded, clenching her mind.

Chris was glancing at her rewritten paragraph. Had he been Edmund, she would have minded. My brother Rob Frayn was a radio personality, well-known locally for Of all the men I've known I was fondest of Although many people listened to his record show, few people really knew Maybe it's because I know all his faults that "Chris," she said from the doorway.

"Yeah," he said, laying aside the page after a last glance.

She shouldn't have made him look up. Now her speech was blocked. She was struggling to think of something else when it spilled out. "There was a bloke I went out with years ago," she said rapidly. "He used to call me Stumpy-legs. Do I look like that to you?"

"So that's where you got that stuff about being deformed. You mean you think I see you that way?"

"I just wanted to hear whether you did."

"Shit, no," he said impatiently.

She felt very light as she walked across the room, very natural. She sat down smiling opposite him. "I didn't think so," she said.

She poured coffee. "Listen, when all this business peters

out," she said, "we don't want to lose touch, do we?" Her
instinct told her they'd seen the last of Edmund. Rob and Kelly
had retreated to a comfortable distance in her mind. (One
terrible hasty thought: Rob's arm was still somewhere.) "I
want you to come to our school," she said. "With the group,
the TTG."

"Yeah, I'll talk to them, see what they say."

"You know," she said, "in a way I'm glad it's ending like
this. I wouldn't like to think of Edmund getting hold of Kelly.
I just don't like that man. Whatever Kelly did, I don't think
he deserves Edmund." She sucked in her cheek, shaking her
head. "I think he's had enough, what with that teacher and his
grandmother. No wonder he went the way he did, with them to
contend with. I'm sure it was she who gave him this thing
about Mulgrave Street by telling him about it, a psychological
thing, a fixation. I mean, of course he'll have to be caught,"
she said. "For his own good as much as anyone's."

That was an awful cliché. But she meant it; she could look
at Kelly that way now, in her newfound ease. She could forgive
him, because it hadn't really been his fault. She gazed at Chris,
anxious to be sure he didn't think she was being insincere.

She was gazing at him. Oh Christ, Chris thought. She knows.

By the time he reached his flat, Chris was no longer sure of
anything. He was even unsure why he'd joined Edmund's hunt.

His plan had seemed brilliantly simple. As soon as he'd read
the newspaper report about Edmund he had known what to do.
When he'd rung the newspaper for Edmund's address, everything the reporter said had confirmed his plan. By joining
Edmund he wouldn't only be able to divert the hunt, if it
came too close; he would be invisible. in the last place they'd
think to look.

An empty, blank-faced bus passed on Princes Road. As he reached the house he felt Mulgrave Street plucking restlessly at him. He hurried into the resounding hall. Now he wondered if he'd joined the hunt so as to trace the house in Mulgrave Street.

The stairs thumped dully beneath him. The sound nagged at his confusion. He hadn't been so confused since his moment of panic when he'd recognized Edmund. The hotel bedroom door had opened, and there was the boy who had watched him and Cyril. Chris had felt hollow with panic. Then he'd realized that the man didn't know him. At once he'd felt flattered that Edmund wanted to write a book about him, after all this time. He'd strode into the hotel room, toward the girl's voice: a star's entrance. He was going to enjoy himself.

The girl had been Clare. That had doubled his delight. She was fine, despite the car crash. He need feel no guilt at all. He ground his teeth as he ground the key in the lock of his flat. It was his delight with Clare that had tricked him.

He'd been dazzled by her gesture of bringing him back into the hunt. He had taken his performance too far in stalking out of Edmund's room; it had seemed the only way to play the scene, but he'd acted himself out of the hunt. He shouldn't have let himself react so strongly—Edmund reminded him of nothing so much as an ineffectual Cyril. He'd tried to think of a way to rejoin the hunt, in vain. Then Clare had come to him in Church Street and had handed him the answer. He'd felt overwhelmingly fond of her.

He had enjoyed that day. He had been spilling his delight. He'd enjoyed the game in the launderette most of all, pretending to be gay so that Mrs. Laird wouldn't recognize him, pretending not to know she had the same doctor as his grandmother, so that Clare could see him find that out for Edmund. He'd enjoyed himself too much, because he'd betrayed himself to Clare. Then he'd betrayed himself doubly, because he'd thought she hadn't noticed.

He slammed the door viciously. Even here in his flat he could feel the plucking, feeble but relentless, like an old man refusing to die. He was sure it had grown stronger since George had told them about the black magic. As soon as George had mentioned the magician's dolls, Chris had felt he'd always known about them.

Then Clare had suggested searching Mulgrave Street. Chris had tried alone, later in the week. But he'd been unable to bear the sense of sinking helplessly into himself, into darkness, into the earth; he'd fled. He had almost refused to join Clare, except that a refusal might have seemed suspicious. As it happened, in the car he'd had no sense of the house at all; Clare's presence had swamped it.

As their search had run down he had become progressively less sure why he wanted to find the house. She had been confusing him deliberately, that was why. It was lucky for her they hadn't found the house and gone in. He bared his teeth: her presence wouldn't have been able to swamp it then.

Back at her flat she'd revealed that she knew who he was. She had only pretended not to notice what he'd said outside the launderette. She had noticed that he'd mentioned St. Joseph's, though she hadn't named the school.

For a moment he had wanted to tell her she was right. He had been sure, as she gazed at him, that she was willing him to tell her. Then he'd seen that she had been playing a game with him ever since the launderette. Getting him invited to the Pughs' house, making sure he was confronted with his grandmother, taking him to Mulgrave Street—everything had been a game, aimed at forcing him to betray himself. Perhaps she had suspected him earlier; perhaps that was why she'd come to him in Church Street. He'd gazed blindly into the coffee; it had scalded his throat, startling him to his feet. "I've got to go," he'd said, and had fled before he attacked her in his mounting fury.

Nothing was sure now. Everything safe was giving way

beneath him. She had done that. He stabbed the kitchen table; the knife stood trembling. Clare, and Maggie, the girl in TTG.

He didn't even feel safe in TTG now. Of everything, it was the theatre, acting, that had made him feel most secure. He'd learned that at school, the only thing he'd thought worth learning. He had been friendly with a boy in the Vale School Players; they'd masturbated each other a few times. His friend had liked dressing up. He'd invited Chris to rehearsals; perhaps he'd wanted to see him dressed up too, perhaps he wanted them to spend more time together. The master had asked Chris to act a small part. He'd done as he was told, as he generally did at school, indifferently.

He'd struggled with the part, frustrated. He had become furious with himself, with his ineptness, with the watchers. "Don't force it," the master had said. "You're trying too hard. Let yourself go, just let yourself relax into the part." Eventually he'd asked if Chris wanted to give up, but by then Chris was furiously determined.

The day after he'd realized there was no God, Chris had let himself go into the part without even trying.

He couldn't have imagined how easy it was. The lightness and relief he'd felt on the way to school, free of his guilt, had been nothing to the ease he'd felt while acting. Later, if he ever felt uneasy with himself, it helped him; what he did to people was only acting, after all; it was only something he did, not the whole of him. Except for the day he'd returned to St. Joseph's with the Vale School Players, when the cat had distracted the audience from him, he had never felt easier than when acting, or with actors.

Until Maggie had begun to nag him. The people in TTG left him alone when he wanted to be, didn't probe. But Maggie had been different, more aggressive. She'd given him hash cake to eat with the rest of them, in her flat. He hadn't been sure he wanted to eat it; he blamed her. Then for hours he'd kept sinking into himself as if into thick mud; he'd pulled himself free with a start like the start of awakening, except that each time he began sinking again at once; no light had seemed to reach him; the others were far away, cut off from him by the gaps that widened in his consciousness. It seemed impossible that he would ever escape.

Eventually he'd fled to catch a bus downtown, anywhere, to try to leave behind what was happening. Voices rose from the crowd on the bus, hurtling at him; everyone knew he'd been eating hash. He'd taken refuge in *Bonnie and Clyde*, which was showing again, but he'd had to leave when the first of the Barrow gang was shot, face exploding into blood. By then the worst of his experience was over. Later, when he'd moved to this flat, he found he felt very much like that near Mulgrave Street at night. Another time Maggie had offered him acid, but he'd never touched drugs again.

She'd kept asking to come to his flat. TTG met at one another's homes for drinks or a smoke. Chris had managed to avoid inviting them; he felt safest of all in his flat, where he could always make problems come right in his mind. In his flat he didn't even need to act being easy with people, he need only be himself. Then Maggie had begun: "When are we coming up to yours?" One of these days she'd try to get in without an invitation. He couldn't even be sure of his flat now.

He slammed the plate of cheese salad on the table; the plate cracked. Of all the things his grandmother had hung on him, vegetarianism was the one he hadn't slipped off—that, and his first name, which he'd always assumed his mother had given him. Vegetarianism showed he didn't *need* to eat anything else.

His toenails scraped at his sandals, nervous from the restless plucking. He knew where it came from now: the magician's house, somewhere up Mulgrave Street. It reached into his flat for him. He took off his spectacles, but then the walls were insubstantial as fog; he put on his spectacles hastily.

He had been returning toward that house ever since he'd left

Liverpool. When he'd left his grandmother he had gone at once to London, to stay with the actor who had introduced him to the Vale School Players. After that he'd worked with various theatre groups, always nearer Liverpool. Once back in Liverpool, he had begun moving closer to the house.

He chewed. His salads weren't as good as Diane's. He'd lived with her for a year or so; she had made most of his clothes. Her thighs had gripped him softly, her cunt gulped him; he'd thought he might have that with Clare. When his restlessness had grown imperative he'd left Diane. "Tell me why. Just tell me why," she'd pleaded, but she was just a voice; since the day his grandmother had screamed him out of the house when he'd offered to help her get used to her blindness, pleas and sympathy were things he didn't bother with. From Diane's he had moved here. He found he could hardly remember anything about her now.

After he'd moved here everything was good, until he'd met Clare.

He shoved his plate away and spat a mouthful of salad toward it. The plucking nagged at him. He felt enclosed; he would feel enclosed even if he went out. He wrenched up the window over the fire escape and gazed down into the backyard, the blearing twilight.

His cat was the nearest he'd come to regret. Killing Mrs. Pugh's fat dog had been like a revenge; he had enjoyed it all the more. His cat had been a stray he'd brought home from the Arts Centre, under his jacket. After the car crash he'd realized the police might question everyone in the area. He'd lain in bed pondering how to deal with them. Suddenly he'd seen that he could head them off: he could make himself a victim. He'd leapt out of bed to grab the cat and hurl her down at the yard wall. She'd made no sound except a thump and a soft crack. Five minutes later he had gone down into the silence to make sure. The cobblestones of the alley were black glistening boils; black plastic sacks of rubbish squirmed feebly in a breeze, rustling. He had lifted the broken cat toward his face.

He gazed down into the yard. He was sure of one thing: Clare would have told nobody what she'd realized. He bared his teeth at the alley below. He was beginning to hope she would find the house and take him there.

Edmund leaned back, patting his stomach. That had been a bloody good meal. It had been worth lingering over; the hotel restaurant was almost empty. The Scandinavian blonde he'd begun to chat up in the lift passed his table, and he smiled and half rose before he noticed the man with her. Never mind, at least he'd had a good dinner. It proved they took trouble once you showed them you knew about food.

But as the forelegs of his chair touched the floor his contentment faded. Now he'd eaten, what was he going to do?

His fingertips stood and galloped on the tablecloth. Bloody waiters. He'd been kept waiting minutes. He signalled the head waiter, who ordered at once, "Bring Mr. Hall's check."

"You're doing a good job there. Have one on me later," Edmund said, stuffing a pound note into the head waiter's hand. He was all right, the head waiter. Edmund wouldn't have minded a drink and a chat with him, except that the hotel management might disapprove.

Hold on. The man was only a waiter, after all. Edmund wasn't so hard up for company. He could ring George Pugh. George was all nerves with that cinema of his; he needed taking out for a break. Edmund signed the check and was halfway to the telephones when he halted, frowning. No doubt that wife of George's would object; she didn't like Edmund.

And George was the type who would give in to her. Edmund headed for the residents' bar, thwarted. He hated interfering women.

The bar was as full of polite hushed conversations as a hospital ward at visiting time. A thin blanket of piped music shifted behind the conversations, occasionally trailing through them, elusive as mist. Edmund drained his bourbon and held out the glass for a refill. He would have gone to a nightclub, but a dozen of Liverpool's weren't worth one of London's.

He felt frustrated, helpless. He hadn't felt so much on edge since his first year in London, when he'd written most of *Secrets of the Psychopaths* in Frank Baxter's two-roomed flat, using a board laid over the sink as a table. Frank had been a friend of his at school. He had never asked Edmund to contribute more to the rent than he'd offered; he'd never remarked how Edmund's bank balance was growing. Still, even Frank had sometimes distracted him from his writing. But he was all right, Frank: Edmund always sent him his books, and he always wrote back that he'd enjoyed them. Edmund hoped he'd enjoy *Satan's Cannibal*, formerly *The Flesh Eater,* when it was finished.

If it was finished. He should have known not to base his hopes on anything in Liverpool. He'd known what he was doing when he had got out; he shouldn't have let anything entice him back.

Working at the newspaper in Liverpool had been the worst time of his life. He'd gone there to learn how to write; it had nearly turned him off writing for good. After they'd encouraged his writing throughout his childhood, his parents—who had both had small pieces published, who had even called him Edmund because it sounded literary—had pleaded with him not to embark on full-time writing: it was too insecure. Journalism, that was secure. His teachers, the youth-employment officer, had backed them up. He'd given in.

At least he'd learned from the experience—learned never to let himself be used again: not by a boss, not by the fatuous people he had had to interview at any hour that suited them. He'd learned contempt—for his colleagues, their pettiness and spite and pathetic eagerness to compromise. He'd learned efficiency of writing; he could thank his parents for that, at least. But if he hadn't been researching and writing *Secrets of the Psychopaths* in his spare time he could never have stood the newspaper. When he'd seen the advertisement in a trade paper, he had written to the new publisher at once; then he'd begun to pack his luggage, already sure *Secrets of the Psychopaths* was what the publisher needed.

He would never have come back to Liverpool, except that his parents refused to move. He had room for them in his house in Surrey, but they'd too many friends here, they said. Even when he had them to stay they wouldn't be persuaded. He couldn't imagine how they stood Liverpool after Surrey.

If he hadn't come back to visit them he might never have heard of Kelly's reappearance. But on one of his visits a young writer had invited him to a party, where he'd met Desmond Harris, a newspaper reporter. Desmond had eagerly offered to keep him supplied with reports of any crimes he might be able to use. At the time, the man's eagerness had seemed as pathetic as the rest of the party, the provincialism, the second-hand trendiness, the ludicrous civic pride they expected him to share. But months later, when Edmund had forgotten his name, Desmond rang him to describe the car crash and its aftermath. The third incident near Mulgrave Street convinced Edmund that they were worth a book; the second had already made him expectant, for he'd always been sure he must hear more of Kelly.

He had been sure since the incident with Cyril. It had linked him with Kelly, for he'd wished Kelly on Cyril, as revenge for his broken nose. Though he'd beaten Cyril, that broken nose had hurt; he had felt Cyril should suffer more. But he didn't intend himself to be harmed further; he wouldn't take that risk again—his nose had been agonizing.

When Cyril had begun baiting Kelly he'd watched and hoped. He was sure that if Kelly lost control Cyril would be sorry. But when it was over he'd felt there should have been more; he had waited to hear of a sequel. Maybe that had made him overestimate it when it came. And maybe he'd felt Liverpool owed him a bestseller.

The bar was crowded now; the murmur was louder, more annoying. He downed his bourbon and went to his room. For a moment, gazing at the neat deserted room, he wished he'd stayed with his parents. But he needed to be central and available; they didn't even have a phone.

Enough of this. No use getting depressed. He still had a salable book, even if events had hindered the one he'd planned. He had made sure Desmond Harris would ring him as soon as he heard they'd caught Kelly. But it wouldn't be the same as being there at the arrest; it wouldn't be the same as confronting Kelly. Perhaps the police would let him interview Kelly. Books had been written that way, after all.

When he'd poured a bourbon he switched on the radio for pop and uncovered his typewriter. At least he could write up the people he'd met so far. He was sure that was one reason why his books sold—that he understood people.

If you tell George Pugh the family is out of date you'd better stand well back. He's a big man, and he knows what he thinks.

If it were out of date George wouldn't care, because he's an independent man. The cinema he owns and runs is independent too. In these days of big faceless organizations it's good to meet a man like George.

He enjoys his job, maybe too much so to relax. But then his job is people as well as entertainment. That's why he wouldn't join a cinema chain, because where he is he knows his clientele. His Saturday-morning shows are the biggest and happiest family you'll see for miles.

That's George all right, Edmund thought, paragraphing.

But George's family is smaller now, and you can see that hurts. It's been smaller since the night he said goodbye to his mother and rode

George's mother. George hadn't written her up yet. You couldn't put a deadline on something like that, but nevertheless it would hold up the chapter. Maybe after all he should talk to George about her, then write her up himself.

His fingers typed invisible curses on the table. Everything in this book was balked. Most of all he was frustrated by his ignorance of the black magician's name. If he knew that, he was sure he could research an extra chapter or two; black magic sold books. Only Mrs. Kelly's stubbornness was thwarting him. Again he thought of giving her address to the police. If he could be sure they'd agree to letting him watch the arrest, or at least let him interview Kelly—

He ripped the page out of the typewriter and shoved it in his folder. Come on. Write something. The publishers would soon be getting uneasy about the advance they'd paid him. "Clare Frayn," he typed.

And halted. He wasn't sure about her any more. He'd thought she was open and straightforward, the kind of girl he liked— not too aggressive, not trying to compete with him, not too proud to show she needed men: feminine, in fact. But he'd come to suspect her of using him deceitfully, of pretending she only wanted to help him when really she was furthering her relationship with Chris Barrow. How she could care for someone like him, Edmund didn't know. One thing was sure: he wouldn't appear in Edmund's book. He wasn't worth the paper.

He hurled the crumpled page at the waste bin. No good. He couldn't concentrate: too much bourbon. He'd get to bed soon, and in the morning write up Mrs. Kelly. Who else? Dr. Miller

—no, he'd been helpful; he'd earned anonymity. But what he'd told George deserved a chapter. A thought was struggling at the back of Edmund's mind. He turned down the three-chord pounding of the radio.

The bourbon washed back down the bottle; the bottle's mouth hung dripping over the glass. Dr. Miller. Mrs. Kelly. Dr. Miller—

Edmund barely caught the bottle from smashing the glass. My God, he thought, my God! He'd almost missed seeing it. He snatched up the telephone receiver. Hold on, it's only an idea, let's be sure before writing any cheques. But he was sure already. "Get me the Newsham Cinema," he told the girl. He was back in business. George would get him what he needed. He would have his black magic, after all.

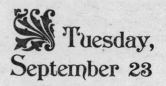# Tuesday, September 23

"There's a man on the phone for you, Miss Frayn."

Three more of Clare's little girls were waiting outside the staffroom to watch her reaction. "Thank you, Debbie," she said, and saw them glimpse her eagerness.

Why were there so many stairs? Her mind counted her footfalls, forty-eight loud hollow blows on stone, retarded by the duller clunks of her hurry across four landings. Why couldn't they have a phone in the staffroom? The playground dazzled her. "John and Trevor are fighting, Miss Frayn," Lynn shouted.

"They hadn't better be when I come back." She hurried past screams of glee, hurtling footballs, impromptu Morris dancers and morose watchers, but her kids were converging from various directions. "Have a sweet, Miss Frayn."

"Oh, thank you, Susie." She popped the boiled sweet in her mouth and almost running (Susie, or was it Yvonne?) swallowed it whole. Oh *no*, she groaned. The sweet bulged her throat as she tried to choke it up; it felt enormous. She could only keep hurrying upstairs. The sweet slipped down into her chest, held immobile and painfully hard for a moment before slipping further, beyond discomfort. She stumbled into the office, gasping her thanks to the deputy head, and picked up the receiver tenderly. But it wasn't Chris. It was George.

"I've booked you a show," he said. "Next month, the morning of Friday the twenty-fourth. *The Amazing Mr. Blunden*."

"Oh, great. Thank you, George. The kids will be pleased." She wished she felt more so. "Have you seen Edmund lately?" she said, to say something.

"He's been in touch with me."

"We had a row. Anyway, I think Chris and I have done all we can to help. We went looking for the magician's house on Sunday. A bit pointless, really."

"Didn't you find it? We have, nearly."

"What do you mean?"

"Well, we'd missed something. Ted only realized on Sunday. Mrs. Kelly told Dr. Miller the magician's name when she took the boy to see him. I went to ask him yesterday, and he didn't mind telling. The magician's name was John Strong. John Strong!" he repeated incredulously. "Ted is getting his address from the Local History library. I should stay out of it now, my dear," he said. "We'll deal with it."

She went to her classroom instead of the staffroom, to think. The walls looked less bare now; they were beginning to accumulate paintings and stories. John Strong could be a reason to ring Chris.

Her class crowded in, chattering, then calmed down. Yvonne Lo was less tidily dressed than Susie Lo; Susie was tidying her hair. So there was a way to tell them apart; good. Debbie and her friends gazed at Clare, speculating. John Strong. It must be a false name. It would be useless.

They had to calm down again when she announced George's film. "Now we're going to do division," she said, and they groaned. She hadn't understood division either, at their age—it was the hardest arithmetic to grasp; they had to be reminded of it constantly. Soon they'd be faced with long division, poor kids. "John Strong" didn't sound like a magician, but what did magicians sound like? Wouldn't he have wanted to sound unremarkable, except to his victims?

David and Trevor and Margery didn't understand what she'd said so far; she began again. At least Trevor and Margery were good readers. She was getting a sense of the class: she'd tested their reading ages and sorted them out a reading scheme each. John and Mark were fighters. Sandra and Ranjit tended to sit apart and mope, and had to be encouraged to work in groups. Half the kids had unstable family backgrounds.

She wanted to get in touch with Chris; she wanted to know why he'd left so abruptly on Sunday. Had he been offended because she'd made excuses for Kelly? He was so unpredictable: she remembered how his feelings about his cat had changed. Had her excuses reminded him what Kelly had done to his cat? Surely he wouldn't still feel offended. She could ring him about TTG, but he hadn't seemed too interested when she'd mentioned that. She knew he was interested in John Strong's house. The children struggled with division, tongues squeezed out, pencils awry. She mustn't lose touch with Chris.

At the end of the afternoon Debbie said, "Did you speak to the man, Miss Frayn?"

"Yes, Debbie, I did." Her own smile took her by surprise, and grew.

When she reached Ringo she knew where she was going. She drove downtown. Small white clouds were scattered low on the blue sky, like elaborate shells. In the city centre, homebound cars were beginning to slow one another down; at last a driver let Clare slip through their ranks. She parked near the columns of the museum's Corinthian portico. Past more columns, a semicircle standing forward from the rotunda of the Picton Reading Room, she hurried through the entrance to the libraries.

"Tally," said a uniformed man behind a counter.

He was thrusting a cardboard rectangle at her. "Oh, thanks," she said.

She was several steps away when he said, "Bag."

"I beg your pardon?"

"Your bag. You can't take that in with you."

"Oh, I see. All right then." In exchange for the bag he gave her a plastic tab fitted with a rattling metal ring, but wouldn't take back the cardboard tally. Released at last, she hurried away. A notice directed her to the fifth floor for Local History. A long-haired young man was emerging from a lift; she slipped past the closing door. The dull-green metal box, which felt crowded with her alone, creaked up to the fifth floor.

The Local History library was a long room full of tables; sunlight poured through portholes in the ceiling. A woman in her thirties came to the counter at once, smiling. "I'm trying to find someone's address from about twenty years ago," Clare said. "John Strong, his name is. Probably in Mulgrave Street."

"Good heavens. Is there a John Strong revival?"

"I don't think so," Clare said, confused.

"How strange. It's just that you're the second person to ask for his address today. I won't be a moment." She returned with a bound volume of voters' lists, and rapidly found the page. "John Strong. Twenty-one Amberley Street. That's just off Mulgrave, or it was. I'll be surprised if it's still standing. Are you researching his book too?"

"That's right." In a moment she realized what they were talking about: if Edmund had read this book, whatever it was, so would she. "Have you a copy here?"

"There's one down in Picton. It's restricted, not on public access. But they'll give it to you if you ask." She scribbled on a piece of paper. "Just fill in these details on one of their forms and you'll have it in no time."

133.0924 Strong: *Glimpses of Absolute Power.* "He used to come in here, you know," the librarian said.

"What was he like?" Clare said eagerly.

"Well, I wasn't here myself. Mr. Carrick is off today; he was here then. If you come in again you could ask him what he remembers, if you're interested."

"Yes, I might. What sort of thing, do you know?"

"Well—the trouble is, there's no photograph of him on the book, and it sounds silly when you say it, but people used to say he had a horribly beautiful face. As if someone had put eyes inside a statue. Mr. Carrick does say he had the most perfect complexion he's ever seen, and he never seemed to look any older. Of course he was getting older really; they could see him slowing down the last few times he came in here. But that thing about being horribly beautiful—there were people on the staff who couldn't bear to look at him, really, couldn't bear to be alone at the counter if he was here, even on a day like this. One girl used to say seeing him in daylight made it worse. As if someone had made a statue walk about and pretend to be alive. And yet his clothes were rags, more or less, as if they didn't matter. I wish there were a photograph, don't you?"

A man walked by outside the window. On the fifth floor— but he was an overalled workman on scaffolding. "I'll tell you what Mr. Carrick told me," the librarian said. "John Strong always used to talk to you at the counter, unless you got away. It was all rubbish—nobody could understand it, like his book. But Mr. Carrick used to have a feeling that the words didn't matter; it was the way he said it, the sound of his voice, the cadences. Like a song hidden under the words. I remember, he said it reminded him of the music a snake-charmer plays. He always used to get rid of John Strong as soon as he could, and call away anyone who was listening. Sometimes Strong would talk to readers in the library and they'd go out with him. I expect they were friends of his, don't you?"

All Clare thought, not quite soberly, was that he sounded even less like a John Strong. She hurried back to call the lift. A stringy man emerged from it. "Book lift," he snapped.

"Pardon?"

"Book lift, book lift." He rapped the words on the closing door with his knuckles: BOOK LIFT ONLY.

He was carrying no books. Nevertheless, she used the stairs, green stone speckled with darker green and white, like a pointillist painting. The Picton Reading Room was two floors down; at the top of the dome a round window spilled dazzling sunlight over the stone rim. Clare found a wad of forms in a pigeonhole among the catalogues that walled the curve. At the counter, a girl handed Clare's completed form to a younger girl, who went away swinging a key to let out the book.

"I should watch out if I were you," said an invisible man beside her.

It took her a while to locate him: whispering to a young librarian, a hundred feet away across the diameter. The dome was full of acoustic tricks. She gave in her tally for the book and carried it out beneath the dome; the echoes of her footsteps on the green carpet thumped distantly, like a heart.

She opened the book on one of the tables. The clack of its cover fluttered high in the dome; readers glanced up reprovingly—some of them did little else, glaring at the shrill of a telephone, frowning at the clank of footsteps on iron balconies around the dome, full of bookcases. They should sit elsewhere, Clare thought.

John Strong had published the book himself. Half the print was askew in the frame of the pages. The ink looked thick as paint; the *p*'s and *d*'s and others were stoppered with ink, as if the print were breaking out in crotchets. The grey paper was full of splinters. The book had been a fat pamphlet, bound later by the library. *Glimpses of Absolute Power*, set down and published by John Strong. Clare turned the page.

"I have undertaken this work late in life, for it was no part of my design. The truly great man confides his wisdom to a single pupil and companion, rather than publish it to the paws of the mass.

"But the truly great man is always at bay. Perhaps the mass may claim a petty victory in robbing me of my intended pupil; though it shall come to pass that my power rescinds that theft. Yet I shall set my knowledge down, in the certainty that it speaks to none save him who will dare to test it. Perhaps, among the mass that fumble over these pages, one may read who, glimpsing my way dimly, will set himself to follow.

"My age spans many generations. The loud incredulity of my beholders cannot shout down that calm truth. Of my birth I shall say nothing. Does a man reminisce fondly of the dung-smeared apes that were his forebears?"

God, was it all like this? Clare turned pages impatiently. To think he'd written this in the 1950s. Incredible. Artistic skills come readily to the man whose aim is absolute power. She flipped through occult terms. The true relation of all things in the Universe— That caught her eye, but its context read like gabble. Sometimes, in its evolution, the Universe bears a mind that will grasp and wield its unity; such a mind is mine. Clare clucked her tongue. Tut tut tut, the dome said. Pages later, her gaze snagged on what looked like narrative.

"Once, on a whim, I allowed a few of them to pit themselves against my power. I displayed myself to them, engorged thick and stiffly raised as a club, and challenged them to move me. Some turned their eyes timidly aside, and shrank back when I granted them permission to touch me. Yet at the last all had worked upon me, upon themselves and upon each other, and lay exhausted while I stood laughing and unmoved. Some seemed cast down, and perhaps they glimpsed themselves as I had seen them, grovelling upon the earth in their eagerness to please me. All understood my meaning well when I spoke of the wand of my power."

So that was what it was all about; oh dear. Clare couldn't see how his fantasies—surely they were only that—related to Christopher Kelly. There was no terror here; the book was just dull and repulsive. A cough reverberated under the dome, sharp as a blow.

"Before snuffing out the life she carried—"

That image plucked at Clare; she turned back. The paper

rustled loudly, dryly, like an insect; its echoes rustled as she tried to hush it; it rustled.

"Before snuffing out the life she carried, it occurred to me to see her dance. I am sure even her fellows must have been amused, in their dull way. With her swollen belly she looked like nothing so much as a boil essaying the waltz."

Clare stared about, to free herself of the book. The library looked distant, unnaturally bright; it offered her no support at all. Whispers drifted close around her; a cough clapped together like hands. Sounds nagged at her, insistent and intolerably sharp, as if she had fever. If what she'd just read was a fantasy, he had infected others with it; Dr. Miller had told it to George. The man had had the power to impose his nastiness on others, after all.

She riffled the pages, glancing warily. They fluttered dryly, rustling. She was searching only for references to Kelly. But images rose from the thick style as if swelling up from a marsh, dragging down her gaze.

"At first she pressed her lips together, and choked and sobbed. But shortly she was imitating her doll perfectly, and enjoying the sweetmeat as if it were drugged. One of her fellows puked and gazed at me in fear, knowing that her response had singled her out to be next."

The words clung oppressively to her, like feverish heat. She made to turn to the previous page, to discover what the passage was about, then she shuddered and riffled on. Iron clanked, footsteps thumped softly, whispers sibilated.

"But she knew that nothing could take back her promise, not even death."

Clare started. She was back in the flickering orange room; Mrs. Kelly was speaking almost the same words. Her heart thudded in her ears, cut off from the echoes. Get it over with. She read.

"—not even death. She knew that should she take her own

life she would feel, beneath the ebbing of her spirit, the movements of the promised child within her, preparing to cheat her cheating and make its way to me."

Clare glared before her. Bright sunlight and echoes. She could see the dying woman in the cave, could feel her engulfing terror as she remembered John Strong's words. In a world where a man could believe he was achieving such horror, anything was possible. She could see the woman gazing down at herself in feeble helpless incredulity.

Abruptly she pushed back her chair. A suite of them clattered under the dome. She strode across the carpet, filling the dome with footsteps, and threw the book on the counter. "You should burn that," she said. On the green stairs she had to close her eyes for a while, for the flecks of colour were crawling on the stone.

The porter gave back her bag in exchange for the plastic tab, but she'd left her tally in the Picton. "You can't leave without handing in your tally," he said.

"You just watch me." When she reached Ringo she slowed, resting one hand on his hot roof. Should she abandon the search? She wanted no more of John Strong. But after all, his words were him; his house was only where he'd lived. It wasn't as if it would be haunted; he'd died in his bed. Besides, it was an excuse to see Chris. Stupid, she thought: she'd no reason to be frightened of the house. After all, she would be with Chris.

At the Arts Centre Clare met the actress who had wanted to be invited to Chris's flat. She was making a long-fanged green monster, man-size. Once she'd stared at Clare her eyes ignored her. Her footsteps resounded loudly on the floorboards, claiming them as her stage. No, Chris hadn't been in today. No, she didn't know where he was. Yes, she knew his address. Clare had to ask before she would release it.

Clare drove away down Mulgrave Street. It wasn't worth feeling resentful. The girl had just been jealous. Clare and her kids could have made a better monster. When she reached Princes Avenue she realized that she must have driven past John Strong's house, if it was still standing. Never mind, she'd save it for when she went with Chris.

She drove through a gap in the reservation and parked in North Hill Street, at the end of the alley behind Princes Road. Above the carriageway the lamps were dull hooks on the evening; beyond the ranks of trees Christ looked shrivelled.

Chris lived in one of the three-storey Georgian houses. The front lawn was ragged; chunks of brick crushed the grass. A girl in a kaftan emerged from the house as Clare reached it. "The fair-haired guy? I don't think he's in. Left on the first floor, if he is." Clare looked for a bell-push, but it was missing from its plastic socket.

Next to the pay telephone on the hall wall was pinned a large advertisement for a taxi firm—friends of the landlady, no doubt. A skinny strip of thick green carpet trailed down the middle of the stairs; when Clare's heels slipped from it they knocked on wood. Otherwise the house was silent.

She knocked at Chris's door. She knocked again. Down the landing stood a dressing table, one of its drawers splintered outward like the coffin in that television film she hadn't been able to switch off in time. She could just see herself in the oval mirror, struggling feebly beneath grime. As she knocked, something moved in the room—only the ghost of her knock. At last she walked downstairs, dispirited. Well, she'd tried.

She was cleaning Ringo's offside window when she glanced up and saw the alley doorway.

The doorway from the backyard of the house into the alley was empty. Its rotten door lay beside it in pieces. Clare gazed from the doorway to the fire escape, climbing the back of the house outside Chris's window. She stuffed her keys back in her bag and hurried into the alley.

Outside the doorway she halted, beside a crowd of fat plastic bags of garbage. She wasn't really going to do it; it was silly. But she only wanted to look through his window. Suppose she were caught in the act! Then Chris would have to rescue her, tell them who she was. What romantic nonsense. All she wanted was to see his flat. She liked the way he hadn't tried to entice her up there; it was part of his appeal. But now she wanted to see. She remembered the way the actress had stared at her. At once she strode into the yard.

It was full of dustbins, overflowing with garbage; she slithered on a piece of fish and almost knocked over the bins. The heat of the evening flooded her, thudding. She must be careful, even though she was sure the house was empty. The empty windows threatened to fill as she stepped carefully to the fire escape.

She tiptoed up. The iron creaked; the ground fell away through the mesh. At least Chris's was the only window she would encounter. The bricks of the house wall jerked down in steps, close to her face. She reached Chris's window and gasped.

She had thought he was being polite when he'd implied his flat was untidier than hers. But it looked like a burgled boutique. Clothes were heaped on the floor, an overturned mug had dribbled coffee on the floorboards, part of a newspaper poked out from beneath clothes, rolls of rug were unrolling near the walls. Oh, Chris, she thought. He really needed looking after. Men!

FOUND MUTILATED. That was all she could read of the newspaper. She frowned, peering, gripping the windowsill through the gap beneath the sash. The newspaper was yellowing. Why had he kept it? What did it say?

She was pondering when she realized what she was holding on to. The sash was ajar. She glanced about sharply. In the yard, dustbins glistened; opposite her above the yards, windows were blank. Chris wouldn't mind; it was just that he'd never had the chance to invite her up. She only wanted to know what the newspaper said. She wanted to know. She raised the sash and climbed over the sill.

CAT FOUND MUTILATED. She should have known. No wonder she'd upset him. He was sensitive about his cat, after all. He had been trying to hide that. But it was morbid, keeping the newspaper. He needed a new companion, she thought, someone he could trust.

She glanced about the large room. Oh, what a mess. Next to an old record deck a pile of records had toppled, slipping from their sleeves. Several yellowing newspapers nested beneath the front window, beside a stolen DANGER sign. The bed—she couldn't control her giggles—the sheets looked like a burrow Chris must slide out of in the mornings, a tunnel into darkness.

She muzzled her giggles with her hand. She was sure she'd heard a door open downstairs.

She imagined someone standing in the hall, staring up toward the giggling they'd heard. Her nose snorted painfully within her hand. Silence. Perhaps they were easing the door closed, to fool her. When she'd subsided she let go of her face, and saw what she had been staring at for minutes.

Over the end of the bed an old drab sweater and jeans were carefully laid. She frowned. She'd seen Chris wearing them. When he was acting? No, that had been the patchwork. She must be mistaken. It was just that they looked odd, laid there so carefully among the scattered clothes. She suppressed a giggle. He must wear them in the flat, to feel comfortable; that was why he treasured them. Just like a man.

She could tell that the wardrobe and couple of easy chairs came with the flat; the whole place felt second-hand. The green flowers of the wallpaper had nothing to do with Chris. A poster for *Bonnie and Clyde* was taped to one door of the wardrobe. Didn't he keep anything in the wardrobe? There was a second lock on the door of the flat, and a chain. Although she'd sensed his vulnerability, she hadn't realized he was so insecure.

Beyond a partition was the kitchen area. The first thing she saw was the cat's dish, smashed against the wall. She could imagine his dismayed fury. If only he hadn't hidden his feelings she would never have upset him! Perhaps in time he would let her see his feelings. On the table, old salad lay on and beside a cracked plate. She glanced at the stove.

Oh, *Chris*. She wrinkled her nose. He was more helpless than any other man she'd met. How could he stand it? Well, she couldn't. He needed looking after, and she'd start now. The stove looked like a full day's job, but at least she could tidy up.

She picked up clothes and laid them on the bed, squashing the burrow of sheets. Handling the patchwork trousers, she felt a twinge of jealousy. Maybe she couldn't have made them, but she wondered how well the girl he'd lived with had looked after him. Too well, maybe. Well, finding his flat tidied might shock him into improving. She hung clothes over her arm and went to the wardrobe.

The door wouldn't budge. She tugged at it; the wardrobe's stumpy legs pawed at the floor. Something rolled about inside, but the door stayed clamped. She laid the clothes on the bed again and tugged two-handed. The wardrobe nodded forward, and she had to let it fall back with a thud; its contents rolled and thumped against its back. She put one hand on the poster and wrenched at the doorknob with the other. But the swollen wood was firm in its frame; only her hand slipped on the poster, and Clyde Barrow's face tore.

Oh *no*, Clare thought. Oh, where was the tape? Could she tape the back of the tear? She was glancing about in distress when she heard the door slam downstairs.

"Mr. Barrow?" A woman was hurrying upstairs. "Mr. Barrow, is that you?" The landing thundered; a key struggled in the lock. Clare forced herself to move, over the sill, slamming the sash, down the clanking fire escape, skidding past the dustbins, along the alley and out. She didn't dare look back at the window.

As she drove home through the terraced side streets, slowly after her headlong first few hundred yards, she felt light-headed. Children ran across the streets, shrieking. Oh dear, poor Chris. Tomorrow she'd look for a poster for him. But halfway home she had to stop the car, to giggle. She was wondering what he would do when he saw what had happened to his flat.

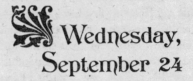 **Wednesday,
September 24**

Mary Kelly lay very still. What had wakened her? Heat hung about her, close and immobile. The house creaked, but it always did; that wasn't what she'd heard. The silence didn't fool her. She had heard something.

Her eyes were full of the feeling of light, grey. When she raised her eyelids it remained, pressing close as thumbs. She held the rest of herself still. The silence feigned innocence. She heard her heart; it sounded starved and feeble.

Perhaps she'd heard a cat, or one of the young drunks who made a row at all hours, with no thought for anyone. It was early morning: the television her neighbours played thoughtlessly past midnight was silent; there was no traffic; no birds were greeting dawn. Perhaps she'd heard a police car hunting criminals, howling. She reached for her handbag and pulled it into bed with her.

She'd not sleep again tonight. Since the writer and his cronies had upset her she had hardly slept at all. They'd succeeded there, though she hadn't let them see. Since losing her sight she hadn't had a single night of unbroken sleep. Last night, tired out, she had hoped to sleep. She shouldn't allow herself hope in this world. It only made God test her, every time.

The heat stood over her. Heavy weather always felt like an

intruder. She remembered the weeks after he, Cissy's creature, had gone—when she couldn't be sure that he'd actually left: groping in her new blindness, she had sensed the oppressive hulking heat everywhere before her, and she had been sure it was him, playing a sadistic game. The heat had blocked her path these last few nights. Only the heat. If he dared show his face here, God would punish him for anything he did to her.

The heat surrounded her bed with presences. They stooped toward her, thrust their grinning faces within an inch of hers, waiting for her to have to touch them. She closed her eyelids and began to pray.

She prayed loudly. Her neighbours had complained that she kept them awake. They'd do better to pray themselves, instead of complaining. She offered up her soul to God. She prayed for Cissy; let God in His mercy grant her a place in Heaven. Again she offered up her own soul, more loudly, for her voice sounded muffled—by the heat, of course. After a pause she prayed for Christopher. Let God in His infinite mercy save him. Perhaps, after all, Christopher should not be blamed for what he was.

Nor should she be blamed. She had been a woman alone, trying to fend for herself and a child. In her letter Cissy had told her the Satanist's name and address, but what could she have done? If he had been caught she would have had to give evidence—what might the Devil have done to her, to the child? She didn't think God could condemn her fear, and she didn't care what anyone else thought. Anyway, she could have changed nothing; the child had already been what he was, the monster he'd become. She shuddered and offered up her soul a last time.

When the silence returned she knew she was not alone in the house.

The house was holding itself still, waiting for her to be fooled. Suddenly she kicked off the sheets, to feel the floor solid underfoot. She wasn't going to lie there like Pearl White.

Once she'd searched the house, she might at least be able to rest. If anyone was there, they wouldn't stop her screaming.

She put on her dressing gown and slippers. Grasping her handbag, she made slowly for the door. Her legs creaked painfully, like sticks swollen a little in sockets. Her movements sounded oddly muffled. By the heat. Her footfalls were enclosed by the wall, then fell out onto the landing. At least nobody could hide behind a door. The house was colder without its doors, but she felt more secure; she'd told Mr. Wright so when he'd argued.

The backs of her fingers ticked across ridged strips of the wallpaper. Her other hand closed on the knob at the top of the banister; its paint was chill. Her footfalls were open and hollow now, but the heat still crowded her; the grey feeling of light pressed into her face like a constant threat. Let anyone try to threaten her. Go on, let them hurt her. God would catch up with them.

The banister cracked loudly beneath her grip. That would startle any lurkers. She smiled bitterly, though her thin blood was rushing faster in her ears. In the hall she stopped to rest, then shuffled to the front door.

The lock and bolts were fastened. Beyond the door she could hear a dog scrabbling at litter, whining. She moved along the hall. Dust-furred grease from the kitchen walls gathered on her nails. The back door was locked and bolted too; the key was still in the lock, just beneath the bolt. All the windows that could have been opened were nailed shut.

The kitchen table flitted vaguely on the greyness. Objects often did that; people, seldom. Its flitting startled her; suddenly she was afraid. She groped for the table drawer. But it was shut, and the knives were all there. In any case, most of them were blunt. She had almost closed the drawer when she reached in and chose the sharpest knife. She would carry that in future.

In the front room her movements sounded padded; the grey

seemed thicker. The presence of chairs loomed at her; there were no other presences—her oppression had lifted somewhat. The fire-irons rattled as she checked them. They were the only potential weapons. Ash whispered dryly beside her face, crumbling. No, there were the photographs; their corners were sharp. She unfolded painfully from squatting. Her hand trembled as it gripped the mantelpiece. She shuffled to the table in the alcove.

One of the photographs was gone.

It was the larger one, the family group. It was nowhere on the table, which was rough with dust; nor on the floor, nor in the corners of the alcove among the ropes of dust. Her tension pulled her to her feet; her whole body shook. She clung to her handbag with one hand; the other gripped the trembling knife.

Mrs. Laird must have moved the photograph. The woman had been interfering lately. She wasn't satisfied just to read out the newspapers to her; she had to keep going outside to the toilet, so she could see how bad the kitchen looked. Let her take herself back to the launderette if she was going to interfere, her and her oily soapy smell. She'd been dusting the house surreptitiously, Mary Kelly was sure.

Or perhaps that interfering teacher had moved the photograph—the one who had come with the writer. Or Mr. Wright —he'd come the other day, pretending to make sure the wiring was safe. They were all taking advantage of her. Well, let them. God would see to them. He'd protect her.

But she knew none of them would have moved only one photograph. Cissy's creature had been here. He must have come with the writer; she'd let no other strangers in. They had all been playing a game with her. They must all have been his friends, helping him.

He was welcome to the photograph. See if it did him any good. She had her memories of Cissy—they had been a happy family; they would be again, in Heaven. God in His mercy would allow that. Claws scraped the window, something snarled at her: the dog. That wouldn't frighten her, however hard it tried.

She trudged upstairs. Her handbag hung from her elbow; her hand on the banister still held the knife. Before she returned to bed she would put that knife in her bag. The heat loomed at her, grey. It muffled her footsteps again as she entered her room.

But heat didn't do that.

It could pretend to be presences, but it never played with sounds like that. Only a real presence could do so: the presence of someone standing absolutely still in her room, someone who'd been standing still ever since she'd awakened, waiting for her beyond the grey. She froze, but her foot had touched something.

It hadn't been there before. She stooped; the heat bent menacingly toward her, at her back. She brandished the knife at it. The object on the floor was sharp-edged, square, glass. The photograph—no, a pane of glass with a handhold of putty stuck to it. It could only have come from the back door. There had been no breeze to show her the gap. He had put the pane there to let her know how he had got in.

"What do you want?" she demanded. She wouldn't let him frighten her.

His voice came from beyond the grey, against the wall; he made no other sound. "The letter my mother wrote you," he said.

She recognized his voice now, its coldness, lack of feeling; it had sounded like that when he had told her he was leaving. He'd disguised it when he had come with the writer. "You want that to remember your mother by, do you?" she said. "To remind you of your birth, eh? Try and get it, then. Just try!"

"I already have."

"You don't even know where it is," she sneered.

"It was in your handbag."

He was only guessing, only trying to make her betray herself. But she was already feeling in her handbag, searching, scrabbling; one of her nails cracked. The letter was gone.

"You'd take that as well, would you, you thief?" she screamed. "You monster, you devil! God help you!" She launched herself at the place where his voice had been, lashing out with the knife.

He hadn't moved. She felt the knife slice his arm, like butter, like a maggot. In a moment he had knocked the knife from her hand. At once she knew he had been waiting for her attack, to give him an excuse to kill her.

She heard him switch on the radio. Pop music spilled out, jangling and thumping. That was to drown her screams. Well, they wouldn't be drowned so easily. She opened her mouth to draw breath. But she had made no sound when the music came rushing toward her face, and the corner of the radio smashed her mouth.

She fell heavily. Her lips began to swell around the hideous pain. Her mouth no longer felt like a mouth; it felt and tasted like broken rusty stone. She could feel nothing else. She heard the music raised high in the air above her, distorting and blurring; then it came rushing down at her. God help me, she thought through the pain.

She knew that killing was only the start of what he planned for her.

Dear Chris,

Just a hasty one before the post!

I've found out about the black magician. His name was John Strong (John Strong! Incredible, isn't it? He sounds more like a wrestler. But I read some of his book in the library, and that's actually very nasty, you can believe anything about him.

Help, I can't get out of these brackets) and he lived at 21 Amberley Street, just off Mulgrave. Will you phone me if you're going to look, so I can go too? I'm not doing anything on Wednesday, the day you should get this.

Now I'm running to the post. See you!

Love,
Clare
XXX

He hadn't intended to kill Clare.

On Monday he'd realized he was trapping himself. He should leave Liverpool at once. To wait for Clare to go to the house on Mulgrave Street, or even to lure her there, would only be wasting time. He should escape while she was keeping quiet about him.

He'd zipped some clothes into a bag and had hurried out, running for a bus. Each minute seemed longer. Red lights snapped into place at intersections; the bus dawdled for passengers to board. His nails had torn at the seat beneath him.

At Lime Street Station he'd found he had left his purse in the flat. He would have tried for the London train with a platform ticket, but nobody would give him change for the ticket machine. The tail of the train had been drawn away leisurely. Half the walk back to his flat had been steeply uphill. The heavy heat had paced him. It had felt more intolerable than his endless trip on hash cake.

He was on the bus again before he'd noticed he had left his bag in the flat. He'd run back, all his body prickling with heat and rage. There was something else that he'd forgotten. He'd searched for half an hour, then with a snarl of rage had wrenched himself away. But he'd walked down Princes Road slowly, more slowly, halting. He couldn't leave until— He couldn't leave. Gazing across at Mulgrave Street, he'd known why. The knowledge had lain dully on his mind.

The worst thing was, he no longer felt free—less so than in his childhood. He'd had little sleep that night. He lay beneath the house, waiting; the earth was full of crawling babies. His grandmother must have told him the story the doctor had told George; he'd forgotten, that was all.

On Tuesday he'd had to get out of the flat. He had walked in the parks. He'd dozed on benches, but children were chattering, birds were babbling. In Sefton Park the light on the lake attacked his eyes jaggedly; in Otterspool Park the path sank among trees, alive with the sound of traffic above on the main road. He had been trying to edge away from Mulgrave Street, pretending he was only strolling. He'd had nothing but his purse and the clothes he was wearing, but that didn't matter: he was only strolling. But he couldn't pretend to himself, and the clearer his purpose had become, the more certain he'd been that he would fail. He was only strolling, and time gathered on him like thick wax, more suffocating than the heat.

When at last he'd returned to his flat, defeated, the landlady was waiting. "Mr. Barrow, I think somebody's been in your flat. I haven't been able to check. Have you had a new lock put on?"

"Yeah, right." In his confusion he'd neglected to lock the window, and someone had got in. Maggie? The police?

"You know very well you should have asked me. Will you check your flat now, please?"

She'd come in with him, blocking the door as he'd made to close her out; she stared suspiciously at his eyes—looking for evidence of acid, no doubt. His clothes had been moved. His bed had been disturbed. Nothing had been taken—but someone had torn his poster. They'd wanted him to know they had got in.

"Miss Fraser says someone was asking for you. A short girl, a brunette. Not much more than five feet tall. She was here shortly before I heard the intruder."

"Yeah, I know her. It was her in here."

"Please tell her it was still burglary, even if she is a friend of yours. For her own sake she had better not do it again.

Please let me have a copy of your key tomorrow. And for heaven's sake, Mr. Barrow," she'd said from the door, "tidy up this flat. I've been meaning to tell you for weeks."

Which meant she'd been getting in too. He had suspected as much; that was why he'd bought the lock. It didn't matter now. His flat wasn't safe any more. He wasn't safe. Clare must be in league with Edmund, after all.

He needed to gain an advantage before he was trapped. He needed the address on Mulgrave Street. It was in his mother's letter; his grandmother had shown him once, then she'd snatched it away, and he couldn't recall it. He didn't dare let the pull lead him to the house. Knowing where it was would give him an advantage. He'd hurried out to buy a glass-cutter and putty. Once he knew where the house was, he would know what to do.

But killing his grandmother had made him less free. In her house he'd felt the pull grasp him, through the walls. Now the killing was something else to flee; it would strengthen the hunt for him. Back at his flat he had tried to sleep, but the sheets had felt unfamiliar. Whenever he'd touched sleep he had felt surrounded by earth that threatened to collapse and suffocate him.

His eyes were gritty embers. Sounds crawled on him. The shallow knife slash on his forearm throbbed beneath plaster. He felt as if the daylight weren't reaching him. The landlady would be here soon, for her key. He was preparing dully to go to the house, hoping that would show him why he needed to go, when Clare's letter arrived.

He gazed at it. She had been trying to drive him into confusion; now she expected him to betray himself by refusing to go to the house. Or perhaps she thought his performance would break down in the house, with Edmund and George in the wings, waiting to pounce. She was sure the house was crucial to him. And suddenly he knew she was right. Suddenly he saw what he must do.

Something about the house was trapping him in Liverpool. He must destroy the house. Now, in daylight. That was why he'd needed the address, the advantage. The house, or what remained of its influence from his childhood, had been confusing him.

He put on his old clothes, to be less conspicuous. He took a box of matches from the kitchen. He could buy petrol if he needed it. It was a pity to leave all his clothes, but he could buy more; his purse was in his pocket. He threw his keys on the bed. He wouldn't need them again.

He strode across the reservation and into a side street, toward Mulgrave Street.

Most of the windows in the terrace were full of planks or doors, like an infection. A few houses had resisted; cars stood outside. Trees were stuck in the pavements; a decaying handbag hung from a branch, a bicycle tyre drooped from another. A rag-and-bone man passed him, wheeling a cart, with a thick, wailing, incomprehensible shout. In one of the occupied houses a broken window was backed with a piece of cardboard: EGGS, it said in the frame of jagged glass. The cart clattered away. The man shouted thickly at the houses.

Chris emerged onto Mulgrave Street. The deep blue sky fell open; around him white clouds lay tangled on the horizon, like convoluted bones. The sunlight accumulated on the back of his neck; for a moment the landscape stirred restlessly. He gazed along Mulgrave Street, at its crossroads on the waste. St. Joseph's School stood alone, surrounded by railings. A master was gesturing ranks of boys into the school. Chris knew his face.

It was the man who'd grabbed him the day he had come here with the Vale School Players. His hands clawed at themselves. If only he could lure that man to the house! A black cat with ragged plastered fur fled past, glancing fearfully aside at him. Never mind: his rage would do for Clare, if she dared come near the house. It was her fault he had killed his grandmother. He would enjoy taking revenge for that, as he had on that dog for the death of his cat.

None of the streets toward the school was Amberley. He walked toward Upper Parliament Street. Lamp standards stooped long concrete necks over the roadway; trees sprouted from the rubbly pavements of levelled side streets. Beyond a corrugated tin wall a mechanical shovel howled and spewed bricks. A lorry laden with spades and pickaxes stood outside the wall.

The pull felt less urgent, too generalized for him to locate. He neared a terrace. This must be it: but it wasn't. A lone postbox said WACK and FUCK. It must be the next terrace—that was the only one left standing. He stumbled off the pavement, which was cracked like ice, onto the waste. The wooden bones of an armchair showed through its torn plastic skin.

The terrace wasn't Amberley Street. He gazed at the tin that filled the windows, bewildered. Beyond the houses a doll whose cracked mouth was stuffed with mud sat in a pram without wheels. Beyond that he saw a single house, its yard walls still intact. A streetlamp stood outside; there was even a street plaque on the house wall. He began to run. AMBERLEY STREET. Hot dust puffed out beneath his sandals.

It was a grey three-storey house. The windows were full of shattered holes, but curtains panted feebly within, colourless as vegetation trapped beneath stone. One sash was almost blind with boards; beneath its glass a curtain stirred. Small attic windows hung with grey curtains stood forward from the slate roof.

The front yard was cramped close to the house. Tufts of grass and weeds sprouted through a scattering of glass and slate. The basement windows were nearly buried; the brows of their sashes stood emptily above the surface of the yard.

Three steps led up to the front door, which was dull brown, partly charred and blistered. The flap of the letter slot hung askew beside a large rusty doorknob. As he approached, Chris glanced at the adjoining set of steps. Above them an intact front door was displayed in a jagged frame of brick. Beyond it a hall with flowered wallpaper led out onto rubbly waste.

He took hold of the doorknob, which felt like a stone rolled in grit, and went into the house.

The hall seemed hung thickly with dust; most of that was the light. Great damp stains bulged the dim wallpaper; one pregnant swelling was covered with pale green patches, like ancient bread.

He moved stealthily along the hall. On his right a closed door led to the room with the almost-boarded window. A floorboard began to shift beneath him, but he redistributed his weight before it creaked. Above his head the posts of the banister faded into colourless vagueness. Someone was moving up there. He crept along the hall, though he hardly needed to: now he was in the house he need fear nobody.

In the wall beneath the stairs he found a door. He turned the knob, which squealed reluctantly, and tugged. The door had clearly not been opened for a long time. Its wood bulged from the doorframe; its moist lock was scaly with rust.

He thrust one foot against the wall and tugged with both hands at the knob. Something creaked faintly, but his foot slithered on a patch of mould. He wedged his foot again and tugged; the slash on his arm was throbbing. He felt movement —it might be the knob working loose in its socket.

He rested. He knew he must reach the basement. That was where John Strong had used his power on his victims. Whatever he had used to control them, he must have kept it down there, safe from them; they would never have dared the basement. The source of John Strong's power was there.

Chris braced both hands on the doorknob. It was dim and slimy. He jammed his feet against the wall and heaved at the knob, heaved until his shoulders ached. Pain pounded in his arm. The door was creaking. It was giving. With a loud crack it sprang open, gasping a thick smell of earth at him.

Peering down, he made out a large room. Slivers of light through the choked slits at the tops of the windows lay stranded, glistening. There was no furniture, only the dully glistening floor: it looked like a marsh at twilight.

He didn't want to go down there. It was too much like something he feared, that darkness. But he had to. There was nowhere else he could go. He struck a match clumsily and ventured onto the stone steps.

Though the basement was large, he felt penned in. The flickering darkness shifted close to him; he was going down into crumbling earth. His sandals rang dully on the steps. On the bottom step he halted, fumbling for another match. The spent match hissed briefly, somewhere in the dark. He stepped out into the basement, and his footsteps became a moist whisper.

There was no floor, only earth. It closed on his sandals like lips; it squeezed moistly over them, licking his feet. The darkness crumbled toward him. There was nothing but earth and a number of flat stones scattered near the walls. Above him the ceiling hovered fluttering, vague and huge; a drop of moisture blinked, then fell.

The flame crept toward his fingers. He had to let in the dark before he could light another match. He dropped the match before it burned him; the earth hissed as it put out the flame. The darkness caved in around him. He scrabbled at the matchbox, and its drawer fell out, spilling all the matches on the wet earth. As his feet moved in panic, the earth seemed to stir wakefully beneath him. The darkness filled his eyes and mouth triumphantly, choking off his scream. It filled him.

And did nothing. It was no threat. It was hardly dark at all. His eyes grew used to the light seeping through the slits of windows. The earth glistened, crawling with dim light. What he needed was beneath that earth. There was nowhere else John Strong could have hidden it. He must dig. He stooped, hands ready. But the slash on his arm began to sting, and he remembered something.

Outside the house, the sunlight hurt his eyes. It made him more anxious to get back to the basement. He hurried to the tin wall where the mechanical shovel howled. Nobody was in sight. He grabbed a spade from the lorry and ran back toward the house.

He had almost reached the house when he saw the car turning into Mulgrave Street.

It had no business here, it looked too expensive. He clambered over the rubble beside the house and listened. When he heard the car halt at the corner of Amberley Street he dodged into a room of the next house that had remained almost intact —only its fourth wall was scattered over its floor.

He heard Edmund say, "This is it."

"Couldn't they knock it down?" George said. "Why leave just this one?"

Clare wasn't with them. Chris listened to their approaching footsteps, crunching over broken glass. They'd go straight in; he'd left the front door open. They had no reason to come round here. They'd better not. He lifted the spade; its sharp edge glittered.

Flies swarmed near him. He slapped them away with the spade. The swarm drifted away, then returned. They weren't drawn to him. They were drawn to something in the rubble. He looked down.

He was running from the car crash, hands full. The man was chasing him. He ran into Mulgrave Street. He heard the man's footsteps, pounding along a side terrace. He glanced along the side streets, looking for a hiding place. Someone might look out of one of the houses at the noise. He caught sight of a house standing by itself, probably abandoned. He ran around it and hurled his burden into the rubble, throwing a few chunks of brick on top of it. Then he ran toward Princes Avenue.

Chris gazed down at the swarming rubble. Emotion welled up in him. He let it come; he mustn't struggle now, with his pursuers in earshot. Slowly he began to grin. He was home at last. He'd been home before and hadn't known it. At last he felt completely safe, free, calm. There was no struggle at all within him. Whatever happened now, he would be all right.

He leaned against the wall, grinning. He heard George and Edmund reach the house. Perhaps Clare wasn't working with them, after all. He hoped she would come to the house by herself while he was there, since she liked playing games with him. He'd just thought of a game he would enjoy playing.

Surely nobody could live here, George thought. The hall was damply chill; it smelled of earth and wet stone and paper— it smelled like a ruin sinking into a marsh. There was no place for life here; it would suffocate.

"We'll start at the top," Edmund said.

Beneath the stairs a door stood ajar. George had assumed they would head for the basement, but he followed. The staircase was even colder than the hall. Each stair gave a separate sharp creak. A strip of wallpaper had flopped across the stairs. Small pale grubs squirmed on its underside; some had been trampled. George imagined groping upstairs here at night.

The first floor stank of urine. A flex like a rat's tail dangled above the landing. In the dimness George failed to see that the floorboards were scattered with plaster; he slithered. "Hell is murky"—but for once Shakespeare couldn't sum up the situation. The underbelly of the ceiling hung down, grey and sweating.

A trickle of strained sunlight lay across the hall: a door was ajar. Beside it the wall had broken out in pale pimples of chewing gum. The lower half of the door was covered with trails of urine. Edmund reached out gingerly and pushed the door open.

The curtains were drawn, warding off most of the sunlight. In the room a young woman sat on a collapsed bed. George was sure she was young, but her breast in the baby's mouth was withered. She gazed out of the room at them, indifferently.

When George stepped forward, startled and horrified, she hurried forward and kicked the door shut. George saw that her pupils were huge and moist, but lifeless. He heard her dragging something against the door. "Junkie," Edmund explained, shaking his head.

George was about to demand what they were going to do about the baby when he realized they were being watched.

He whirled, grabbing at the wall; fallen plaster shifted in its cradle of wallpaper. The man was standing at the top of the stairs to the attics. His small body stooped as he peered at George with one eye; the other socket was bright pink. He wore a raincoat the colour of the dim light. One sleeve was missing; his bare arm hung slackly almost to the floor. He drooled. As soon as Edmund gazed up at him the man burst into tears and scuttled back into an attic.

"Jesus," Edmund said. George gazed at where the man had been. From the edge of his eye he glimpsed sunlight creeping out behind them, into the hall. The other first-floor door was opening.

A burly man stood there. The bib of his faded overalls was thick with old food. He hefted an iron bar above his head as he advanced toward them. His face was smooth and bland as an infant's, but his eyes were those of a man backed into a corner, defending it, although he hardly knew why. Behind him George could see the room he was defending. Except for a pile of old newspapers against the wall, it was completely bare.

"It's all right," Edmund reassured the man. "We've got permission to look round."

The man kept advancing. That wasn't the way to handle him,

George thought scornfully. He stood his ground. "Just you put that down," he told the man. The two of them could handle him. He was glad to have something to confront at last, something more solid than the suffocating atmosphere of depression.

But Edmund was plucking at his elbow. "It's all right. Leave it, George. We'll talk outside."

Suddenly George knew why Edmund had asked him to come: not for help in the search, but for reassurance. Edmund was a coward; he hadn't even known anyone lived here. George let himself be urged out of the house.

The man followed them at the bar's length. He kept the bar poised above his head. He waited on the front steps while Edmund and George got into the car, then he retreated into the house. George glimpsed his face as the door closed; he looked more trapped than before.

"Well, that's that," George said.

Edmund was pondering. "Maybe not," he said. "We didn't look right. We couldn't live in a place like that. But you know someone who wouldn't look like an intruder? Chris Barrow." He started the car. "There's an Arts Centre somewhere near here," he said. "They'll know where he lives."

Everyone had a partner but Ranjit. "Now, you do something," Clare told him, "and I must copy it exactly." Around them in the hall the children were being mirrors of each other. Ranjit lifted his right hand timidly; so did Clare. He lifted his right leg; so did she. He looked as if he felt awkward and foolish; so did she, probably.

When there was an odd child out in the warm-up games Clare would partner him. It was always the self-conscious one nobody else wanted to play with; Clare was skilled in helping the odd ones, for she had to lose her self-consciousness too.

But today she felt foolish as well. She had been foolish, incredibly foolish, at Chris's flat.

She hadn't dared go back to explain. After dinner she'd decided to write to him. But she couldn't think of words to explain her behaviour; she was exhausted after school and her adventure. She had torn one letter up, had scribbled the note asking him to phone her. When she saw him she'd be able to explain.

Ranjit made a face; so did she, and he laughed. He was gaining confidence. "Now you copy me," she said. As soon as she'd woken this morning she had remembered what she'd done. She could hardly believe she had been so idiotic. What must poor Chris have thought, finding his flat burgled, his poster torn?

She smiled encouragement at Ranjit as he joined the others. They were being trees dying of pollution: their own idea. Pollution was the term project. She watched them, glad to relax for a while. During the night she had seen someone lying under a sheet. As she'd approached, the feet—or what she had taken to be feet—stirred and scuttled out from beneath the sheet, leaving a spreading stain at the ends of the legs.

The children improvised in groups, dropping litter, lecturing each other. John was trying to turn his group into a fight. Earlier he had been sobbing. "They've taken his granma away," Hilary had told her. Clare joined the group and began to drop litter, so that John had to shout at her and exhaust some of his feelings.

She only wished Chris would ring, so that she could tell him how sorry she was. Not over the phone—she'd arrange to meet him. Margery's group improvised, then Tommy's. "English people always pick up litter," Tommy told Ranjit. A phone was ringing.

Clare glanced uneasily at Ranjit, but he retorted, "You more litter to pick up."

He grinned when everyone else laughed. The phone had

stopped. Someone was hurrying toward the hall. Clare gazed at the door, but the deputy head had hurried by. Oh, why didn't Chris phone? Had her burglary made him feel so vulnerable that he didn't trust anyone? Was he sitting in his flat, brooding?

She gasped. Sandra's group faltered, glancing at her. "No, it's all right," she said, flustered. "Go on." She had just realized how much of a fool she was. Chris knew she had been the intruder. The girl in the kaftan must have described her to him. Clare's letter must have read like a deception, a trick. That was why he wouldn't phone.

Sandra had spontaneously become a piece of litter, fluttering around on the floor. If Chris wouldn't phone, she must phone him, insist on meeting him. He mustn't think she was trying to trick him. Sandra was rolling at people's legs, showing off. "Now, Sandra," Clare said, "that was good. Don't spoil it." Hurry up, twelve o'clock, hurry up.

Mrs. Allen, the deputy head, was in her office. "Of course you may use the phone, dear. Is everything all right?"

"Yes, I think so." But Chris wasn't at the Arts Centre; no, he hadn't been in for days. "Thank you," Clare said, cutting her off hastily; she hadn't much time. "If anyone wants me I'll be back after lunch," she told Mrs. Allen.

"All right, dear. Off to see your boyfriend?"

Despite everything, Clare found herself smiling. "Yes, that's right," she said.

They couldn't find Chris's name among the doorbells; a wire sprouted from an unnamed socket. "Let's see if he's upstairs," Edmund said, nudging the front door further open.

George pulled his sleeve impatiently back from his watch. Nearly quarter to one. They'd had to wait an hour for someone to arrive at the Arts Centre. He wanted to get back to the Newsham; next week's posters were supposed to arrive on Wednesday now, so that he could check them. But he didn't want Edmund exploiting the boy's good nature. He followed.

A door on the first floor was ajar. Glancing in, George saw a torn poster for *Bonnie and Clyde*. "That might be him," he said. "He liked that film."

Edmund strode in. "He's probably only gone out for a minute," he said. "We'll wait."

He strolled about. "That's stolen," he said, kicking a DANGER sign. "I don't understand his kind at all. They don't care. They're all criminals." He pointed to a pair of patchwork trousers lying on a heap of clothes: "This is him all right. God, look at all this. Could you live in this?"

He seemed furious with the disorder. George disliked it too, but not so vehemently; it was up to Chris how he lived, after all. "He's got a bloody wardrobe, for God's sake," Edmund said. "Why the devil can't he use it?"

He tugged at the wardrobe door; something rolled, something bumped. "I'll bet it's nearly empty. Here you are, George, give me a hand."

"No, I don't think I will. Leave the man's wardrobe alone."

"This mess annoys me. I'll tell him so when I see him. It's typical of him." He wrenched at the door; the wardrobe rocked back, and the door burst open. Something rolled out onto the floor—a metal rod for hanging hangers.

George hoped that was worth Edmund's trouble. But Edmund had stooped into the wardrobe. "My God," he said, muffled.

The tone of his voice penetrated the wood. George turned apprehensively to watch what he was lifting out. It was a framed photograph. Two of the faces were blotted out by stars of smashed glass, but between them was the face of Christopher Kelly's mother.

Edmund sat back on his bent feet, as if he couldn't feel their aching. He gazed at the poster on the wardrobe. "Barrow," he said. "Chris Barrow. My God. With all his fat gone—yes, I should have seen it. And he did need glasses, after all. He's a good actor, I'll give him that. He nearly fooled me."

He pointed to the photograph, speaking to George now. "You can see him when you look, can't you? There, in her face."

Still hoping he hadn't understood Edmund, George began to see Chris almost hidden in the outlines of the woman's face. Oh God. "I've got to phone my wife," he blurted.

"Go ahead. I won't be going anywhere." Edmund was poking through a heap of clothes; his growing eagerness seemed almost hysterical. "My God!" he said. "Do you realize, we might have wasted our time in Mulgrave Street!" He was laughing.

At the phone, George thought for a giddy moment that he had no change. After a long time Alice answered. "Just when I'm making dinner," she rebuked. "Did you go to the house?"

"It was awful. There was a girl trying to feed her baby in that place. But there's something worse. We've found out who killed my mother. It was Chris Barrow, the boy who came to our house."

After a silence she said, "Oh, George," in what might have been sadness or disbelief.

"It was!" he said, his voice cracking with bewilderment. "We've found a photograph he stole from his grandmother!"

"All right, George. Thank God, at least they'll catch him now. Come home now, George. Don't stay there, please."

"I've got to see what Edmund's going to do." She didn't seem to understand why he had phoned. "Don't you realize," he shouted, "he knows where we live!"

"Yes, that's true. But I don't think he'd hurt us. I'm sure he wouldn't." She was silent for a long time. "There's one good thing," she said.

"Good!" he shouted angrily. "What's so good?"

"Well, I was just thinking. Clare will be at school. At least she's out of this."

✝

Twenty past twelve. She was wasting her time sitting here. Clare got out of the car. She didn't dare go into the house, but she couldn't wait all day in the hope that Chris would look out and see her. She picked up a handful of gravel from the reservation and, venturing into the garden, pelted his window. She was glad there was no response; she retreated hastily to the car.

There was one more place he might be. She drove to a gap in the reservation, drove back to Mulgrave Street. Boys were playing outside St. Joseph's; footballs rang on stone, over the loud whirring of her car.

John Strong's house stood sharply grey against the blue sky. She and Chris must have driven past it several times; it seemed incredible that they hadn't noticed. But of course there were other houses isolated by the desolation. She halted Ringo outside the house; the echoes of the engine faded across the waste. The sun blinked dully in cramped attic windows.

She pulled her emergency torch from its nest beneath the dashboard. Was the house occupied? Curtains drooped behind grimy panes, behind boards. If Chris wasn't inside she would come out quickly. At least the front door was ajar. The blistered paint crumbled beneath her fingers as she pushed the door.

The sunlight failed almost as soon as she entered the hall; dimness came at her; she stumbled over something. The dankness that had closed around her didn't fall back as she switched on her torch.

An iron bar was propped against the wall at her feet. That was stupid, dangerous. It might have hurt someone. She carried it out and dropped it clanking into the gutter, near her car.

She probed her way into the hall with her torch-beam. If she hadn't been worried that the house was occupied she would have called to Chris. Shadows burst from swellings in the wall-paper; green spots glimmered. Shadows slid out from the posts of the banister, a rank of them swaying down the moist wall above the stairs. Beneath the stairs a door swung further open, moved by shadow.

The basement. That was where John Strong had taken his victims. It was dark; Chris couldn't be down there. She shone her torch through the doorway. Bare plaster glistened on the wide walls. A spade, a new spade, stood in the earth of the floor. Hanging from the handle by a drawstring was the purse from which Chris had bought her lunch. He must have left the purse as a sign that he'd be back soon. She would wait outside.

She stood by Ringo. How could Chris have left her a sign when he didn't know she was coming to the house? Maybe he'd meant it for George and Edmund. If they were here, she would have to make sure of seeing Chris alone.

She gazed about. A burly man in discoloured overalls was plodding away across the waste. Cars hastened along the bared roads, but otherwise there were no people. On the exposed wall of a demolished house wallpaper lolled, feebly stirring. The basement windows of the nearest street were choked with rubble; the front steps of the houses were thick with shattered slate. The sun hung brightly above the waste. Boys shouted in the school playground. She glanced toward them.

God! She stumbled hastily around the house. She was all right; he hadn't seen her. She would have to stay hidden as long as she waited for Chris. The master she had tricked was on playground duty. He would be there all lunch-hour.

She surveyed the area beside the house. The surrounding earth was a network of bulldozer tracks. If anyone lived in the house, he must have sat in it to prevent demolition. Why would anyone want to protect it? Because he had nowhere else to go, she supposed.

Rubble scraped beneath her feet. In the remnants of a room of the adjoining house, flies gathered over fallen brick. She touched the bricks with her foot, then drew back. She gazed at the side of John Strong's house.

Pieces of ruin clung to it: rusty struts that had held a bath, a line of tiles above the struts, a fireplace with a metal cowl, collages of layers of wallpaper. Fallen slabs of floor surrounded her. At the first-floor level a thick rusty girder protruded for yards. Rope was wrapped around the girder. Sharp bricks were piled on the girder, above the rope. Something lay under the bricks. Eyes. A face. A cat tied to the girder, pelted to death.

Clare flinched. This was stupid, lurking here behind the house. Twenty-five to one. She was wasting her time here. But Chris might be back soon. She didn't mind waiting; she just wanted something to do.

An ice-cream van was playing in the side streets, like a giant rusty musical box. That decided her. It was broad daylight: why was she skulking timidly when she could be helping Chris? Maybe she could finish his digging before he came back, find whatever evidence of John Strong he was looking for. Helping him might make it easier for her to talk about the burglary. She secured the torch by its metal tab to her belt and hurried into the house.

At the top of the basement steps she hesitated. Walls and earth shifted as the torch-beam touched them. A moist chill floated up at her. The ice-cream van boomed, worn and blurred. It sounded like a familiar old toy, rusty with playing. Come on now. She descended the steps. At least her sandals wouldn't be spoilt by the mud; she'd walked through worse with the kids. The torch nudged her stomach companionably. The cold mud reached for her bare feet.

The basement shook around her. Walls advanced to the light and shrank back. The torch-beam scooped the mud into the light, let it rush back into darkness. This was no good. The torch would be even less steady while she was digging.

Where could she rest it? Its rubber cover was meant to be waterproof, but she didn't want to chance the mud. She could lay it on a stone—flat stones were scattered on the mud, near the walls. What were these stones, anyway? She put Chris's purse in the pocket of her dress; it nestled against her breast. Then she pulled the spade out of the shallow pit and went toward the stones.

Were they tiles? Had they fallen from the walls? She couldn't see any patches they might have fallen from. They had been carefully carved: smooth grey stones about nine inches square, perhaps a quarter of an inch thick. But they weren't smooth underneath. They lay raised a little from the mud, on shadow. She slipped the spade beneath the nearest and levered it up.

Movement caught her eye first, wriggling off the underside of the stone and into the earth: a fat pink-and-grey worm. Something with numerous legs scuttled glistening behind the stone. But Clare was gazing at the face she had turned up from the mud.

The high domed forehead was smooth: neither wrinkles nor eyebrows. Mud dribbled from the deep eyes and the mouth, revealing them. The cheeks were long smooth hollows; the long blunt nose was absolutely straight. The thin lips were set in an aloof cold smile.

To Clare it looked rather as if the face were trying to pretend that it hadn't been found in the mud. She turned over the next stone. She and the torch peered closer; the dark wall stood over them.

The stone showed a tableau. A woman knelt, mouth open. A man stood above her, holding a swarming handful of insects. Clare pulled the spade away convulsively; the light brought the wall nodding toward her. When she'd recovered she poked at the next stone, defying it to disturb her. The same smooth face came up, smiling thinly with contempt.

Something moved beside her on the mud. A shadow. She whirled toward the slits of windows. Something was still there:

chunks of rubble. It must have been a cloud across the sun. Come on, stupid.

By the time she'd turned up all the stones she felt a little sick. Most of them depicted men or more often women being used for various purposes, frequently by animals. As they turned up they added to the room's thick smell of earth; parts of the tableaux crawled back into the soil. Every few stones the smiling perfect face came up again, like a card trick.

Beneath the oozing mud the attention to detail in the carvings was astonishing. Their art made them all the more disturbing—that and the fact that they didn't seem to relate to sex. Clare might have understood that, but they looked as if the artist had hated anything remotely human.

Something peered in the window slits. Rubble, stupid. The bottom step into the basement was in fact two stones; she turned them up, a kneeling woman whose mouth was being hammered full of a brick, the smiling face. She stood up, glad to have finished.

She had been bending too rapidly, too often. The darkness filled with orange light. She staggered dizzily toward the pit Chris had been digging. She closed her eyes and leaned on the spade. When she opened her eyes she saw that she was encircled by the upturned stones. She would have to step over them to get out of the cellar, and she didn't like the idea at all.

Why on earth not? They were only stones. John Strong had carved things on them to frighten his victims, but they didn't frighten her—they just disgusted her. Why should she want to step over them now? She could if she wanted to. She was supposed to be digging. It was only ten to one. Chris would be back shortly. She hoped he'd hurry.

A dog was chasing the ice-cream van, which played on obliviously; the dog tried to shout it down. Clare smiled. Daylight was only yards away; splinters of sunlight lay between the pit and the stones. She rested the torch on the edge of the pit nearest the steps, pointing down where she intended to dig.

She didn't want it lying on any of the stones. It had better be waterproof, that was all.

The pit robbed her height of a few inches. It was all right for Chris, but it made her feel like a child lost in a huge dark bedroom. How silly. So long as the sides of the pit didn't cave in on her poor old sandals. The crumbling edges tumbled down the sides.

The pit was several feet square, on the way to six inches deep. The earth was harder than the mud had looked. Should she widen the pit? But Chris might have had some reason for digging in this spot. It looked as attractive as anywhere else in the basement.

She dug. The torch gazed brightly at the thrusts of her spade; above the torch, at the top of the steps, was the dim rectangle of the doorway. She hurled spadefuls of earth toward the stones—most of which had propped themselves up when she'd turned them, rather than falling: John Strong must have meant them to do that. She dug vigorously. She'd show Chris. Too vigorously: all at once she felt her exhaustion and lack of lunch—prickling heat poured over her amid the chill of the basement; the darkness throbbed orange; she had to support herself with the spade. After that she dug more slowly. Five to one. Come on, Chris.

Earth stirred moistly on her spade. She hoped it wouldn't wriggle, slough off its crumbling skin of earth. But the earth seemed free of crawlers here, and felt comfortingly solid underfoot. She threw the spadeful wide, spattering the stones. If she was burying them, good. Let Edmund dig them up if he wanted them. No doubt they were the sort of thing that would interest him.

Someone was moving upstairs. She glanced up at the hovering dark ceiling. There was movement on its underside, running along the ceiling in the dark, falling near her: moisture. But she'd heard someone upstairs. She felt the spade rest in soft yielding earth at the side of the pit as she listened.

A baby. A baby crying. It couldn't be, not in this house. But the sound was certainly overhead. Of course, it must be a cat. When her pulse grew less insistent she recommenced digging. For heaven's sake, wasn't Chris ever going to come?

She threw earth. The room was less dark now, her eyes were adjusting. She found she'd preferred the dark. Grey light gathered very slowly on the stones; the basement filled with the same dim smiling face, watching her from every side, watching her dig herself deeper into the earth. She threw a spadeful straight in one of the faces. Go on, piss off. He'd disturbed her with his book; he wouldn't disturb her again.

The dim light accumulated on the walls, the ceiling, the shifting drops of moisture. It brought the room closer, made it more difficult to ignore. She was a little girl lying in bed, surrounded by six, seven, eight smiling faces almost as vague as the dark, waiting for her to cry out. Oh no she wasn't. She hurled earth at them. The next thrust of the spade touched something.

She gazed at the torchlit patch of earth. Perhaps it was only a stone. She pushed the spade down gently, timidly. She didn't want to break her find, if it was worth having. She wasn't scared of what it might be, she wasn't. She dug the spade beneath the object. Come on, get it over with. She heaved.

The earth cracked, glistening in the torchlight. The crack caved in. The spade levered up, spilling earth. In the mound of earth on the spade she could see a small pale form. She could see its tiny whitish bald head.

She couldn't touch it. She shook the spade gently, so that the mound fell away from the figure. Earth crumbled from the head. In the torchlight she saw the tiny perfect face, smiling contemptuously up at her. The first time she had turned up the face she'd known it was John Strong.

He was naked: pale grey, and smooth as an infant. His erect penis reached up beyond his belly. He lay smiling up from the spadeful of earth. Had he needed to bury this doll to preserve himself? Unimpressed now, Clare pushed at the doll with her finger. As it rolled over, a slug squeezed out between its legs.

She hurled the doll away. It flew from the spade and broke on her torch. Clay limbs fell apart on the mud. The head landed upside-down, smiling. She shoved it further from her with her spade. Then she pulled the torch away from it, closer to her.

Well, that was that. If John Strong had left any of his power here, she'd destroyed it. And good riddance. She picked up the torch and poked its light at his faces. They came forward at once, still smiling; their eyes filled with shadow, gazing at her; their mouths worked. The light flinched away from them, toward the steps.

A fly buzzed beyond the steps, in the hall. Distant cars whispered. Otherwise the house was still; the ice-cream van had moved on. The chill of the basement settled on Clare. Drops of moisture shifted overhead, glinting dully, not quite falling.

She'd wait outside, after all. She would have to be heading back to school soon. She'd be catching cold if she wasn't careful; her feet were cold already. At the top of the steps the doorway swayed restlessly. She made her torch glance away from that into the pit, to show her there was nothing crawling on the spade.

She had uncovered something else besides the doll of John Strong.

It was pale grey, a swelling in the earth. A stone. But it was exactly the colour of the doll. The spade hovered over it. She'd seen the worst, and smashed it. Whatever this was, it couldn't be as bad, but it might be important. The grey bulge swelled up toward her, gathering light, swaying feebly.

She must go, or she'd be late for school. The faces peered out of the dimness; the grains of the dimness swarmed. Flies buzzed in the hall, which sounded full of them. Oh, all right. She would just see what the object was, quickly, without digging it up. She began to scrape the earth away.

It was a doll. A woman. Her face was large, the lips full. The woman was gazing down at herself in appalled panic. Clare knew the face, from the photographs at Mrs. Kelly's. She hesitated; the face gazed down in immobilized panic, trapped in the light; flies bumbled in the hall. Clare scraped the earth from the rest of the doll.

The woman was pregnant. Her belly swelled between her hands, which clawed at the earth. That was all. There was nothing more to see, only a small patch of earth stuck to the doll. But it was dragging Clare down to peer closer, to be certain. It wasn't a patch. The earth had collected in a hole in the belly of the doll: a mouth.

Clare stood up too quickly. The basement rocked unsteadily about her, orange. She closed her eyes, waiting for the orange to drain. She was intensely aware of the doll at her feet. For the first time she was convinced of the power of John Strong. He must have been able to do everything he said he could. The pregnant doll made her feel that his power was still here.

She kept her eyes closed. She must be calm, mustn't flee in panic; she might fall. The orange faded. Pick up her torch, the spade; Chris's purse was safe in her pocket. But the sound of the flies distracted her. Her ears seemed full of it.

It was nearer than the hall. It was at the top of the steps. It was coming down into the basement, buzzing. It was coming toward her, covered with flies, to take its revenge for what she'd done in the basement. Even when she'd swung the torch beam toward the steps, it took her a long time to open her eyes.

"Oh, Chris," she said. "You fool."

Oh, poor Chris. She'd come to explain and apologize; that was a fine way to begin! But her relief was so great that she couldn't have contained her exclamation. "Oh, I'm sorry, Chris," she said, laughing, safe now. "Come and see what I've found."

He didn't move. He stood halfway down the steps. His hair hung lank beside his cheeks; his spectacles glared with torchlight. He was wearing old clothes, for the digging—the clothes she'd seen laid on the bed. Flies circled him. He held out one arm before him, stiffly.

"Oh, don't play now, Chris. It's nasty down here, don't. I've got to go in a minute," she said.

He was descending the steps, slowly, silently. He was pretending to be John Strong or someone. Perhaps he actually wanted to scare her, for intruding into his flat. His long pointed face was paler than she'd ever seen it, intent, unmoving. "Chris," she said sharply.

He had reached the bottom step, still holding one arm stiffly toward her. It looked paler than his face. "Don't," she said. She dropped the torch beam toward the stiff arm. He was holding it in both hands. It wasn't his arm at all.

It was one of those things they sold in joke shops; it was rubber. He'd bought it to make sure she was frightened. But she could see the flies. She could see the clothes Chris was wearing, and at last she recognized them.

At last she saw Rob, his raw shoulder pressed against the passenger door. She saw Chris gazing in at him, at her, his orange face at the window. She saw him running into the mirror, stooping to the explosion of blood on the gravel, standing up triumphantly, hands full. The worst thing wasn't what Chris had done, but the sight of Chris. Chris.

He left the steps and came toward her, throwing his burden carelessly toward the wall. Now that the light had left his spectacles, she could see his eyes gazing at her. They were as dead as a doll's.

She must get past him. But he was between her and the steps. She must defend herself, with the spade. But she felt as if she and the spade were stuck in a marsh. Why couldn't she move? Why couldn't she pull up the spade?

Because if she did she would fall. Only the spade was holding her up. She felt exactly as she had just before she'd fainted at the hospital.

She mustn't. If she fainted she would be at his mercy. But

the spade was slipping, she was tottering sideways. She threw herself back and lunged for the far edge of the pit. She could hear him behind her, approaching softly across the mud. His sounds were softer, they were rushing away from her, they had rushed into the distance, leaving her with no support at all, poised on the edge of darkness. She fell.

†

Chris tossed his toy into a corner, where the flies followed it. He had finished playing now. He moved toward Clare. The torchlight had left his face; the grey light of the basement settled comfortably around him.

She knew what he was going to do. She'd given up trying to talk him out of it, trying to make him feel he knew her. She was just someone staring at him as his grandmother had used to. Her mouth was opening, like his grandmother's when she had tried to scream. He'd stop that. There was the sharp edge of the spade.

But she was turning. She had pushed the spade away. She twisted in the pit and moved toward the far side, moving as though she couldn't stop herself. He watched as she fell across the side with a squelching thud. Light spilled from the torch ahead of her, across the mud.

She lay unmoving. As he gazed at her he felt his first emotion for a while. He was going to enjoy himself. She had made it easier for him. He moved leisurely toward her.

He was nearly at the pit when his foot slipped. It slithered on a small round object near the edge, like a stone. He was skidding toward the pit.

The earth gaped at him, its lips crumbled, glistening. At the bottom he could see a doll. It was a woman with a swollen belly. A mouth was emerging from the belly. At once he knew it was him in his mother.

He couldn't keep his balance on the edge. He was falling

toward the doll. He managed to take most of the fall on his left foot, but his right came down on the doll. Beneath his weight he felt the doll sink into the earth.

It was taking him down with it. It was dragging him down into his dream, to lie beneath the earth. He heard earth falling behind him, into the pit. Soon he wouldn't be able to see even the dimness, only the earth packed on his eyes. His mouth and nose would be full of earth; his ears would be plugged with it. In sudden panic he wrenched up his foot and stamped the doll into fragments.

He stood in the pit. The earth had ceased falling. He stared at the grey fragments around his feet. They had been him and his mother. He had been lying there in the earth; he'd broken himself in pieces. He couldn't understand what that meant. He gazed down.

At last the torchlight attracted his gaze. Clare lay near it. That confused him more. What was he going to do about her? The others—her brother, Mrs. Pugh—had been dead before he'd done anything. His grandmother had struggled to protect herself; he'd enjoyed that. But Clare lay breathing, yet still. It bewildered him.

He would wait until she moved, so that he could stop her. He climbed out of the pit and turned the torch to show her face in the mud, her breathing torso. Then he stepped back to watch for movement.

He was still watching when he heard someone creeping along the hall.

He turned toward the steps. Sunlight from a window slit fell across his face. He watched the grey rectangle of the hall. A figure appeared, peering down. The figure came forward into the doorway, stood at the top of the steps, staring at him. It was Alice, George Pugh's wife.

The sunlight clung to his face as she scrutinized him. She was trembling, trying to conceal it. Let her come down if she wanted to. He had nothing against her.

At last she came down the steps, as if there were nothing else she could do. Her face was set hard; it looked in danger of breaking, releasing a flood of emotion. She swatted flies viciously away as they rose toward her. She passed him on the far side of the pit, gazing at him all the while, and went to Clare.

He turned to watch. She was thrusting the torch at Clare's face. Breath slabbered in the mud at Clare's mouth. Alice was slapping her face as she lay in the mud. She stooped further and tried to drag Clare to her feet. After an effort she let her fall back and stood panting.

She'd never do it. He could help. But as he went forward Alice brandished the torch at him, battering his face with light. "Don't you come near," she said. She crouched over the girl, like a cat protecting her kitten.

He hadn't done anything; he hadn't touched Clare. He wasn't going to hurt her now. He'd show Alice. "I'll help," he said; his voice seemed distant. He stooped to Clare, gazing up at Alice.

She shone the torch into his face. All he could see was the glare, aching in his eyes. At last he heard her say, "All right, you carry her." She sounded weary, helpless.

She shone the light on him as he picked up Clare's small body and carried her easily toward the steps. The knife wound stung. As he passed the pit he kicked earth down on the grey fragments. Near the pit, a small grey face smiled upside-down at him from the mud.

Clare's head felt brimming with liquid, liquid that swayed. Leather burned on her back; her shoulder rested against metal. She felt painted with heat. She only hoped she wouldn't be sick. She opened her eyes.

She was sitting in Ringo, outside the house. She was in the front passenger seat. Through the windscreen she saw Alice and Chris, standing on the pavement with their backs to her. When she saw Chris she wound the windows closed more tightly and locked the doors. Something touched her breast: the purse. Ripping her pocket in her haste, she hurled the purse out onto the rubble and screwed the window tight again. Then she sank back against the hot leather. She felt faint. She just wanted to rest.

Alice and Chris stood aimlessly. They glanced unseeing at the fall of the purse. Alice's bicycle leaned against the yard wall. Through the glass Clare heard Alice chattering. "I rang Clare at school. I wanted to meet her, to tell her something. I thought it might be best if she heard it from me. It doesn't matter now. They told me she was looking for you. I thought she'd probably come here." Clare could tell she was talking so as not to think.

Alice fell silent. At last she said, "Chris, will you come with me?"

"Where?" he said dully.

"To the police station."

In a voice in which there was no life at all he said, "Yeah, all right."

A lorry left the corrugated tin wall, flashing sunlight. The sun hung near the grey house. Alice stood irresolute, now that she had charge of Chris. There was movement down Mulgrave Street, at Princes Avenue. A tiny George had appeared there.

He was hurrying toward the house. Edmund appeared behind him, small as a doll; he looked as if he were trying to call George back, gesticulating. Clare watched Edmund see Chris.

He halted, then he ran. He ran past George, toward Clare, growing, growing faster. She watched him grow. She wondered whether Chris would see him.

"Shit, no," Chris said. Some life had returned to his voice.

Alice glanced where he was staring. "It's all right, Chris, I'll talk to him. It's all right!" she cried. But he'd grabbed her bicycle and was astride it. He shoved himself away from the wall; the bicycle wobbled past Clare. She turned to watch him, slowly, holding her head steady on her neck. By the time he reached Mulgrave Street he had his balance and was pedalling.

Edmund came running toward the car. He glanced about frantically, at Clare, at the rubble. His face brightened. He stooped to the gutter behind the car; she heard metal scrape. Then he was running after Chris. "No!" Alice cried, starting after him. But he'd hurled the iron bar.

It struck the back wheel of the bicycle and caught in the spokes. The bicycle fell, throwing Chris across the roadway. All four wheels of the lorry went over him.

When Alice reached Edmund she slapped his face as hard as she could.

Around them, empty houses clapped. The lorry driver climbed down from his cab, gazing in disbelief. George had reached Alice and Edmund; he stared at them, bewildered. They were standing close together, but had turned away from each other. George looked back as a baby started crying in the house. Then they went toward Chris.

 Saturday,
April 17

If I hadn't followed George in case he needed help, Kelly might be at large today.

But we did more than stop a criminal from committing further horrors. George went back to the house to rescue that baby, and George does what he sets out to do. I like to think that by starting the search for Kelly, I helped save that baby. I think that makes everything worthwhile.

The End
of a book by Edmund Hall
Coming soon: *The Terrible Terrorists*

The switchboard was winking at Dorothy. "BBC Radio Merseyside," she said, and sent the call to its extension. Rain rushed at the window; it reminded her of a car-wash. Across the roofs, the Liver Building looked like a bedraggled charcoal sketch. Someone was waiting at the reception counter. She turned and saw Clare.

Clare was early, unexpected. Dorothy made a hasty grab to hide *Satan's Cannibal*, too late. "It's all right, Dorothy," Clare said, smiling slightly. "I've read it."

"Oh, that's good." She was glad Clare felt able to. "That's a good handbag," she said while she regained her poise.

"Haven't you seen it before? No, you wouldn't have. It's the one my parents bought me last year."

The wind hurled rain at the windows. "We won't want to go far for lunch," Dorothy said. "Do you fancy the Master Mariner's?"

After a silence Clare said abruptly, "Yes, all right."

"We'll go somewhere else if you'd rather."

"No," Clare said. "We'd better go there."

Carol arrived to take over the switchboard. "I'll just be a minute, Clare," Dorothy said, and hurried to Studio 2. As she opened the door Bob's voice boomed out. "Now here's a real working-class sound; you can tell he knows what he's got in his head."

"Will you put that tape in my pigeonhole when you've finished with it?" Dorothy said.

"All right, love," Billy Butler said. When Dorothy turned she saw that the door from Reception hadn't closed behind her; Clare had heard Bob's voice.

The lift's door winced away from Clare's foot. Dorothy followed Clare's expressionless back. "Bill asked to listen to that tape," she explained. "He wants to trace a record Bob played."

"Do you listen to Rob's tapes?"

Clare would never call him Bob. Well, Bob was hers too; if calling him Rob made her memories more secure, Dorothy wasn't going to argue. "I listen sometimes," she said. "I used to enjoy listening to his shows. They sounded as though he'd never let anyone tell him what to say. But now I don't know; he sounds as if he's just talking to himself, not to us at all."

"All his fibs about the working class, you mean." The lift halted at the second floor, yawned, recommenced sinking. "I mean, some of the parents of my kids are thieves. Some of the women live with more than one man; the kids don't know who their parents are. Some didn't want their kids at all and still don't," Clare said. "And Rob was trying to idealize all that. They're only people; it does no good to blur them into something else. It's funny, Rob was trying not to sound class-conscious. He never realized that was exactly how it made him sound."

Though the rain was abating, the crowds sheltered; Dorothy and Clare had a clear path. Puddles bubbled with the last raindrops, as if the pavement were full of fish. "I'll tell you what annoyed me," Dorothy said. "Some of the things Edmund Hall says, I never told him. All that about how I put up with Bob's artistic temperament, that's silly. Bob just didn't want anyone to know how unsure of himself he was. He didn't like my knowing. That's why we had rows. But I still loved him."

Puddles frowned at a breeze; jigsaw pieces of window displays glided by beneath the water. In Williamson Square the cloudy sky tossed and turned underfoot. A man with a handful of pamphlets came at Clare, but she eluded him, almost running. "There's another way the book's unfair," she said as they entered St. John's Precinct. "To Chris."

She had never mentioned Chris before. "How, unfair?" Dorothy asked.

Chairs sat in windows, waiting to be bought. "Edmund makes it sound as if Chris were just trying to trick us," Clare said. "Edmund never liked him. But Chris never really lied to me. And when he did lie it wasn't deliberate; he couldn't help himself. It was that thing in the house."

"Do you think so?"

"I know so, Dorothy." People gazed through plate glass at a mute newsreader, multiplied by televisions; he was red-faced, green-faced, grey. "Edmund mentions the doll of John Strong," Clare said, "and all the dolls they dug up later. But there's one he never saw, because it was broken. It was Chris's mother, and him coming out of her. Chris broke it," she said, moist-eyed, "because it would have made him kill me."

They crossed the balcony above the market. Dorothy gazed down at the stalls. "Oh, look at that dress," she said, but Clare hurried ahead as if she hadn't heard, into the restaurant. Dorothy followed.

She chose a plate of salad. Clare was staring at it. "I'm on a diet," Dorothy explained, but Clare kept staring; then she looked away. She was certainly in an odd mood. Today she'd been walking more naturally than Dorothy had ever seen her walk before; now she was stumping to the cash desk like an old vagrant woman tramping the streets.

Dorothy was wending her way to a booth when she saw Tim. He was collecting scripts into his briefcase from among the things that crowded his table—a bowl with a tidemark of soup, a lone chip on a plate, a poetry anthology. "There's Tim Forbes," she told Clare. "He does our poetry series. Shall we sit with him?"

"I don't feel like meeting people just now," Clare said curtly.

"I must introduce you sometime. See you, Tim." At her call he glanced up from poking contents into his briefcase. He brushed his flopping hair back ineffectually with one hand, and smiled so widely that she suspected he'd forgotten who she was.

She slid into a booth overlooking the street. The escalator carried fresh tiers of shoppers upward constantly. "Are you all right, Clare?" she said.

"Yes, perfectly." But her tone wasn't. She sounded as if she thought Dorothy had been matchmaking, perhaps even that she'd known Tim would be here. Dorothy made to tell her how wrong she was—but it wasn't worth the unpleasantness. In fact she would like to see Tim married; he seemed gentle, and rather lonely.

Dorothy searched for a change of subject. "Oh, something else in Edmund's book," she said. "He says Bob caused all our rows. That isn't what I told him. Some of the people I used to invite round, that I knew Bob couldn't stand—Bob was right, they were terribly posy. I only kept inviting them because he said I shouldn't. I never see them now."

Clare's expression made her falter. She was staring, as if she'd just realized she had lost something. No, it was worse than that—as if she'd seen there had been no reason at all for

207

her to lose it. She looked as if she were about to speak, then her lips pinched shut.

Obviously she didn't want to talk about Bob. "Is George Pugh's cinema still going?" Dorothy said.

"Yes."

"Does he still put on films for your kids?"

"Yes," Clare said even more abruptly, and filled her mouth with food, leaving no room for conversation.

Wasn't Dorothy supposed to say anything at all? At this rate she might as well have stayed at Radio Merseyside and eaten sandwiches—and not got wet, either. It wasn't just that Clare disliked to be reminded of Bob. She hadn't minded before, when they were walking. But since they'd reached the restaurant Clare had been increasingly unfriendly. Deep down, Dorothy thought, it was simply that Clare didn't like her very much.

She never had; she had always held herself back from Dorothy, had been inexplicably wary of her. But she had never been as bad as this. Now she seemed to be doing it deliberately, to want Dorothy to notice—to make Dorothy feel somehow guilty. This was the last lunch she would have with Clare, Dorothy decided. And the last time they'd arrange to meet, if she had her way. She had been kind to Clare, because of all that the woman had gone through. Well, Clare had had her chance.

A sudden glittering beyond the window distracted Dorothy from her growing anger. Sunlight had flooded the city. A bus was passing, raindrops trembling on its roof; the sun scattered a rainbow among them, pinpricks of brilliant colour quivering in the wind. Clare watched too, and when the bus had passed she continued staring out of the window.

Dorothy glanced where she was looking. It was an old cinema, now a chapel. The marquee said, "Come to Me, all you that labour and are burdened, and I will give you rest." After a moment Clare's reflection in the window came clear. Two enormous tears were running slowly down her cheeks.

At once Dorothy felt in control again; this was a situation she could handle. "What's wrong, Clare?" she asked gently.

Clare's face stayed on the glass, a silent portrait of misery. Her shoulders began to shake; her mouth opened loosely, and Dorothy heard her sobbing. She turned back and forth on the seat, trying to hide. "What is it, Clare?" Dorothy said.

"Oh, everything," she said indistinctly. "It goes back so far."

Dorothy was about to respond when she caught sight of the clock. "Look, Clare, I'm sorry—I've got to go back to work in a minute. Come to dinner tonight, and you can tell me everything."

Clare drew in a long shuddering breath, interrupted by a sob. "There's so much of it," she said. Then she was rubbing her eyes viciously. "It's all right, Dorothy. Thank you, but I'm going to be busy tonight."

"Do it tomorrow, whatever it is. You need to talk, you know you do. Please come tonight. And promise you'll tell me. Please."

"You don't want to hear my troubles," Clare said, smiling to show she was over them now.

"Yes, I do. Please come." Dorothy gazed at her. "I get lonely sometimes," she said.

After a pause Clare said, "All right." She sounded weary, rather helpless.

As they emerged from St. John's Precinct the first drops of a new rain were feeling out the pavement. "I'll see you about eight," Dorothy said. Clare nodded slightly, unsmiling, and hurried away. Dorothy watched her small figure dwindling into the crowd. She looked aimless, like a lost child. In a few moments the crowd had engulfed her, and Dorothy could see only the taller heads. Now that she had been able to cry, Dorothy hoped she would be able to talk. Dorothy began to run, to outdistance the rain.

THRILLERS

0352   Star

397012	Georges Arnaud **WAGES OF FEAR**	75p ♦
395184	David Axton **PRISON OF ICE**	85p
396474	Paul Boncarrère **ULTIMATUM**	75p
396962	William F. Buckley Jr. **SAVING THE QUEEN**	60p*
396059	Richard Butler **WHERE ALL THE GIRLS ARE SWEETER**	60p
300523	Henry Denker **A PLACE FOR THE MIGHTY**	75p*
398582	Burt Hirschfeld **FATHER PIG**	60p*
395176	**SECRETS**	85p*
398590	**MOMENT OF POWER**	75p*
398604	**BEHOLD ZION**	85p*
396253	Tony Kenrick **THE SEVEN DAY SOLDIERS**	60p
396849	Hugh C. McDonald **THE HOUR OF THE BLUE FOX**	60p*
395982	Graham Masterton **PLAGUE**	75p
396911	**FIREFLASH 5**	60p
395818	Michael Maguire **SCRATCHPROOF**	70p
397853	**SLAUGHTER HORSE** (also see Tandem Thrillers)	70p
300078	Lawrence Sanders **THE FIRST DEADLY SIN**	95p

GENERAL FICTION

Wyndham Books are obtainable from many booksellers and newsagents. If you have any difficulty please send purchase price plus postage on the scale below to:

Wyndham Cash Sales
P.O. Box 11
Falmouth
Cornwall
OR
Star Book Service,
G.P.O. Box 29,
Douglas,
Isle of Man,
British Isles.

While every effort is made to keep prices low, it is sometimes necessary to increase prices at short notice. Wyndham Books reserve the right to show new retail prices on covers which may differ from those advertised in the text or elsewhere.

Postage and Packing Rate

UK: 22p for the first book, plus 10p per copy for each additional book ordered to a maximum charge of 82p. **BFPO and Eire:** 22p for the first book, plus 10p per copy for the next 6 books and thereafter 4p per book. **Overseas:** 30p for the first book and 10p per copy for each additional book.

These charges are subject to Post Office charge fluctuations.